An Enchanting Kiss

Captivating Kisses
Book 5

Alexa Aston

Dragonblade Publishing, Inc.

ARE YOU SIGNED UP FOR DRAGONBLADE'S BLOG?

You'll get the latest news and information on exclusive giveaways, exclusive excerpts, coming releases, sales, free books, cover reveals and more.

Check out our complete list of authors, too!

No spam, no junk. That's a promise!

Sign Up Here

www.dragonbladepublishing.com

Dearest Reader;

Thank you for your support of a small press. At Dragonblade Publishing, we strive to bring you the highest quality Historical Romance from some of the best authors in the business. Without your support, there is no 'us', so we sincerely hope you adore these stories and find some new favorite authors along the way.

Happy Reading!

CEO, Dragonblade Publishing

Additional Dragonblade books by Author Alexa Aston

Captivating Kisses Series
An Unexpected Kiss (Book 1)
An Impulsive Kiss (Book 2)
An Innocent Kiss (Book 3)
An Unforeseen Kiss (Book 4)
An Enchanting Kiss (Book 5)

The Strongs of Shadowcrest Series
The Duke's Unexpected Love (Book 1)
The Perks of Loving a Viscount (Book 2)
Falling for the Marquess (Book 3)
The Captain and the Duchess (Book 4)
Courtship at Shadowcrest (Book 5)
The Marquess' Quest for Love (Book 6)
The Duke's Guide to Winning a Lady (Book 7)

Suddenly a Duke Series
Portrait of the Duke (Book 1)
Music for the Duke (Book 2)
Polishing the Duke (Book 3)
Designs on the Duke (Book 4)
Fashioning the Duke (Book 5)
Love Blooms with the Duke (Book 6)
Training the Duke (Book 7)
Investigating the Duke (Book 8)

Second Sons of London Series
Educated By The Earl (Book 1)
Debating With The Duke (Book 2)
Empowered By The Earl (Book 3)
Made for the Marquess (Book 4)

Dubious about the Duke (Book 5)
Valued by the Viscount (Book 6)
Meant for the Marquess (Book 7)

Dukes Done Wrong Series
Discouraging the Duke (Book 1)
Deflecting the Duke (Book 2)
Disrupting the Duke (Book 3)
Delighting the Duke (Book 4)
Destiny with a Duke (Book 5)

Dukes of Distinction Series
Duke of Renown (Book 1)
Duke of Charm (Book 2)
Duke of Disrepute (Book 3)
Duke of Arrogance (Book 4)
Duke of Honor (Book 5)
The Duke That I Want (Book 6)

The St. Clairs Series
Devoted to the Duke (Book 1)
Midnight with the Marquess (Book 2)
Embracing the Earl (Book 3)
Defending the Duke (Book 4)
Suddenly a St. Clair (Book 5)
Starlight Night (Novella)
The Twelve Days of Love (Novella)

Soldiers & Soulmates Series
To Heal an Earl (Book 1)
To Tame a Rogue (Book 2)
To Trust a Duke (Book 3)
To Save a Love (Book 4)
To Win a Widow (Book 5)
Yuletide at Gillingham (Novella)

King's Cousins Series
The Pawn (Book 1)
The Heir (Book 2)

The Bastard (Book 3)

Medieval Runaway Wives
Song of the Heart (Book 1)
A Promise of Tomorrow (Book 2)
Destined for Love (Book 3)

Knights of Honor Series
Word of Honor (Book 1)
Marked by Honor (Book 2)
Code of Honor (Book 3)
Journey to Honor (Book 4)
Heart of Honor (Book 5)
Bold in Honor (Book 6)
Love and Honor (Book 7)
Gift of Honor (Book 8)
Path to Honor (Book 9)
Return to Honor (Book 10)

The Lyon's Den Series
The Lyon's Lady Love

Pirates of Britannia Series
God of the Seas

De Wolfe Pack: The Series
Rise of de Wolfe

The de Wolfes of Esterley Castle
Diana
Derek
Thea

Also from Alexa Aston
The Bridge to Love (Novella)
One Magic Night

CHAPTER ONE

September 1807

"M AJOR! MAJOR!"
Rupert Cummings slowed his stride and turned, seeing a soldier chase after him. It surprised him that the lad had recognized him since he wore civilian clothing similar to what a French peasant would wear, and a beard now covered his usually clean-shaven face. His latest spy mission had lasted almost four months, and he was eager to rid himself of the itchy beard, as well as have his hair trimmed to a respectable length.

"What is it?" he asked.

"For you." The soldier handed a letter to him. "Good day to you, Major."

He looked at the letter, his name scrawled across it, having no idea who might have written to him. In his eight years serving in His Majesty's army, this was the first piece of correspondence Rupert had ever received.

Flipping it over, he broke the seal, only to find a single line in the message.

Sell your commission. Return home at once.

Cressley

His blood began to boil. Why on earth would his brother demand that he resign from the army and return home? To what? Second sons were destined for the army for life. Nothing awaited Rupert. He had no intention of obeying a command from a man he was, for all intents and purposes, estranged from.

They had never been close, even before he had taken up his commission. Perceval was fifteen years his senior. The only thing they had in common was a father who had been cold to them both, and a mother whom Rupert had never known. She had died giving birth to him. He was raised by servants and could count on one hand the times he had even spoken to his brother. Their father had died during Rupert's first year at university. No one had thought to inform him, and he only learned of the death when he came home at the end of the first term. He remained year-round at Oxford after that, not wishing to be alone in an empty house at Crestbrook. Perceval preferred town to country and was never in residence at his country estate in Cumberland. He also had never invited Rupert to visit him in London.

His anger simmered as he jammed the note into his pocket and headed to his commanding officer's tent. The sentry took a moment to study him, and Rupert quickly gave his name and rank. Only after hearing his voice did the sentry seem to relax, allowing him to pass. Grime still clung to him, thanks to weeks without a decent bath, but he knew Bond would want a full report immediately. His commanding officer had become not only a mentor, but also the kind of older brother Rupert had always hoped to have, and he did everything he could to please the man. That had meant going on one dangerous assignment after another, but the information he brought back was vital to Britain's war effort.

He stepped inside the tent, where another sentry stood, and he nodded to the soldier. Bond was deep in thought, focused on what he wrote, and Rupert held back until the officer set down his quill. Only then did he step forward.

"Lieutenant-General Bond." He saluted the officer, and Bond returned the salute. The older man looked to the sentry and nodded curtly, causing him to step out of the tent.

"You look a bit haggard, Major Cummings," Bond observed.

"I am sorry I did not pretty myself up for you, but I do have news."

For the next half-hour, Rupert gave his report, Bond taking copious notes as Rupert did so. This would be the written record of his most recent espionage activities. For his safety, he never committed anything to paper, relying on his keen memory. The decision to do so had saved his hide on more than one occasion, along with his excellent command of French and exceptional forged papers.

Bond asked him several clarifying questions, and then he sat back, looking satisfied.

"It is as I feared, Major," his superior confided. "Britain held Bonaparte off at Trafalgar two years ago, and that lulled us into a false sense of security, thinking our superior navy would protect us from invasion. Bonaparte is far from finished with us—or the rest of Europe. The information you gleaned in your recent mission tells me as much."

The lieutenant-general shook his head sadly. "I fear from other reports we have received, ones which have been shared at the highest of levels, that we are in for many more years at war."

Rupert believed the same, which led him to remember Perceval's note. He withdrew it and said, "Might I ask some advice of you, Lieutenant-General?"

He handed over the folded page, watching as Bond opened it and read the sparse message within. Then their gazes met.

"I assume Cressley is the brother whom you have mentioned to me."

"It is. We have had no communication in all my years serving in the military. I saw Cressley the day he authorized my commission to be purchased through the family solicitor. There has been no contact since them. Until this." Frustrated, he asked, "Why should I act upon some order from someone who is practically a stranger to me?"

"It is terse," Bond agreed. "Ironically, to me, that speaks volumes." He paused, collecting his thoughts for a moment. "If your brother wishes for you to sell out, there is good reason for you to do so. My gut tells me Cressley is dying—and needs you at home."

Rupert's thoughts had only been concerned with himself and how he resented the notion of being told to sell out. He had taken Cressley's note literally, not reading anything into it. He had learned, however, that Bond's gut feelings proved accurate a majority of the time.

"How old are your brother's children now?" Bond asked.

He shrugged. "How should I know? When I joined the army, I had no idea if Cressley had ever wed, much less had children. That is how little I knew about him even then."

"In my opinion, a man does not write this kind of note unless he is desperate. I believe your brother is dying, Major Cummings, and it is your duty to go home and become the guardian to his children. Run his country estate. Manage his holdings until his heir is of legal age to do so himself."

Ire filled him. "Why should I have to give up the life I have built for myself for someone I have only seen a handful of times?"

"Because he is family—and he is asking for you to do so. We cannot choose our family, Major. We can, however, act as men of honor when called upon."

Bond rose and began pacing about the tent. Rupert had never seen his commanding officer agitated.

"Your report is one of several we have gathered over the last few months. The war is going to accelerate considerably, as early as next year. Englishmen will die by the thousands until this conflict is over. The Little Corporal is a greedy bastard. He is not satisfied with what he has already taken."

Bond returned to his seat. "I share this with you in confidence. Intelligence we have received has caused a decision to be made. The bulk of the British army will soon travel to Spain."

"Spain? Why Spain?"

"The Spanish government is headed for disaster. Our reports tell of immense corruption, and King Charles IV's leadership is questionable, at best. All indications point to Bonaparte's plans to remove the Spanish king and his son and install his brother Joseph on the throne. Naturally, this will lead to civil unrest. Even war.

Britain will not stand for this. The battles will be bloody. Frankly, your brother's message may be a blessing in disguise."

"But I want to fight for my king and country," he insisted.

Bond shook his head sadly. "That is no longer possible. You are an honorable man, Major Cummings. It seems your brother's character is less than exemplary. If you can guide the family in the right fashion and assist his sons in developing integrity, you will make your mark on the next generation of Englishmen." He smiled. "Not to mention the fact that you could wed and start a family of your own."

The idea of marriage and children seemed foreign to him. He had known, going into the army as a second son, that this would be his adult life.

"I can handle the sale of your commission for you if you would like me to do so. Give me the name of your family's solicitor and his address, and I will see the funds from the sale sent to him. Arrange for transportation for yourself to leave camp as soon as possible."

Bond rose and came to him. Rupert also stood as the older man offered his hand.

"It has been a pleasure serving with you, Major Cummings. I wish you all the best." Bond paused. "I would ask that you write to me. Not when you reach home and learn of the situation. Wait a year and then write to me. By then, you will have settled into whatever role has been designated for you. I would like to know where you land and how you are. Will you do this for me?"

His throat swelled with emotion, and he swallowed it down. "I will do so, sir. Thank you. For everything. Your leadership and guidance have been inspiring. I hope I can emulate the lessons you have passed on to me."

Rupert left the tent, the life he had known and loved abruptly coming to an end. He returned to his quarters to pack and knew he would need to seek transportation to London, all the while wondering what his future might hold.

HE LEFT THE bustling London docks and decided to stretch his legs for a few minutes before hailing a hansom cab. As he walked, it struck him that he did not even know where his brother's townhouse was located. His father had never brought him to town. The only time he had visited London was when he had come to meet his brother at Mr. Ousley's offices. The solicitor had handled the purchase of Rupert's commission. He supposed he would go there now and discover the lay of the land and ask for his brother's address.

After walking for several blocks and having no clue where he was, he signaled a hansom cab driver and gave him Ousley's address.

"I'll get you there in no time, Major," the man told him.

Rupert sat back, taking in all the sights until they pulled up in front of a building. When he tried to pay the driver, the man waved him off.

"My own boy is in uniform, Major. Left us a year ago. We are terribly proud of him. It's the least I can do, giving you a ride."

"Thank you, sir."

He entered the building and went to the desk where a clerk sat, announcing, "I am Major Rupert Cummings. I wish to speak with Mr. Ousley at his earliest convenience."

"Do you have an appointment, sir?"

"I do not. I am willing to wait for as long as it takes."

"One moment, please."

The clerk vanished and then returned in less than a minute, looking a bit sheepish.

"Mr. Ousley is most eager to meet with you, Major Cummings. If you will follow me."

He was taken to a large office and recognized the solicitor, now a man in his late forties, with graying hair and wearing a dark gray suit. Ousley rose and greeted him.

"Ah, Major Cummings. What has it been—six—seven years?"

"Eight, actually, Mr. Ousley."

"May I have my clerk bring you anything? Tea or coffee, perhaps?"

Though he was both hungry and thirsty, Rupert did not wish to delay matters. "None for me, thank you."

The solicitor nodded brusquely to his clerk, who left them, closing the door behind him.

"Have a seat," Ousley offered, and he took one in front of the desk as the solicitor sat behind it.

He removed his brother's note from his pocket and set it on the desk. "Open it."

The older man did so, shaking his head. "It is just like Lord Cressley. Not revealing a thing to you. Frankly, I am surprised you did as he asked with so little information provided to you."

"I am walking into this situation blind, Mr. Ousley. In fact, I came to you simply because I haven't a clue as to where my brother even lives. You have to know that we have never been close. Over the years, we have barely spoken to one another, much less been in one another's presence for any length of time. I suspect he is gravely ill, and that is why he has asked me to come home. Do you know if he is dying? Am I to be named a guardian to his children?"

"You are right about the dying, Major. Lord Cressley is grievously ill. Reaping what he has sown."

Rupert thought the solicitor's words cryptic, but did not interrupt.

"The viscount never wed," Ousley explained. "I will be brutally honest with you, Major, and tell you that Lord Cressley has one of the worst reputations in all of Polite Society. He has always run with a fast group of friends. Gambling. Drinking. Wenching. This is common knowledge."

He winced involuntarily. "You are telling me that *I* am his heir apparent."

"That is correct," the solicitor confirmed. "Men such as Cressley eventually wed and produce an heir. In this case, it is too late for him to do so, which is why he has summoned you home." The solicitor cleared his throat. "Since you are the heir apparent, I am treating you accordingly now. I would like to give you a full accounting of the estate you will shortly inherit, as well as your other holdings."

For the next hour, Ousley walked Rupert through the financial situation of the viscountcy. Besides Crestbrook, which was a profitable estate, his brother had investments in everything from coal to shipping to silk.

"You mentioned gambling," he said when the solicitor finally came to a close. "How large are Cressley's debts?"

"I cannot say for certain, Major. Those who hold his markers will come out of the woodwork upon Cressley's death. I will say that your brother's reputation is one of a winner, however. It seems he has won much more over the years than he ever lost. Even after you pay off any debts he may have, you will be in excellent financial shape."

Everything he had heard during this past hour had changed his life radically. Instead of helping to manage Crestbrook and his brother's investments, along with seeing to the care and education of his nieces and nephews, Rupert would be the only Cummings left standing once Perceval passed.

"I suppose it is time I go to see Lord Cressley. Might you provide his address to me?"

Ousley did so and encouraged Rupert to let him know when the viscount was gone. Then, he said, "I am here for you, Major Cummings. That is, if you wish to retain my services."

"I will most certainly do so. You have been a faithful retainer to my family for years. I appreciate how you have looked after our interests, and I look forward to working closely with you in the future."

He left the solicitor's offices and hailed another hansom cab, giving the driver an address in Mayfair. As they came closer to his final destination, he could see this area was most likely the most desirable in London. His mind swirled at everything he had been told. One thing Rupert was certain of, however, was that he would not squander his life the way his brother had. He was obliged to wed and provide an heir and keep the family holdings secure for all future Viscount Cressleys.

When they arrived, he paid his driver and then approached the door to the large townhouse. Knocking briskly, he was faced with a footman who answered his knock.

"I am Major Cummings, here to see my brother. Lord Cressley," he added, watching the footman's eyes go wide.

"C-Come in, Major," he said, clearly thrown by Rupert's sudden appearance.

Rupert stepped inside, looking about the foyer, seeing nothing had changed. He had been a different man when he last set foot here.

The footman closed the door, still looking a bit flustered. "Please wait in the foyer a moment if you would, Major."

He gazed about the foyer, seeing two beautiful paintings hanging on the wall. One was a landscape. The other was of a woman, richly dressed. He wondered if she might be his mother.

"All this will be mine," he said in wonder, still finding it hard to comprehend how quickly things were changing in his life.

The footman appeared with an older man in tow, and he gave them his attention.

"Good day, Major. I am Bowers, Lord Cressley's butler. His lordship is with his physician now. If you will accompany me to the drawing room, I will let Dr. Thayer know you are here and wish to speak with him." The butler paused. "Will you be staying with us?"

"I will. Lord Cressley asked that I sell my commission and come to him. I assume with him being ill that he needs my assistance."

A shadow crossed the butler's face. "His lordship is gravely ill, Major. I will have a room made up for you. Now, if you would follow me."

Rupert was taken to a drawing room. He wandered about it for a few minutes, taking in the furnishings, and then turning his gaze out the window, which overlooked the square the house sat upon. Then he sensed a presence and glanced toward the door, seeing a thin, tall man entering. He moved toward him.

"I am Dr. Thayer, Major Cummings. Might we sit?"

"Of course."

Once they were situated, the physician said, "Lord Cressley is suffering from venereal distemper."

Immediately, he asked, "Is it the pox? Or the clap?" The two diseases ran rampant in London, which was why many titled gentlemen preferred taking one mistress rather than risking their health with infected partners.

Dr. Thayer frowned. "The pox, I am afraid. The clap would have been much easier to treat. His lordship had the typical signs of discomfort at the beginning. Pain during urination. A slight rash. Foolishly, he did not come to me and instead bought some pills and potions a friend of his recommended. There is a huge market for these so-called remedies." Thayer snorted. "They do absolutely nothing."

"By the time I was called in, Lord Cressley had begun suffering from high fevers and debilitating pain. He begged me for something to help ease his pain. After examining him, I realized what he suffered from and could offer him no hope of recovery." The doctor paused. "That is when he begged me for the mercury treatment."

Rupert frowned. "I am unfamiliar with this."

"It simply does not work," the physician said emphatically. "It is hogwash, and I refused to put Lord Cressley through it. He took it anyway, against my advice."

"What does it involve?"

"The purpose is to stimulate the patient to salivate to excess, which supposedly rids the body of the impurities of the pox. The treatments can last for well over a month. Lord Cressley made it through three weeks and by the time he returned home, he was suffering from brutal side effects. Loss of a good number of his teeth. Painful mouth ulcers. Extreme fatigue and weight loss."

"What is his prognosis?" Rupert asked.

"Death," the physician said bluntly. "At any time now. His hair has fallen out. He suffers from constant fever and muscle aches. He is almost totally blind. His heart has been damaged beyond repair. Frankly, I am surprised Lord Cressley has managed to last as long as he has."

Shock filled him, but he reined in his feelings. "Might I see him?" It was the last thing he wanted to do, but he felt he owed it to Perceval.

"Of course. I will go with you. The moment I heard you had returned home, I knew I must speak candidly with you so that you were to understand the severity of the situation."

They left the drawing room and went down the corridor to its end, entering without knocking. The drapes were pulled, and the room was quite dark, save for a lone candle burning. A servant sat by the bed, and he rose as they entered.

"Damsley, this is Major Cummings, Lord Cressley's brother," Dr. Thayer said. He turned to Rupert. "Damsley is the viscount's valet and most faithful attendant."

"I do my best to keep Lord Cressley comfortable," Damsley said.

"Thank you for all you have done for my brother," he told the valet.

"Leave," a weak voice said from the bed.

Rupert had avoided looking there and forced himself to do so now. His eyes took in the frail frame of his once vibrant brother. Perceval was ghostly white, his eyes sunk far into his skull. He looked as someone who might have been starved for weeks. As he gave Rupert a tentative smile, Rupert could see the gaps where teeth had once been.

Leaning toward the bed, he asked, "Do you want all of us to leave, Cressley?"

"You. Stay."

He straightened. "If you would please leave us." When Damsley looked upset, he added, "Just for a few minutes. I will spend a brief time with my brother and then leave to allow him to get some rest."

The physician and valet exited the room, and Rupert took the chair Damsley had vacated, scooting it closer to the bed. He took one of his brother's hands, which looked as if it belonged to a man of eighty.

"I would ask how you are, but I can tell you are in no shape to speak much," he began. "I have done what you asked, Cressley. My commission is being sold. I have returned to take care of you and Crestbrook."

Perceval wheezed and then made a gurgling sound. Rupert felt so helpless. He watched in horror as his brother finally gained control once more.

"They say . . . a night with Venus . . . a lifetime . . . with mercury."

"Why did you not take a mistress, Perceval?" he asked. "At least when you are with but a single woman, you have a better chance of not contracting disease."

One corner of his brother's mouth turned up in an attempt to smile. "And leave all . . . those women untouched?" Perceval coughed, the strain of such a simple act looking like agony on his face. "I was foolish, Rupert. So . . . so foolish. And those whom I called friends? They . . . abandoned me long ago."

They sat in silence a few minutes. He doubted Perceval had the strength to continue their conversation.

Then his brother rallied. "You are . . . my heir. No wife or sons from me. Dr. Thayer . . . says not long now." His eyes cut to a table on the bedside. "Some of . . . the laudanum. Now."

"How much?" he asked.

"Drops. On . . . my tongue. Helps."

Picking up the bottle, he squeezed the dropper, bringing the laudanum into it. Rupert brought it to his brother's mouth. Perceval opened his lips, and he placed a drop on his brother's tongue.

"More."

He added two additional drops before returning the dropper to the bottle. Then he waited.

Finally, Perceval said, "Be better than I was. Be . . . strong. Kind. Not like . . . me."

He took the bony hand. "I will. I promise." He remained standing, watching over his brother, feeling absolutely helpless because he could do nothing. Then the wheezing began again.

"I will fetch Dr. Thayer."

Rupert rushed to the door and opened it, finding both Thayer and Damsley outside the door.

"Lord Cressley's breathing is labored. Come quickly."

Both men rushed past him, and Rupert followed. The doctor lifted Perceval's wrist, pressing a finger to it.

"His pulse is weak. Barely fluttering. Administer a drop of the laudanum, Damsley."

"I have already done so," he informed them, worried that he had given Perceval three drops, while the doctor called for only one. "He asked for me to do so."

All three men stood, their gazes on the shriveled form in the bed, what was left of the man Perceval Cummings had once been. Then the labored breathing ceased. Again, the doctor took his patient's wrist. He frowned. Placed two fingers on Perceval's throat. Then he nodded slowly.

"He is gone," Dr. Thayer told them.

Guilt flooded Rupert.

Had he administered the dose which had killed his own brother?

The doctor looked to Damsley. "Go and tell Bowers. He knows what to do."

Once the valet left, Rupert had to ask, "How much laudanum had you been giving him?"

The physician shrugged. "It varied. Usually, a couple of drops."

"Would three . . . have been too much?" he asked anxiously.

Dr. Thayer shook his head. "No, my lord. Not at this point."

He started to correct the man and then it struck him.

He was now Viscount Cressley.

"Thank you for all you did for my brother. While I did not truly know him, I am in anguish, seeing how much he suffered in the end."

"Lord Cressley told me a week ago that he had no regrets. That he lived his life as he saw fit." Dr. Thayer paused. "The viscountcy is now yours to do with as you choose, my lord."

Rupert vowed he would be the best man he could be and restore the reputation of his family's name.

The doctor left, and he stayed with Perceval until Bowers and Damsley appeared. A woman accompanied them, and he suspected she was the housekeeper.

"We will care for his lordship now, my lord," the valet assured him.

"Mrs. Bowers has prepared a temporary room for you, my lord," the butler added, indicating the woman. "Of course, as soon as possible, these rooms will be cleaned and aired for your benefit."

He couldn't imagine lying in the same bed where his dead brother now lay.

"There is no rush. I will be happy wherever Mrs. Bowers has placed me. Has the vicar been sent for?"

"Yes. He will wish to discuss the funeral with you," Bowers said.

He hadn't a clue what Perceval would have preferred and decided he would let the vicar take the lead. The same went for who should be notified of the death. Rupert had no idea who his brother's friends were, although from what he had gathered, there were no true friends at all.

"I suppose I will take Lord Cressley back to be buried at Kidsgrove," he said.

"His lordship made arrangements to be buried here in town," the butler shared.

"I see. I will stay until the service is held, and then I will go to Crestbrook. I am certain there are things to be seen to there."

"Good," Mrs. Bowers said, looking relieved. "Because you will need to see to Miss Celia."

"Who?" he asked, having never heard the name, wondering if this was some elderly aunt or cousin he had never met, who his brother had taken in.

Mrs. Bowers looked at him almost apologetically. "Miss Celia is Lord Cressley's bastard daughter."

CHAPTER TWO

Millvale, Kent

L IA WORTHINGTON SAT at breakfast with her brother and new sister-in-law. She would miss Val and Eden terribly, but she was looking forward to visiting the Lake District with Mama and Tia.

Her come-out—and her twin, Tia's—had not gone as planned. Their father had collapsed on the verge of the Season, dying hours later, and it had plunged their family into mourning. Tia had been vocally resentful, and Lia could not blame her sister. Their father had never valued his three daughters, only paying attention to his heir apparent. Even Val had not garnered much attention from their frequently absent father. She knew Val would make for an excellent Duke of Millbrooke, especially now that he had wed Eden. The former governess would keep her charming brother in line.

They were a love match, just as her older sister Ariadne had made with the Marquess of Aldridge. The couple now had a six-month-old daughter, Penelope, and Val had shared with them how Julian melted at the sight of his wife and daughter.

A love match was something Lia hoped for, but she knew these were rare within the *ton*. Her practical nature would be quite happy with a kind husband who gave her an abundance of children. She hoped she would grow to love him over time, but that would not be something she needed or expected. She had been brought up to run a household and bear children, and she eagerly looked forward to both once she and her twin made their come-outs next spring.

They were in for a bit of adventure, though, since they departed today for Cumberland. Aunt Agnes, a favorite amongst all the cousins, had been her mother's closest friend for decades, since they had made their own come-outs together. When Papa had died suddenly, Aunt Agnes had accompanied them back to Millvale. Knowing she would need to stay a while, she had sent for her daughters. Having Verina and Justina here the past few months had made mourning bearable.

Now, however, Mama had decided the three of them would accompany Aunt Agnes back to Traywick Manor, where they would stay for a few months. Lia thought it was because Val and Eden were newlyweds, and Mama was trying to give them time together. She had overheard Mama talking to Aunt Agnes, saying that it was important that the servants start looking to Eden as the Duchess of Millbrooke and transfer their loyalties to her, instead of keeping them with Mama, who was now the dowager duchess.

No matter the reason, it would be exciting to travel to the northwestern part of England. Lia had read some of Mr. Wordsworth's poetry, and he had lived nearby to where Traywick Manor stood. She had always been fond of poetry and couldn't wait to see in person the places which had inspired the poet. It would be nice to pass some time in Cumberland as they awaited their come-outs.

"Try a little of the scrambled eggs," Val urged his wife, who shook her head.

"You know I do not like to eat before ten o'clock. Let me sip my tea in peace."

Eden was in the early stages of increasing. So far, she had trouble keeping food down in the mornings, and she retched several times a day.

"I worry about you," her brother said, taking his wife's hand and kissing her fingers tenderly.

"Ariadne—and even your mother—told me that this will not

last forever. That I will soon regain my appetite. Before you know it, I will be eating you out of house and home," Eden teased. She looked to Lia. "Tell him."

She smiled. "I can tell him all day, but my brother can be stubborn. He will have to see for himself."

"I will miss your practicality, Lia," her sister-in-law said. "But I know you will have a wonderful time in Cumberland. It is so scenic. There is such majesty to behold."

Eden had served as governess to Verina and Justina and had lived at Traywick Manor for five years before coming to Kent and falling in love with the duke.

"Do not tell me you miss it," Val said.

Eden smiled tenderly at her husband. "How can I miss anything when I only have eyes for you, my darling?"

She decided to slip away, her breakfast finished and leave the two in private. Going up to the bedchamber she shared with Tia, she saw two maids bustling about, adding the last of things to her sister's trunk. Lia's trunk had already been packed for two days, which grated on Tia to no end.

"Did you eat?" she asked her twin.

"Bessie brought me some tea and toast points," Tia said absently, looking about the bedchamber. "I hope I have not forgotten anything."

"If you have, you may borrow whatever you need from me or our cousins. Or we can stop and purchase it along the way."

Tia stepped closer to Lia. Throwing her arms around her, she said, "You are right. I need to relax and stop worrying."

"I am going to see if our cousins are ready," she said, heading across the hallway and entering the bedchamber since the door was already open.

Everything was neat as a pin, not a trunk in sight. Verina stood gazing out the window, and Lia came to her, slipping her arm about her cousin's waist.

"Did you enjoy your stay at Millvale?" she asked.

"It was wonderful. It was so good to see you, Tia, and Val

after so many years."

The ten cousins had been brought together in town about a decade ago. While the Worthingtons lived in Kent, the Alingtons resided in Somerset, and the Fultons in Cumberland. Because of the great distance between the three families, that had been the only time everyone in the three related families had been together. Having Aunt Agnes bring Verina and Justina to Millvale had been a terrific treat.

"Well, I cannot wait to see Traywick Manor. And reintroduce myself to Tray."

Her cousin had become the Earl of Traywick at the tender age of ten when his father and brother had been killed in a carriage accident. Hadrian, as he had been called from birth, changed his name to reflect his title. Justina told Lia that Tray had hated his given name. The ten cousins had all been named for various Roman and Byzantine emperors and empresses. While some of them, such as Verina and Justina, kept their original names, several of the cousins had opted for a more diminutive form. She was Cornelia and Tia was Thermantia, but Val had trouble saying their names, being so young. He was the one who had given them their nicknames, and they had stuck.

"Since I see no baggage, I assume everything has been taken downstairs by our footmen."

"Yes," Verina said. "Justina went to supervise them. Not that they needed it, but she likes to assert herself."

"Come, let us go downstairs. The time to depart grows near."

They walked, arm-in-arm, down to the foyer. Justina was already there, and Val and Eden joined them. Tia came bounding down the stairs.

"I haven't missed anything, have I?" her twin asked anxiously.

"We have gossiped about you incessantly," Eden teased.

Laughing, Tia said, "Then I suppose it will help prepare me for next year's Season. Mama has warned us that there are vipers within Polite Society who like nothing better than to tear others down, especially attractive young ladies making their come-outs.

Lia and I will not let them bother us. Our behavior will be impeccable."

Justina laughed. "I think you will have trouble behaving yourself, Tia. And I should know. We are too much alike."

Her cousin was right. Where Lia and Verina were more soft-spoken and unassuming, Tia and Justina were curious and outgoing. She was glad that she and her twin had such different temperaments. Although they favored one another in the face, she was a few inches shorter than her sister. Tia also had strawberry blond hair, while Lia's was auburn. Despite being so different from one another, she loved her twin more than anyone in the world.

Finally, Mama and Aunt Agnes made their appearances. Mama, ever dignified, glided down the stairs without effort. Aunt Agnes, who was still girlish at her age, smiled widely at everyone.

"Are we ready to head for Cumberland?" Aunt Agnes asked.

"Yes!" cried all four girls.

Then Eden began weeping. She gathered Justina and Verina to her. "I know these tears are because I am increasing. Everything seems to make me cry these days, but I will miss the two of you so much."

"We will miss you, too, Miss Snow," Verina said. "I mean, Your Grace."

Eden wiped the tears from her cheeks. "It was not that long ago that I was your Miss Snow."

Val slipped an arm about his wife's waist. "She is now *my* Miss Snow. An utter tyrant who orders me about all day long." He kissed Eden softly. "And I would not have it any other way."

Eden embraced Aunt Agnes. "I would say I am sorry for abandoning my post, but Val was simply too hard to resist."

"I am happy for you, my dear. You were an excellent governess, but you will be an even better duchess and mother."

The dowager duchess hugged her daughter-in-law. "Take good care of Millbrooke, Eden. He is not far removed from being one of London's rakes."

Eden smiled. "They do say reformed rakes make for the best husbands."

Val beamed. "Then I will be the best husband in all of England," he declared.

The duke and duchess walked them outside. While Val had pressed his mother to take the ducal carriage, she refused, saying it should be for his and his duchess' use. They were taking the family's second carriage, which was almost as grand and nearly as large. It was a good thing because there would be six of them inside it. Another carriage would follow with the rest of their trunks and a couple of maids.

A footman opened the coach's door, and Val handed up each of them. Lia went last.

"Take care of everyone," her brother urged. "You are the one I trust the most because you have the best head on your shoulders. Enjoy the Lake District and your time away from Millvale."

"We will be home long before Christmas," she assured him. "Mama said we will leave in mid-November. I know the roads might not be the best then, but we can take our time." She looked to Eden. "And I plan to start a journal of my own on this trip. I will record my impressions and everything I see."

As a governess, Eden had her charges write in a journal. Lia had read some of the entries in both Verina's and Justina's and thought it an excellent idea. She would be seeing so many new things and gathering new experiences, both on the journey to and from Cumberland and at Traywick Manor itself. It would be a good way to reflect upon them and have a record of her thoughts and impressions in lasting form.

She settled herself inside the carriage as Val closed the door. He signaled the coachman, and the vehicle began rolling.

Eden ran alongside the coach briefly, shouting, "Write to us! Have fun!"

Then the carriage picked up speed, and she stopped, waving madly at them, Val by her side.

"It is good to know we are leaving Millbrooke in such good hands," Aunt Agnes said. "Eden is perfect for him."

She looked at Mama, whose eyes were misted with tears. "I will miss the both of them. Millbrooke is already becoming a better duke than his father ever was. With Eden by his side, he will be a great one." She smiled. "And I cannot wait to be a grandmother again when they have children."

Mama's words surprised Lia. She, like Papa, had not spent much time with her daughters. Polite Society's view was that first sons were to be exalted and other sons and all daughters, for the most part, ignored. Yet Mama had grown closer to Ariadne during her come-out Season. Perhaps the same would be true when she and Tia made their come-outs. Her mother was usually so stern. If having grandchildren softened her a bit, Lia thought that would be a good thing.

It took almost ten days to reach Traywick Manor. By the time they arrived, Lia was tired of riding in the bumpy carriage, but she had thoroughly enjoyed the scenery during their entire journey. It was fascinating seeing the beauty of different parts of England, and she looked forward to the time they would spend in the Lake District over the next two months, as well as seeing her cousin Tray again.

As she disembarked from the carriage and the housekeeper showed her and Tia to their shared bedchamber, Lia was excited for whatever experiences lay ahead.

CHAPTER THREE

"WHAT!" RUPERT ROARED, seeing both the butler and housekeeper wince. Reining in his emotions, he asked, "When did this happen? How old is the child?"

"It must have been close to five years ago," Mrs. Bowers said. "His lordship arrived with a babe. One look at her, and I knew she had to be his. Most babes are bald, but this one had hair black as night and the same pale blue eyes his lordship did."

A chill ran through him.

"A woman was with them," Bowers continued. "Lord Cressley told me they would be going to Crestbrook the next morning." The butler shook his head. "They left—and we never saw the babe again. His lordship said not one word about her in all these years."

"I only know her name was Celia because I went up to see the woman who was caring for her," Mrs. Bowers added. "I asked if she needed anything. Her name was Newton. She was a bit frightened. When I asked if she might be the child's mother, she grew weepy but told me no, that Celia belonged to another."

"And this Celia has been at Crestbrook all these years? Did Lord Cressley ever go to visit her?"

"No, my lord," the butler said. "He never left town for Crestbrook, and Mrs. Bowers and I have been in service for many years. His lordship always remained in town."

"You can tell me nothing more of the child then?"

Both servants sadly shook their heads.

He wondered why Ousley had not mentioned the child. Then again, the solicitor might not have known of Celia's existence.

Edwards, the vicar, arrived, and Rupert took him to his brother's study. No, *his* study. He was still trying to comprehend that he was now a titled lord, in possession of a fortune.

And a niece.

"I had visited with Lord Cressley," Edwards informed him. "He knew that he was dying. The viscount gave me instructions regarding his service. His lordship wished to be buried here in London."

"Yes, my brother had a great affinity for town," he said non-committedly. "When do you suggest we hold the service?"

The clergyman said, "Two mornings from now would be acceptable," and they set the time for ten o'clock at St. George's, with burial to follow.

He knew he should put a death notice in the newspapers, and so after the vicar left, Rupert quickly wrote out the information they would need, asking Bowers to see it delivered.

"I am off to notify Mr. Ousley about my brother's passing," he told the butler.

"Shall I have your carriage readied for you, my lord?"

The question startled him. He realized he no longer needed to take a hansom cab since he had a carriage and fine team of horses at his disposal.

"Yes, please do so. Let me know when it is ready."

Rupert spent the next few minutes looking through the desk drawers, seeing if could find anything of value or interest. He found a few copies of some of the documents Mr. Ousley had gone over with him jammed haphazardly into drawers. The military had influenced Rupert greatly, and he winced seeing how disorganized Perceval had been. He would need to clean all of this out and organize it in some fashion once he knew what he had.

The trip to his solicitor's office did not take long, and the clerk greeted him by name when he appeared.

"Good afternoon, Major Cummings. Did you forget something this morning?"

Grimly, he said, "It is Lord Cressley now," causing the clerk's eyes to widen.

"Yes, my lord. I will inform Mr. Ousley that you are here."

The solicitor saw him immediately, expressing sympathy for Rupert's loss.

Eyeing the man, he said, "You know it is not a great loss to me. My brother and I were too many years apart to ever have become close, especially with no mother to help us bridge that age gap. All I wish now is do right by the title and my tenants."

He told Ousley when the funeral services would be held at St. George's and requested that he have copies of all pertinent documents, sharing he had found some in the viscount's study but that everything was terribly disorganized.

"I will keep records going forth with military precision," he assured Mr. Ousley. Then Rupert added, "There is another matter I wish to discuss with you. About Celia."

He watched but saw no recognition in the solicitor's eyes.

"I am not familiar with that name, my lord. You are the only person named in Lord Cressley's will. Is this perhaps some distant relative you have become aware of?"

"She is my brother's child."

Ousley gasped.

"Illegitimate," he said, then sharing all he had learned from the Bowers. "What are my responsibilities toward the girl?"

"Legally, none, my lord," Ousley told him. "If this Celia is his lordship's bastard, you can have nothing to do with her if that is your wish. She can be taken to a foundling home. I hear that Oakbrooke Orphanage is an excellent facility."

"No, I will assume responsibility for her," he assured the older man, knowing he could never neglect his responsibilities to a blood relative, even if Celia might have been born on the wrong side of the blanket. "Are there papers to be drawn up regarding guardianship?"

They talked about the situation, and when Rupert left the solicitor's offices, he knew he would see that the girl was educated and cared for.

By the time he arrived home, his brother's body had been placed in the library, washed and dressed by his valet. Damsley now sat beside the body.

He told Damsley, "It is not necessary for you to keep vigil."

"Begging your pardon, my lord, but I want to. From what I gather, his lordship ran off his fair share of valets over the years. I tended to him when the sickness began. I wish to see everything through until the end."

"That is most admirable of you, Damsley. Do you plan to stay on in service to me? Or would you prefer to leave my household? I would be happy to write you a recommendation if that is your choice."

The valet said, "I would be grateful if I could retain my position, Lord Cressley."

"We will make our way to Crestbrook then once the funeral is held. I have very little to be packed. Once we arrive in Cumberland, I will see a tailor and have some civilian clothes made up."

"I will see to his lordship's things being cleared from your rooms, my lord."

"You cannot sit with the body and do that, Damsley. Let Bowers and Mrs. Bowers handle that task."

"Thank you, my lord," the valet said, gratitude in his voice.

He spent the following day familiarizing himself with his new household, meeting all the servants. The Bowers removed all clothing and personal belongings from the viscount's rooms, asking Rupert what he wished done with the clothing. Since he was much taller and leaner than his brother had been before he wasted away, he told them to distribute the clothes however they saw fit.

"Give them to other servants. Sell them. I simply do not care."

The next morning, he breakfasted and went to St. George's. He told Bowers to inform the staff that they were welcome to attend the funeral. The butler frowned deeply.

"If I may be frank, my lord, I doubt anyone will wish to go. His lordship was a harsh master, with never a kind word for anyone. The staff feared him." Hesitating a moment, Bowers added, "I hope you will respect the feelings of the servants and not hold this against them."

"Please let the staff know I would never do something such as that," he assured Bowers.

He took his carriage to the church, Damsley asking if he might ride atop with the coachman to the church. Rupert gave his permission, not wanting the loyal valet to have to spend his hard-earned coin to pay for a hansom cab. When they arrived, the two entered the church together. They were greeted by the vicar, and the valet took a set near the rear of the church. Rupert went to the front, placing his palm on the closed casket.

"This is goodbye, Perceval. I am sorry we were never close. If I am fortunate enough to have sons of my own, I will do everything in my power to see they are close to one another."

Having nothing more to say, he took a seat on the front pew and waited.

No other mourners came.

He knew the death notice had run in the newspapers because he had read them yesterday. Surely, some friends of Perceval's must still be in town even though the Season had already ended. Yet not a single one took the time to come and say goodbye to him. It let Rupert know just what a dissolute life Perceval had led, with no one to mourn him in the end but a distant brother with whom he never spoke.

He returned to his townhouse, Damsley accompanying him again. As he exited the carriage and the valet climbed down from the driver's seat, Rupert said, "Thank you for coming to the service. I am certain it would have meant a great deal to my brother to have you there."

"It was my duty to do so, my lord. Lord Cressley was a hard man, and his illness only made him more difficult. I doubted anyone from the household would come this morning, which is why I needed to be there."

"Loyalty such as yours will not be forgotten, Damsley. Be ready to leave at dawn's first light tomorrow."

They parted, Damsley heading down the stairs to enter the house through the kitchens, while Rupert went through the front door. Sadness filled him, thinking of the life Perceval had wasted. He would choose to be a much different man from his brother.

THEY REACHED KIDSGROVE, a village Rupert had not seen in many years. As a boy, he had liked to walk from Crestbrook to the village, going into the various shops and speaking with the owners. He wondered if any might still remember him, since he had been gone for a decade.

His curiosity about young Celia had grown over the week it had taken to reach Cumberland. Obviously, Perceval had sired the girl, else he would not have taken her in and sent her to his country estate. Rupert wondered what the circumstances had been. Had her mother been Perceval's mistress? Or had she been some Covent Garden nun, one of dozens Perceval might have coupled with? He hoped the nursemaid who had accompanied Celia to the country was still in service caring for the girl. Perhaps she might have answers for him. If not, the truth had died with his brother.

Having never thought he would wed, much less have children, Rupert had no idea what to do with a young girl. She was family, true, but she was also a by-blow. He would have to think carefully regarding her care.

The carriage rolled up the lane, and everything suddenly became so familiar. As a boy, he had wandered these lands, knowing them like the back of his hand. He decided he would remain in the country, at least until next spring when the new Season began. He would not find himself in Perceval's shoes, without a wife or an heir. His goal would be to find a bride and bring her home. Until then, he would learn everything he could about his estate, hoping Williamson still managed it. The steward had been at Crestbrook ever since Rupert was young. Since the records Ousley had shown him proved the estate thrived, he assumed Williamson was still in charge. He wondered if the older man would resent him coming home after so many years and trying to take charge.

The vehicle turned in front of the house, and he saw two lines of servants awaiting him. He had written ahead to let whoever was in charge know of the previous viscount's death, and that the new one would be arriving home soon. Someone must have spied his carriage, and the staff had quickly been assembled to greet their new master.

The coach rolled to a stop, and his footman opened the door. Rupert exited the carriage. A man stepped from the line, and he supposed this was his country butler.

"Lord Cressley, I am Prater. I manage the household here at Crestbrook, along with my wife, Mrs. Prater. She is the house-keeper."

Mrs. Prater joined them. "It is so very good to meet you, my lord. Our condolences on your loss of the viscount."

Neither of the Praters had been in service when he had left over ten years ago, but glancing around, he did recognize a few of the servants.

"Would you please introduce me to my staff?"

The couple took him down each line, giving him the name of each servant and what they did, in the house or on the grounds. He gave a friendly greeting to those he recalled and decided to address the entire group.

"I know the previous viscount did not choose to come to Crestbrook, but that will not be the case with me. I enjoy the country and plan to make Crestbrook my permanent home."

He caught the pleased smiles and continued. "I do plan to attend the Season next spring. Hopefully, I will return with a bride. I want to fill the halls of Crestbrook with children."

A footman whom he'd favored spontaneously began clapping, and suddenly, the entire staff applauded his words.

"Thank you for your service to the previous viscount and to Crestbrook itself. I look forward to getting to know each of you."

The Praters led him into the house, and Mrs. Prater asked if he would like tea.

"I would welcome a cup, Mrs. Prater."

"Your rooms are ready for you, my lord," the butler informed him. "Shall I unpack for you?"

"I brought my valet with me, but there is very little to unpack, Prater. You see that I still am wearing my major's uniform. I will need to make an appointment with the village tailor and have new clothes made up for me."

"I can send word now, my lord. I am sure Mr. Burrows could see you tomorrow morning for a fitting if you so desire."

"Do so," Rupert said, wanting to shed his military clothes and settle into civilian life.

The butler left, and Mrs. Prater asked, "Shall I take you to the drawing room and have your tea sent there, my lord?"

He chuckled. "I remember where the drawing room is," he said with a smile. "After all, I did grow up at Crestbrook."

"Prater and I were not certain of the circumstances. We were hired almost five years ago by an employment agency to come and work here. The previous couple who managed the estate for Lord Cressley were ready to retire."

"Before you leave, Mrs. Prater, I do have one question. Where is Celia? And does the nursemaid she came with still care for her?"

The housekeeper looked apprehensive at his question.

"Newton is still employed to care for the girl, my lord. Miss Celia will be five soon." She paused. "Or she may already have turned five. I am not certain. They were here when we arrived. Newton is very tightlipped, so I can tell you nothing about her or the girl."

"I was disappointed they were not here to greet me."

The housekeeper frowned. "Newton is an odd one, my lord. Something is . . . off about her. She and Miss Celia come and go as they please. Most likely, they are traipsing about somewhere."

Concern filled him, but Rupert gave the housekeeper a pleasant smile. "I, too, loved to roam Crestbrook as a child. I do wish to meet both of them, however. Please bring them to me as soon as they return to the house."

"Yes, my lord."

Rupert made his way up to the drawing room. It seemed to sit forlornly, as if it knew no one ever used it. He hoped to meet his neighbors and become active in the local community. He was not a man to sit idly about, and so he would become involved in the management of his estate and hopefully get to know others in the community.

As he waited for tea to arrive, he wandered about the room, pausing at a globe. He gave it a spin.

Suddenly, a blur flashed before him, and the globe stopped spinning. A young girl had halted its rotation.

"You must be Celia," he said gently, not wishing to frighten her.

"It's mine," she said, stroking the globe possessively.

"Actually," he said lightly, "it is mine. This house is mine. Everything in it is mine."

She frowned, studying him carefully, her light blue eyes serious. Then she asked, "Are you my father?"

CHAPTER FOUR

HER QUESTION STARTLED Rupert. He had never been around children in his life, and he had no idea how to explain to this young girl the very complicated situation she was in.

He looked at her bedraggled appearance, anger seizing him. She was definitely a Cummings. Her black as night hair and unique eye color marked her as a child Perceval had sired. Celia's hair was a tangled mess, however, matted as if it had not been brushed in a week or more, while her gown was stained and too small for her. The Newton woman who had been hired to look after this child had neglected her terribly. He wanted to speak to that servant immediately—and most likely, dismiss her. If he did, however, he would need to immediately hire a new nursemaid. Or perhaps even a governess. He simply did not know who was supposed to look after a five-year-old or what they did with a girl that age.

Celia gazed up at him with solemn eyes, waiting for his reply. He thought it might be better if they could look one another in the eyes, so he knelt before her.

Hoping to redirect their conversation, he asked, "And how old might you be?"

She cocked her head and then said excitedly, "Five! I am five. That's what Newton says."

"Are you certain?" Rupert asked. "Why, I thought you might be forty and five, a very old person with gray in her hair."

She giggled, a sweet sound which tugged at his heart. "Like Mrs. Prater." Celia frowned. "She doesn't like me. She yells at me."

Hearing that upset him. "Does Mrs. Prater help care for you?" he asked, hoping she would actually open up about her relationship with Newton.

Shaking her head, Celia said, "No. I'm not supposed to talk to her. Or any other servants."

He had already been angry at Perceval for sending his daughter away to the country, but now it seemed as if the child were being punished for something she had no control over, being a by-blow, isolated from everyone.

"Who told you not to speak with Mrs. Prater?"

"Bets."

He frowned. "And who exactly is Bets?"

"Bets is really Betsy," Celia confided. "That's her *whole* name. She likes to be called by *part* of her name," the little girl explained very matter-of-factly.

"So, what do you and Betsy do together?"

She shrugged, suddenly going shy, so Rupert decided he would have to guide her responses through gentle questioning. He had done his fair share of interrogating spies. He wondered how much information he might be able to pull from his niece.

"Does Bets help you dress?"

Celia nodded.

"Does she comb your hair?"

She nodded again, offering no new information.

"Hmm. It looks as if Bets forgot to comb it this morning."

"Sometimes, I comb it," Celia said proudly. Then she frowned. "But it is very tangled today. I couldn't get the comb through it."

"Then it seems as if I will need to comb it for you," he suggested.

She brightened. "Would you?"

"I would be happy to do so."

He heard the door open and spied Prater carrying in a tray. The butler's eyes widened when he caught sight of Celia, who ducked under the table the globe stood upon. Quickly, Rupert pulled her out and held her hand firmly as she squirmed next to him.

The butler hurried across the room and set down the tray. "I am sorry, my lord. The girl knows she is not allowed here."

"Why is that?" he asked, glowering at the butler.

"Because . . . she is . . . not. That is how it has always been."

"A new viscount means new rules, Prater," Rupert said sternly. "I will be speaking to you—and the entire staff—about this. For now, fetch a cup of milk for Miss Celia. She can share in my tea with me."

"Yes, my lord," Prater said, scurrying from the room.

Rupert released his hold on his niece, and she scampered away. This time, he held out his hand, giving her a choice, hoping she would take it voluntarily. She came to him and did so, seeming to trust him, and he led her to a settee.

"I have come a long way," he told her. "From London, the largest city in England. It is one of the largest in the entire world. I am very hungry, though. Would you like to share what has been brought?"

Her eyes lit up as she looked at the food upon the tray. It contained a couple of sandwiches, a slice of cake, and two blueberry scones.

"I can?" she asked in wonder, looking at the food.

His belly lurched. She was thin as a rail, and he wondered how often she was being fed. He decided to steer the conversation back to this Bets.

"Here, let me settle you."

He clasped her waist and lifted her to the settee, taking the seat beside her. Taking the plate, he placed one of the sandwiches upon it.

"Here. Try this sandwich first. If you eat all of it, you may have some cake."

Her eyes gleamed. "I promise. I will eat it all. Then I can have cake!"

Rupert placed the plate in her lap, and she tried to pick up the sandwich, which was much too large for her to hold.

He picked up a knife. "Let me cut it in half for you." He did so and separated the halves on her plate.

She looked up at him, her eyes round. "You can have one of these if you want."

It was good to know she had a generous nature. That would be a start.

"Why don't you eat what is on your plate, and I will eat this other sandwich."

She clapped her hands in delight, then she picked up one of the halves and bit into it. He was shocked because her manners proved to be atrocious. She practically shoved food into her mouth and tried to speak to him while her mouth was full.

In a gentle but firm tone, Rupert said, "No talking while food is in your mouth. That is one of the rules you must follow."

"Rules?" she asked, chewing with her mouth open.

"Another rule is to chew with your mouth closed. No one likes to see what your food looks like all mushed up inside your mouth. This is the way to do it. Take a small bite—not a large one—and chew as thus."

Rupert demonstrated and saw she watched him carefully.

"Let me try!" she cried, taking a dainty bite and chewing as he had.

When she swallowed, he praised her, saying, "You learn quickly, Celia. I am very pleased with you. Eat the rest of your sandwich that very same way. And all of your meals in the future."

She looked up at him. "What is learn?"

It appalled him to know she did not know such a simple word.

"Celia, have you been taught your letters? Or numbers?"

"No," she said, looking very small and a bit frightened, as if she had done some wrong.

He didn't know if this Bets could read or write, or if she might be illiterate. Why, she might even be this child's mother, despite having told Mrs. Bowers that she was not. But would a mother treat her own child in such a disgraceful manner, letting her go about looking like a savage, not even teaching her the basics of how to consume food?

Prater appeared with the cup of milk, and he brought it to the table, placing it upon the tray.

Though it was unusual for a servant to be thanked, he wanted his niece to practice her manners. Looking at Celia, Rupert said, "This is where you would say, 'Thank you, Prater,' because he has done something nice for you. It is good for you to appreciate kindness from others."

His niece looked at the butler and parroted Rupert's words. "Thank you, Prater."

For his part, the butler appeared stunned, but he found his voice. "You are welcome." When Rupert eyed the butler stonily, Prater added, "Miss Celia."

"That will be all for now, Prater. Thank you."

The butler left, and he watched his niece eat. As she did, he asked her a few more questions, and she was clever enough to wait until she finished chewing and swallowing each time before replying. Apparently, she remembered lessons taught to her, which was a good thing.

"Where do you think Bets is now?" he asked.

"I don't know. Maybe in the village?" Celia suggested.

"Why would she go to the village and leave you here if she is supposed to watch you?"

Celia shrugged. "She leaves me by myself a lot. Bets tells me to stay in the nursery, but I don't have anything to do there."

"Are there no toys or dolls? No books?"

"A few blocks. The doll has a broken head. And no books."

Anger simmered within him. This child was being sorely neglected. "What do you do when Bets is gone?" he asked gently, not wanting her to be frightened by his growing rage.

"Well, I go inside rooms. I like this room. I like looking at books. The ones with pictures."

"And the globe?"

She frowned, so he pointed in the globe's direction. "Oh, you mean the round ball that spins. I like it a lot."

Over the next several minutes, he got out of her where she went in the house and how she tried to avoid the servants since she was never supposed to leave the nursery.

"I even go outside," she confided. "I like to run and smell flowers."

He could not imagine how limited and boring Celia's life had been up until now. The first thing he would do would be to find her a governess. Of course, he had absolutely no clue how to go about doing so.

By now, she had finished both halves of her sandwich and looked at him expectantly. "Is it time for cake? One time, Bets brought some to the nursery. She let me have a bite of it. It was so good!"

"Yes, you may have the entire slice of cake."

Rupert placed the cake on her plate and returned it to her again. Before he could hand her a utensil to eat it with, she grabbed the cake with her hand.

"No," he said sharply, shocked by her behavior.

Then he saw her wince as she withdrew her hand, her eyes filling with tears.

In a kinder tone, he said, "Cake is very messy, Celia. That is why you must use a fork to eat it."

He demonstrated how to use a fork, the girl watching him carefully all the while. "You try, now," he said, handing her the fork.

"Like this?" she asked, obviously wanting to please him.

"That is exactly right." Then he asked, "Have you ever used a spoon or fork before?"

"Sometimes, I have a spoon, but I haven't seen that before."

Here she was, five years of age, possessing no sense of good manners, simply because someone had been too lazy to teach her properly. It might be hard to find a governess who would take her on in such a state.

At that moment, Rupert decided he would always do right by Celia. He would teach her himself until he could hire a companion for her.

"Let us get the cake off your hand first."

She held up her hand and began licking it, and he kept his face neutral, not wanting her to feel as if she did something wrong. When she finished cleaning it with her tongue, he handed her a napkin.

"Wipe your hand on this. And after every bite or two, wipe your mouth on it. Mouths can get messy when you eat, especially something delicious, such as this chocolate cake."

That earned him another giggle, which was fast becoming the sweetest sound he had ever heard.

After she ate all the cake, Celia asked if she could have one of the scones. It surprised him someone so young and small could eat so much. Then again, he had a suspicion she had not been fed well up until now.

Rupert finally decided to address her question from earlier after she finished her scone, wiping her hands and mouth with the napkin. He taught her to fold it instead of leaving it wadded up.

"Would you like to come sit in my lap?" he asked, thinking his niece had never had any affection shown to her.

Her eyes widened, and then she smiled. "Yes. Please."

Before he could scoop her up, she scrambled into his lap, snuggling against him. A warmth filled him, an odd feeling he had never experienced before. He decided that they had formed an instant bond. Even though he knew next to nothing about Celia, Rupert believed that he already loved her wholeheartedly.

He had never loved anyone before.

Slipping his arms about her, he said, "You asked me before if I might be your father. The answer to your question is no. Your father is Lord Cressley, and I am his brother. That makes you my niece."

He paused, letting her take in that information.

"Then . . . what do I call you?"

Now came the tricky part. "I do have something to tell you, Celia. It may make you sad. Your father has passed recently. I am now Lord Cressley."

He stroked her matted hair. "That means everyone else will be calling me Lord Cressley. You should call me Uncle Rupert, though."

She gazed up at him solemnly. "Uncle . . . what?"

"Rupert. It is my name. Uncle Rupert."

She tested it out. "Uncle Rupert." Celia smiled at him. "Uncle Rupert," she repeated. "I like that."

Then she grew quiet a moment, and he could see her thinking, so he asked, "What is it, Celia? What are you thinking about?"

"Bets said that my mother died. Is that what my father did—die? Are they together now? When do I get to see them?"

"Passed—and died—means that someone is gone forever." Cautiously, not knowing how to tread through these waters, he added, "You will not see them again. If we are good to others, when we die, we go to heaven. That is where your parents now are."

Her brow wrinkled. "Where is heaven?"

"Have you been taken to church before?"

She shook her head.

"Well, you and I will go to church every Sunday. That is a place where you learn about God. He lives in heaven."

Rupert had not graced the inside of a church in over two decades, but he now believed it important to take his niece to Sunday services.

"Bets said she and my mother were friends. She told Bets to look out for me. My father also told Bets that."

Quietly, he asked, "Do you think Bets has done a good job of looking after you? Does she play with you or sing to you? Does she read to you or take you on walks?"

Celia grew thoughtful. "No," she whispered.

"Then it may be time for Bets to go back and live where she did before the two of you came to Crestbrook." He hesitated. "Would you miss seeing her?"

Celia shook her head. "No."

His eyes misted at how this small girl had been treated for the first five years of her life. Rupert kissed the top of her head.

"Why did you do that?" she asked.

"Because I am your uncle, and you are my niece." Then he decided she needed to hear and be shown she was a creature of value. "And because I love you."

"Love me? What is . . . love?"

"It is something that I hope I am going to show you all about."

Rupert rose, Celia still in his arms, and rang for Prater. When the butler appeared, his eyes widened, seeing Celia asleep in Rupert's arms.

"I do not know what has been done to—or for—this child," he said quietly, anger in his tone. "She is my niece, and as the daughter of the previous Viscount Cressley, she will be treated accordingly. Have the kitchens heat water for a bath. She needs to be bathed, and her hair washed. Has this Bets returned?"

Disdain crossed the butler's face. "That one comes and goes as she pleases. I have no idea where she might be, my lord."

"And none of you thought to care for the child because her caretaker was absent all the time? You, Prater, should have written to Lord Cressley and informed him what a terrible disservice this woman was doing to his own child. She is to be dismissed at once—and I intend to be the one to do so."

"I will go to the kitchens now, my lord."

It angered Rupert that his butler ignored everything which had been said. He would have to seriously consider whether or not he wished the Praters to remain in service to him. So far, he did not think either had exercised good judgment, at least as far as Celia was concerned.

At the door, Prater stopped. "There is no bathing tub in the nursery, my lord. When Newton does bathe the child, she does so in the kitchens."

"Have the water sent to my rooms," he instructed. "I will bathe my niece myself."

Shock crossed the butler's face, and his jaw fell open.

"You are dismissed," Rupert said brusquely.

He waited half an hour before heading upstairs, Celia still asleep in his arms. Servants exited his rooms, buckets in hand. They avoided his gaze.

Entering the viscount's rooms, he moved to the bathing chamber, where Mrs. Prater stood, nervously ringing her hands.

"I will supervise Miss Celia's bath, my lord."

"You will assist me," he said, his tone brokering no objections. "And let me say this, Mrs. Prater. I believe you and your husband have been neglectful of my niece."

"But it wasn't our job to—"

"Stop," he ordered. "You saw the girl lacked in supervision. Why, she looks a fright and ate like an animal. This Newton is nowhere to be found. It was your responsibility to see to Celia's proper care. To write to Lord Cressley and describe to him how intolerable the situation was."

Rupert paused. "Your lack of good judgment, along with your husband's, may have cost both of you your positions at Crestbrook."

The housekeeper began trembling. "Please, my lord. Give us another chance. We both were terrified to speak up. The letter his lordship sent with Newton made it quite clear that he wanted nothing to do with the girl. It was left for us by the previous couple who ran Crestbrook. They told us Lord Cressley never came to the country. He cared little for his estate and its staff and tenants. We feared if we contacted him, it would cost us our positions."

Sympathy filled him. "Thank you for explaining the situation to me, Mrs. Prater, but I will tell you now that you both currently walk on thin ice. I expect common sense and good judgment from servants in your position. You lead my staff, and they follow whatever lead you set. I will speak to everyone together, but you and Prater must treat Miss Celia with all the respect a child of a viscount is due." He paused. "Else you will be dismissed without references."

"I understand, my lord."

Gently, he stroked his niece's cheek. "Wake up, Celia. It is time for your bath."

She opened her eyes, stretching sleepily. Then she caught sight of the bathing tub. "Where am I?"

"The kitchens were too busy for you to have your bath there," he said cheerfully. "I brought you to my rooms so that you might use my bathing tub. Does that meet with your approval?"

"Yes," she said timidly.

"Then we shall remove your clothes and place you in this warm water. Mrs. Prater is here, and she will help me bathe you."

He looked to the housekeeper and indicated for her to undress Celia. For his part, Rupert stripped off his coat and rolled up his sleeves to his elbows. Scooping up his niece, he lowered her into the bathing tub.

"Oh, this feels so good," she told him, leading him to question if she had ever bathed in heated water.

He had her tilt back her head, holding her nape in his palm to steady her. "Relax. This will feel good," he said as he poured warm water over her hair, thoroughly wetting it. He was afraid to ask about the last time it had been washed. Then he took the cake of soap and lathered it up, washing her hair as Mrs. Prater scrubbed her limbs.

When she was thoroughly washed, he had her to stand and rinsed the soap from her hair and thin body. The housekeeper held out a bath sheet, and he lifted his niece and allowed the woman to wrap Celia in it.

"Fetch one of Miss Celia's gowns and a comb, Mrs. Prater."

Rupert picked her up and took her into his bedchamber, sitting with her in a chair by the window until the housekeeper returned.

"I can dress and comb her hair, my lord."

"You can do so in the future while I am looking for someone new to care for her. I will take care of my niece now."

"I brought her nightgown, my lord. It must be close to her bedtime."

"Good thinking, Mrs. Prater. That will be all."

Celia piped up, "Thank you, Mrs. Prater," making Rupert's heart swell with pride.

As the housekeeper left, he asked, "What did you thank Mrs. Prater for?"

She thought a moment. "Well, she had water for me. Hot water. And she went and got my comb."

"All good reasons to thank her as you did." He cupped her cheek. "You are a sweet girl, did you know that?"

His niece bit her lip. "Bets says I'm a bad girl."

Blood boiling, he merely smiled. "Bets has been wrong about most everything. You will not be seeing her again."

He slipped the nightgown over her head, and then had Celia sit in the chair while he stood behind her, working on her hair. It took a good hour to untangle the ungodly mess, and he even apologized a few times for being too rough.

"I don't mind, Uncle Rupert," she assured him. "I know you love me."

And he did. He truly did.

When her hair was free of tangles, he picked her up and carried her upstairs to the nursery. It consisted of the nursery itself, a schoolroom, and two bedrooms. Celia showed him her small bed in the nursery, and he placed her upon the mattress.

She leaned up and hugged him. "Thank you for coming here."

"I plan to stay at Crestbrook," he told her. "I will have to go to town—London, the city I told you about—but perhaps you might wish to go with me."

He knew children were never brought to town, but already, this sprite had wriggled her way into Rupert's heart. He could not abandon her next spring and be gone for months during the Season. The bride he selected from the Marriage Mart would be made to understand that she was not only taking on a husband, but she would also have a niece to help raise.

Celia lay back against the pillow. "Goodnight, Uncle Rupert." She yawned.

"Goodnight, Celia." He kissed her brow. "I will see you to-morrow."

Her eyes drooped and then closed. Moments later, she was breathing evenly. He pulled the bedclothes over her and watched her a moment, wondering how Perceval could have exiled this wonderful creature. He had never seen his daughter after sending her to Crestbrook. Rupert only knew he would be a better father figure to this girl than her real father ever had been.

Returning downstairs, Prater lingered in the corridor. Seeing him, the butler hurried to him.

"My lord, Newton has come home."

"Where is she?" he asked, tamping down his temper.

"Waiting in the kitchens."

"Have her come to my study."

CHAPTER FIVE

L IA ALLOWED ESTHER to remove her gown and set it aside. Moving to the jug of hot water that had just been delivered, she poured some into the basin and began to wash. It had been hot in the coach for the second week of September, but Aunt Agnes said things would start to cool rapidly now they were in the Lake District.

"I hope Tray will be here for dinner," Tia said as Esther helped her from her gown. Her twin joined Lia at the basin, wetting a cloth and moving it across her face.

"I heard one of the servants mention that he was out on the estate with his steward," she said. "I am certain he will be here for dinner. He will have been informed that his family has arrived, along with us."

Lia had noticed that Aunt Agnes had quickly learned all the names of the Millvale servants, and she decided it would be something she would do here while at Traywick Manor. Eventually, she would be mistress of her own household, and she believed quickly learning the names of all the servants would be important.

The maid helped her dress in a fresh gown, which had just been unpacked, and she was glad Esther had accompanied them from Kent to Cumberland.

"Do you think you will miss Millvale?" she asked.

"I'm not sure, my lady," Esther replied. "It's a bit exciting going so far and seeing new places. I figure I'll enjoy what I can, but when we get home to Millvale, I think I'll be ready to sleep in my own bed."

That caused Lia to yawn. "My, I hope I will be able to stay awake through dinner."

"The journey to Cumberland was long," Tia said. "I am glad we have come here, however. It was nice of Aunt Agnes to invite us."

"Our being gone will give Eden time to establish herself as the new Duchess of Millbrooke in Mama's absence. Already, everyone at Millvale adores her. Aunt Agnes will need to find a new governess for Justina and Verina, though. I doubt any of them will live up to Eden, however."

Neither twin needed anything done to their hair, and Lia suggested they head to the drawing room, where Aunt Agnes had said to meet before dinner. Upon entering the room, she saw Tray standing at the window. He turned, breaking into a smile.

"Cousins!" Tray came toward them, opening his arms wide and embracing them both. "You have changed so much. I would not have recognized either of you."

"So have you," she said. "You are so incredibly tall, just as your father was. You also have his coloring and deep blue eyes. We were but children when we last saw one another. You were still Hadrian then." Lia paused. "We are very sorry you lost Lucius and your father, Tray. It must have been hard, especially because you were so young."

"It was the most terrible thing," he admitted. "Lucius and I were a little less than two years apart. We were not only brothers. We were the closest of friends. And our entire household revolved around Papa."

"I remember how kind he was," Tia said. "To all the children. We were told that he and Aunt Agnes were a love match."

Tray nodded solemnly. "The light went out of Mama's eyes for a long time. I know it was difficult for her, not only losing a child but also the husband she adored. Fortunately, Mama is made of strong stuff. She knew she still had three other children to raise. We are all very close to one another."

"How long will you be at Traywick Manor?" Lia asked.

"I will be going back to university next week." He smiled. "I am glad I was still here to see the two of you and Aunt Alice. I was afraid I might miss you."

"This is your last year at Cambridge, isn't it?" asked Tia. "What are you studying?"

Tray began speaking of his interests, and Verina and Justina entered the room. He paused to greet his sisters, and Lia could tell how much they loved one another. For a moment, she missed Ariadne and Val terribly. She had hoped to spend time with her older sister during last Season, getting to know Julian and playing with Penelope. Hopefully, things would work out, and she and Tia would be able to make their come-outs next year and see Ariadne often during the Season.

Mama and Aunt Agnes joined them, and Tray warmly greeted his mother and aunt.

"My, Traywick, you have turned into a man," Mama said. "A very tall, large man. Thank you for allowing us to stay at Traywick Manor for a bit."

"My home is open to you at any time, Aunt Alice. I am thrilled you came to visit and that you brought Lia and Tia with you. I am only sorry that Uncle Charles is gone. I know you miss him."

The butler appeared and announced that dinner was ready. They went to the dining room.

"Sit wherever you like," Aunt Agnes said. "We do not stand on formality at Traywick Manor."

The soup course was a brought in, and Aunt Agnes said, "Tell us news of the neighborhood during our absence, Traywick. I left early last march before the Season began in April. It seems as if I have been away from home a very long time."

"The biggest news is that Lord and Lady Roy's daughter accepted an offer of marriage from a viscount. She will be marrying next week at the church in Kidsgrove. And Mr. Peck has been ill recently. From what I gather, he will not see Christmas this year."

Tray continued to mention others in the neighborhood, people that Lia hoped she and Tia might get to meet.

Then Tray said, "How could I forget some of the biggest news of all? Lord Cressley has passed."

"He must have done so in town," Verina said. Turning to Lia and Tia, she said, "Lord Cressley's estate, Crestbrook, is adjacent to Traywick Manor. I have never laid eyes upon him because he never comes to the country."

"Never?" questioned Tia. "That seems odd."

"There are those who favor town over country," Aunt Agnes said. "Viscount Cressley was certainly one of those men who did so." She frowned. "He did not have a pleasant reputation. It is probably best that he left his estate in the care of his steward. Mr. Williamson does a wonderful job managing Crestbrook."

"I agree," Tray said, "He is in frequent contact with our steward. They enjoy sharing ideas."

"Who has claimed his title?" Lia asked, curious.

Aunt Agnes said, "That would be his much younger brother, Rupert Cummings. He went into the army years ago. I suppose Cummings will need to sell out and come home now to take on his duties as the new Viscount Cressley. You cannot have a viscount traipsing about a battlefield, can you?"

"I vaguely recall Rupert," Tray said. "He is several years older than I am, but I would see him in the village occasionally. Then he seemed to vanish."

"From what I gather, he left for university and never returned to Crestbrook," Aunt Agnes said. "There had to be at least a dozen years—if not more—between him and Cressley. They were never close."

She thought it sad for brothers not to be close to one another. She and Tia were close to Val and Ariadne and could not imagine being distant or even estranged from them.

"Well, if he is worth his salt, the new viscount will come to Crestbrook and see how it is being managed, at the very least," Tray declared.

"If he does, we must ask him to dinner, "Aunt Agnes said. "Cressley has no family to support him. It would do him good to meet his neighbors again after so long a time. I hope he will become involved in life in the neighborhood."

The topic turned from the new Lord Cressley to other matters. After dinner, they adjourned to the drawing room. Verina and Justina played and sang for them, wanting their brother to hear some of the musical pieces they had been working on that summer.

"It just struck me," Tray said. "Where is Miss Snow? She always dines with us."

Justina said, "I cannot believe we forgot to tell you. Miss Snow wed our cousin Val!"

"Miss Snow . . . is now a duchess?" Tray said. Then a slow smile crossed his face. "She will do quite well in the position. Miss Snow—that is, Her Grace—is kind and intelligent. Good for her."

Lia liked that her cousin had not been judgmental. Even though Eden's father was a viscount, she believed others might gossip some about her and the fact she had wed such a man of high rank and wealth. Lia liked Cousin Tray all the more for his enthusiastic response to the news regarding Val's marriage.

They made plans to go riding together after breakfast the next day, Tray wanting to show his cousins his estate.

"It is not as grand as that of your ducal brother, but I am proud of Traywick Manor. We will also need to introduce you around the neighborhood."

He looked to both twins. "I have expressed condolences to Aunt Alice, but I neglected to do the same to you. I am sorry you have lost your father."

"Thank you," they said in unison, as they often did when others addressed them.

"It was long journey here. I believe I am ready to retire for the evening," Mama told the group.

"I agree, Alice," Aunt Agnes said. "Goodnight to you all."

All four girls decided they, too, were in need of sleep, and bid Tray goodnight.

Lia was eager to ride out tomorrow and see more of Cumberland. The passing scenery in the carriage had been breathtaking, and she knew she would enjoy their morning ride.

⟫⟫⟫⟪⟪⟪

RUPERT UNDERSTOOD HE must keep his temper in check. He needed to glean as much information as he could from Newton before dismissing her.

A knock sounded at his study's door, and he said, "Come."

Prater stepped inside. "I have Newton for you, my lord."

"Show her in."

He remained seated behind his desk and watched as a woman came through the door. She was dressed better than the average servant and appeared to be in her mid-twenties or a bit older. She was fairly pretty, but he detected a hardness about her.

She came to stand before the desk, and he nodded at Prater and said, "That will be all."

The butler closed the door, leaving him with Newton.

Rupert thought he might get more out of her if she were comfortable in his presence, so he said, "Please take a seat, Newton." As she did so, he added, "Or should I call you Bets?"

She flashed him a flirtatious smile. "Bets is fine, my lord." Batting her lashes at him, she added, "It is short for Betsy, but I've always preferred Bets. A little saucy, don't you think?"

"Your speech is bold for a servant's, Bets."

She cocked her head. "Well, I am not so much a servant as I am someone who . . . looks after one of your family members. I have learned that Lord Cressley is no more. Not directly, of course. Strictly through the gossip of servants." She paused. "You must be the younger brother. Maude mentioned you once to me."

"Maude?" he asked easily, knowing he was getting somewhere now.

"Yes. Maude is Celia's mother. She was my dearest friend in the world."

"I am surprised Cressley did not have Maude accompany Celia and you to Crestbrook."

"That's because she died giving birth to the brat," Bets said brazenly, and then looked contrite. "The girl, my lord."

"You must have been very good friends with Maude to have known about her liaison with my brother."

"Oh, Lord Cressley got a house for us. A bit on the smallish side, but a house, all the same," she said breezily. "He would come and visit Maude there. Gave them some privacy."

"And the viscount approved of you living with Maude? I do not know of many men who keep a mistress *and* a mistress' friend."

"Well, I had fallen on a bit of hard times," Bets revealed. "I was acting as a lady's maid to Maude while she was seeing his lordship."

Rupert doubted the two women had been friends. He believed this woman nothing more than a servant.

"It was gracious of you to volunteer to care for my niece when your friend passed."

"I didn't know what to do," she declared, suddenly agitated. "There was so much blood. The midwife took her time getting there. By the time she arrived, Maude was so weak. Broken. The head was already crowning. The midwife delivered the child, and Maude was no more. I sent word to Lord Cressley. He didn't come for three days!"

Knowing only Newton and Celia had arrived at Crestbrook, he asked, "What of a wet nurse?"

Color quickly flooded her cheeks. "Well, my lord, that was part of the trouble I found myself in. I, too, had a titled gent who got a child on me. He was not half as kind as your brother, though. He washed his hands of me when he learned I carried his child."

He stared at her stonily, not certain he could believe everything this woman said. "What happened to your child?"

"She died," the servant spat out. "And I was glad for it. I lost my good figure because of her. I knew with Maude gone that I would be turned out by Lord Cressley. When he finally came, I told him I'd been nursing his babe to keep her alive. I was the one who told him that *he* needed *me*. That Maude had loved him beyond measure, and he owed it to her to take care of their child. Give it a home. And I came with that."

"So, you served as wet nurse, and the viscount sent you to Crestbrook."

"He did," she said, resentment sounding in her voice. "But I knew nothing about babes. Or children. I've had to figure things out with Celia."

"I do not think you have done anything except abstain from your obligations to my niece, he said coldly.

When she started to protest, he held up a hand to silence her.

"I have only been at Crestbrook a few hours, and I see how neglectful you have been regarding my niece. Celia's clothes are stained. Her hair is like a rat's nest. She had no table manners whatsoever and is left to roam the house and the estate while you are off doing God knows what."

Leaping to her feet, Newton said, "I never wanted to be here this long. I thought his lordship would have come by now and possibly offer another position to me instead."

The coy way she said that made Rupert burst out in laughter. "You were never going to be Cressley's mistress, Newton. If Celia has been an afterthought after all these years, why do you believe he would have thought of you, much less as his mistress?"

She sputtered, her body simmering with anger.

"I did not know of Celia's existence. Neither did our family's solicitor. And you have barely acknowledged the child you were charged to care for."

Rupert rose. "You are dismissed. You have never done a minute's worth of work. You are the last person I wish to be looking after my niece."

She crossed her arms. "You can't simply let me go."

"I just did," he said flatly.

"I am owed. I need to be paid for this quarter. I need coin to leave this horrible place in the middle of nowhere." Her eyes narrowed. "I kept the brat alive when no one else did. I nursed her until my nipples cracked. I could have tossed her out with the rubbish and told Lord Cressley that she and Maude both died. But I didn't do that, my lord."

He would do anything to get this woman as far as possible from Celia and Crestbrook.

"Where do you wish to go?"

"Back to London."

"I will give you adequate funds to purchase a ticket on the mail coach, along with a bit more so that you can have meals along the way. But that is it. Prater!" he called.

The door swung open, and he wondered just how much of the conversation the butler had overheard.

"Yes, my lord?"

"I wish for you to personally escort Newton upstairs and watch while she packs her things. See that she takes nothing which does not belong to her. And do not under any circumstances allow her into Miss Celia's room."

"I understand, my lord."

"After that, she is to be taken into Kidsgrove and left at the inn. Tell the innkeeper that I will pay for one night's stay." He turned to Newton. "Get on that mail coach tomorrow. Is that understood?"

"Yes, *my lord*," the woman snapped, flouncing from the room.

Prater hurried after her, and Rupert opened the top right-hand drawer, where he had found some pound notes and coins. He guessed at the amount needed and took it to Mrs. Prater.

"Newton is packing now under your husband's supervision." He handed the money to the housekeeper. "She is to be given this so she can return to London."

"Thank goodness she will be gone," Mrs. Prater declared. "We have been told by others in the village that Newton spent much of her time at the tavern, drinking the night away."

He wanted to call her out since she had known of Newton's frequent absences and had done nothing to protect Celia. Then again, all this had taken place under his brother's watch, or lack of it. He had told the Praters they were to have a fresh start, and he meant it.

Rupert remained in his study watching out the window until a cart appeared, Newton sitting next to the driver. It moved away from the house. Only then did he feel his niece was finally safe. He then went up to the nursery and sat beside Celia's bed.

Stroking her hair, he said to the sleeping child, "That woman is gone. She will never be seen again. I vow to protect you, Celia. No harm will ever come to you."

CHAPTER SIX

L IA AWOKE, FEELING refreshed by a good night's sleep. Tia was snoring softly, so she slipped from the bed to wash and dress. She didn't have to worry about being quiet. Her twin could sleep through the Second Coming of the Christ. Of the two of them, Tia had always needed more sleep.

She rang for Esther and admitted the servant when she arrived, placing a finger next to her lips to indicate her twin still slept. Esther could be a bit boisterous, and Lia did not want her sister awakened. The maid helped her to dress and then took a seat in the room, waiting for Tia to awaken.

She made her way downstairs to the breakfast room. Aunt Agnes had requested a buffet be set up for the first meal of the day, so everyone could choose whatever they liked. Mama and Aunt Agnes both breakfasted in their bedchambers, so it was just Tray, Verina, and Justina who were in the room when she arrived.

"How are you liking your stay in Cumberland, Cousin?" Tray asked as she filled her plate and took a seat, a footman pouring tea for her.

"I know we have only been here less than a week, but I have fallen in love with the Lake District. Your estate is beautiful, and the surrounding land is so scenic. I wish Millvale had a lake on it as you do."

"Since Tray is leaving in a few days, we should have a picnic by the lake as a farewell," Justina suggested. "We could even take out the rowboats."

"That is an excellent idea," Verina agreed. "I know Mama will not mind us doing so." She looked to her brother. "How would tomorrow afternoon be for you, Tray? Would you be available to take a respite from estate business and play a bit with us?"

"You know I am always up for a picnic," he replied. "Shall we tell Cook about it since we know Mama will approve?"

"I will draw up a menu for us so that Mama does not have to," Verina told them. "You can help me, Justina. Lia, since you and Tia are our guests, we will surprise you. We can decide what to have after breakfast and then meet with Cook."

"I think I am going to go and practice the pianoforte after I finish eating," she told them. "I have neglected it since we arrived and would like to get back to my usual routine. I trust you will include some delicious foods, especially ones which are local favorites here in Cumberland."

"We also need to draw up a list of what we would like in a governess," Justina said. "Mama told me that she plans to write to an employment agency in London to find our next governess."

Curious, Lia asked, "Is that how Aunt Agnes found Eden?"

"It has been too long. I suppose that is what Mama did," Justina said. "I was only ten when she came to us, and that was over five years ago."

"Whoever is hired must be someone who is optimistic and pleasant to be around. Those were some of Eden's best traits," she said. "While I love learning," Verina began, "I almost feel as if I should focus more on readying myself for my come-out in two years. I want a governess who is well-versed in the ways of Polite Society. One who can help me with my dancing, music lessons, and social conversations. It will be important to comport myself in an appropriate manner. Justina is younger, so she will still need a governess who can continue with academic lessons with her."

"Are you both still writing in the journals Eden gave you?" Lia asked.

"Verina is," Justina said. "I have been a bit more haphazard about doing so."

"I do think it is a good idea, to record your thoughts and feelings, whether you are undergoing new experiences or simply living your usual life," she said.

"We have a few blank journals which Eden left behind if you would like one, Lia," Verina offered. "I can put it in your bedchamber if you like. One for Tia, too."

She laughed. "Go ahead and leave one for both of us, but I doubt Tia will take the time to write in hers."

Tray excused himself, saying he had a meeting with one of his tenants. Lia went to the music room and played for an hour. She found some pieces from composers whom she enjoyed, as well as a few new to her. She decided to tackle a new invention written by Bach. It proved to be a bit frustrating, but she knew she would conquer the fingering with enough practice.

Leaving the music room, she went to the drawing room. Neither her sister nor her cousins were there. She thought Verina and Justina might still be meeting with Cook regarding plans for the picnic, so she decided to take a long walk. She had ridden the estate with her cousins each day since their arrival, but walking was something she truly enjoyed. It would be a different way to view things.

She decided to set out for the lake, which they had ridden partially around two days ago. The body of water separated Traywick Manor lands from that of Crestbrook. She thought to walk as far as the boundary between the two estates and enjoy the beauty and peace of the September day. Autumn had now come to Cumberland almost overnight, and she could not wait to see more of the Lake District. Tray had promised to take them on a tour by horseback before he left for university, and Lia looked forward to that excursion.

She continued along the path next to the water, and spied someone ahead of her, sitting on the bank. As she drew closer, she saw it was a man with dark hair, who held a little girl about four years of age in his lap. His hands were wrapped about a fishing pole, and the girl also had her small hands holding the pole. It was a sweet scene, and Lia wondered if he might be Viscount Cressley since she was nearing the border between the two estates.

Lia moved toward them, and the little girl turned her head. "Look! A lady."

The man fixed his gaze upon her, and her heart sped up.

Without a doubt, he was the most handsome man she had ever seen. His hair was dark as midnight, and he had light blue eyes which seemed to see all. His cheekbones were sharp, his lips sensual.

When had she ever looked at a man's lips—much less thought them sensual?

Heat bloomed in her cheeks. She looked away from him, turning her attention to the young girl who obviously was this man's daughter, thanks to her close resemblance to him. She was a beautiful child, with the same dark hair and blue eyes of her father.

"Forgive me if I am intruding, my lord. I do not wish to scare the fish away."

Her words made the child giggle, causing the man to smile. He quickly kissed the top of his daughter's head and said, "The fish have not been biting as of yet. But they did so quite a bit yesterday, didn't they, Celia?"

The little girl nodded. She held up a hand, four fingers showing, and proudly said, "We caught this many fish."

"How many is that?" her father nudged.

She frowned, looking at her fingers and then counted, "One. Two Three, Four. Four! We caught four fish."

"We did," he agreed good-naturedly. Then he turned his attention back to Lia. "Forgive me for not rising to introduce myself. I am Lord Cressley, and this is Celia."

"I am Lady Lia Worthington," she told him. "My cousin is Lord Traywick. I have come all the way from Kent with my mother and sister for a visit."

"It is a delight to meet you, Lady Lia. Might you like to join us for a bit?"

"Yes!" cried Celia. "Please. Come help us talk to the fish."

"All right," she said, going to sit on the bank near them, a closed basket separating her from the viscount.

"When did you arrive at Traywick Manor?" Lord Cressley asked.

"This is our sixth day here. Aunt Agnes had come to visit us in Kent, along with my cousins Verina and Justina. My brother, who is the Duke of Millbrooke, recently wed, and Mama thought it would be good if we gave the newlyweds some time to themselves at Millvale."

"Have you ever been to Cumberland before, my lady?"

"No, my lord. This is our first visit. In fact, it is really our first visit anywhere other than Kent."

"I thought you might have gone to town by now for the Season," he observed. "You look of age."

"Tia and I were to make our come-outs this past spring, but our father suddenly passed prior to the Season. Those circumstances caused us to return to Kent. That is why Aunt Agnes and my cousins came to visit us. They have been a great deal of comfort to Mama. All of us, really." She paused. "Do you attend the Season, my lord?"

"I have never done so," he said. "My older brother also passed recently, so I have not been the viscount for long."

Lia recalled now that Aunt Agnes mentioned he had been in the military. Not wanting him to think he'd been gossiped about at their table, though, she asked politely, "What were you doing before you claimed the title? Did you live in town?"

"No, I was a second son, so I became an officer in His Majesty's army."

"It must have been difficult to leave the army behind. As a second son, you most likely grew up knowing you were destined for a career in the military. I cannot imagine how hard it must be to have to adjust to a radically different kind of life."

"You are most perceptive, Lady Lia. It has been an odd transition, to say the least. A very unexpected turn of events."

Celia was grinning at Lia, and so she said, "I am certain your daughter and wife are happier being in one place instead of always being on the move with the army, especially now that the action with Bonaparte is beginning to heat up."

He smoothed the girl's hair. "Celia is my niece, my late brother's daughter."

"Oh! Forgive me, my lord. There is a strong resemblance between the two of you, and so I assumed the relationship."

Resolve filled his eyes. "Celia is mine in every way now," he said fiercely. "I am the only family she has, and I would protect her with my life."

Not all men would take to having inherited, along with a new title, a small child. Though she knew little of the new Lord Cressley, her opinion of him was already high.

"It seems you and your niece are quite close. She looks most comfortable in your lap."

He kissed the top of Celia's head again. "We have only known each other a few days, but it as if we have always been together," he revealed. "Celia has been living at Crestbrook since shortly after her birth, while I only arrived a week ago."

"Then you must be quite good with children, my lord. Your niece appears happy in your company."

Celia gasped. "Did you feel that, Uncle Rupert? I think it's a fish."

Lia looked and saw the fishing line move.

"Yes. I feel a fish tugging on the line. He is taking our bait," the viscount declared gleefully.

Over the next couple of minutes, she observed the pair as they reeled in the wriggling fish. Obviously, Celia was too young to do this by herself, but her uncle assisted her, making her feel as if she did everything on her own. Again, she was touched by the effort he put into this and the care he had for his niece.

"Lady Lia, if you might open the basket sitting next to you, we will place our fish inside it."

She opened it, finding it empty.

The viscount slipped the fish off the hook and dropped it into the basket, while Celia clapped, her smile wide. Lia closed the basket's lid, securing the flopping fish.

"You have brough good fortune to us, my lady. Do you have time to stay with us a bit longer and see if we might land a few more fish?"

"Certainly, my lord. I was merely out for a walk when I saw the two of you. I have nowhere I need to be at the moment."

Suddenly, Celia scrambled from her uncle's lap and climbed into Lia's. It surprised her, but she slipped her arms about the young child.

"You will have to see if my lap is more comfortable than that of your uncle Rupert's," she said playfully, Celia snuggling closer to her, giggling.

They talked for another hour, Lord Cressley catching four more fish during that time. He told her some about his army experiences and something of Crestbrook, which he mentioned he had not visited since his early days in university. Lia, on the other hand, told him about life at Millvale with her siblings and described the fete recently held on the estate.

"Although Eden was charged to plan the fete, she included my sister and me, along with our two cousins, in the planning."

She elaborated on the types of stalls in which merchants had sold their wares, along with food and drink, explaining how they had contacted each person and convinced them to partake in the fete. Lia gave him details about the games they had held for the children and how they had sought volunteers to oversee these contests.

"There were even competitions for the adults to enter. Eden suggested both archery and riding, but there may be more next year. I helped in designing the obstacle course."

"What is that?" he asked, clearly interested.

She described how they had set fences of varying height into place, along with digging ditches and filling them with water, which competitors then had to jump.

"It was challenging but quite fun. And then, the best part of the day came. Val, my brother, wed Eden in front of everyone at the fete. He had been off visiting his other estates and had stopped in town to purchase a special license so they could wed immediately upon his return."

"I am not clear as to who Eden is," Viscount Cressley said.

Dread filled Lia, and she hoped this man would not judge Eden harshly.

"Eden was Miss Snow before, governess to my cousins Verina and Justina. She had lived here at Traywick Manor, teaching them for five years, and accompanied Aunt Agnes and the girls to Millvale on their visit to us."

Lia carefully watched his reaction, hoping she would not see disdain upon his face. Instead, the viscount smiled, a warm, sunny smile that made her tingle.

"Then it sounds as if His Grace made a love match."

"He most certainly did, my lord. All of us adore Eden. I cannot imagine my brother with anyone else. And my sister Ariadne also made a love match a couple of years ago during her come-out Season. She wed the Marquess of Aldridge, and they have a daughter, my niece Penelope."

The viscount grew thoughtful. "I have heard love matches within the *ton* are rare, my lady. It seems as if your family is destined to find one each time someone weds."

"I will be frank with you. My parents' marriage was an arranged one, and they led very separate lives. Val says our generation can be different, though, than that of Mama and Papa's."

"So, you will make your come-out next spring with your sister?"

"Yes, that is what is planned. We were not close to Papa, but we had to abide by the rules of Polite Society. The *ton* would have been scandalized if Tia and I had ignored our mourning period in order to make our come-outs."

"I know that was not easy for you, delaying something which you had looked forward to your entire life."

"I have been more accepting of it. Tia, my twin, is still angry we had to do so, however." She paused. "Since you now hold a title yourself, my lord, will you consider going to the Season next spring?"

"I will have no choice. I must wed in order to get an heir off my wife. Also, Celia needs the tender care of a loving aunt to help me in raising her."

He smiled at the girl, and Lia looked down, seeing that Celia had fallen asleep in her lap. Her gaze met his and he told her, "I do not mean to overshare, my lady, but my niece has had no love or attention during her five years of existence. She is my brother's by-blow. Perceval sent her to Crestbrook when she was less than a week old. Her mother died giving birth to her, and the woman my brother engaged to care for Celia did a poor job."

The viscount confided the condition he had found his niece in when he arrived the previous week, her hair and clothes a mess, her manners abominable.

"Yet in just a few short days, you can see the difference in her," he declared. "She has thrived with the attention I have given her. Celia was taught nothing of her letters or numbers by this woman. Celia even had few toys to play with and no books to look at. I will need to engage a governess for her. My niece is quite bright. She will learn rapidly when given the chance. I have already started teaching her myself these past few days, and I am amazed at her progress."

"My aunt also needs to find a new governess for my cousins. She has mentioned writing to an employment agency in London. Perhaps the two of you could discuss this matter. I know Aunt Agnes would have some wonderful advice for you. She is very easy to get to know. You would quickly warm to her."

"I would be grateful for an introduction to Lady Traywick. I know nothing about children and am learning every day with Celia. Still, I cannot keep her with me every waking minute of the day. She needs supervision and to be taught under the hand of a loving, gentle governess."

An idea came to Lia.

"We are to have a picnic here tomorrow. At the lake. Traywick will be returning to Cambridge for his last year of studies, and we thought to give him a send-off. Why don't you and Celia come? It would allow you time to talk things over with Aunt Agnes—and even Mama—and you could meet the rest of my family. I am certain you are eager to make the acquaintance of others in the neighborhood. Perhaps there are even young children close to Celia's age whom she might play with."

His smile made her insides do odd things, as her belly seemed to flip in succession several times.

"That is a lovely idea, Lady Lia. Celia and I are most grateful for your invitation. If you do not feel we are putting out your aunt or Traywick, we would be delighted to come to this picnic."

Lia said, "We will come down to the water about one o'clock tomorrow afternoon. It will be on the opposite side of the lake from where we are now. You will find a boathouse nearby where we will set up. I believe we are to take out some of the rowboats on the lake."

"Oh, Celia might like that." He paused. "Only if you would come out with us, my lady. It seems my niece has taken to you."

Glancing down, she placed a soft kiss upon the girl's head, a tenderness welling within her. Lia had always known she wanted a husband and children. This moment told her she had listened to her heart and found she wanted what it did.

"I should return to the house," she said. "I have been gone a good while now, and they will be looking for me." She paused. "One bit of advice before I go, my lord. You are free to take it or ignore it."

"Now, I am curious to hear it, Lady Lia."

"I will hold in confidence what you shared with me about

Celia's birth. You seem to already love her a great deal. I see no point in telling anyone that her parents were not wed and that she is illegitimate. It serves no purpose, and she might be judged harshly for it."

"I had not thought of that," the viscount admitted. "I would never wish to do anything to harm Celia."

"Since she is a girl, naturally, you were your brother's heir. You already claim her as your niece. I would keep quiet about the circumstances of her birth."

He sighed. "I cannot keep my servants from gossiping. They may have already told others in the neighborhood of her origins."

"Ignore that. You can introduce her as Miss Celia while she is young. She will then become Miss Cummings when she is older."

"Not Lady Celia?" he asked, perplexed.

"No, a viscount's daughter is always addressed as a miss. It is only an earl's daughter or a higher rank who receive the title of lady before their Christian name."

He nodded in understanding. "I see. As you can tell, I am not familiar with all the workings of Polite Society. I do believe, though, that you have offered me excellent advice, my lady. I plan to treat Celia as my niece, and I will expect the world to do the same."

Lord Cressley rose and, leaning down, clasped her elbows, bringing her to her feet. Lia held Celia close to her, and the girl mumbled in her sleep. Handing her over to her uncle, he brought Celia close, her head resting on his shoulder. Lia picked up the basket containing the fish and handed it to him, then reached for the rod.

"Oh, dear. Should I keep this for you? You do not have a free hand."

"I can take it." He opened his right hand, and she placed the fishing rod into it. "Thank you for stopping and chatting with us, Lady Lia. You are the first person I have met in the neighborhood, beyond my tenants and staff. I look forward to meeting Traywick and the others tomorrow."

"Until then," Lia said, waving as he turned and headed toward Crestbrook.

She watched until he turned at a curve on the path and was lost to her sight. Only then did Lia head for the house. She knew her aunt would not mind that she had asked their neighbor to come to the picnic. It would be good for Tray to meet the new viscount, as well, especially since their estates were in such close proximity to each other.

Lia began to sing softly to herself as she made her way home, eager for tomorrow to hurry and come so that she might see Lord Cressley and Celia again.

CHAPTER SEVEN

L IA DECIDED TO wait and share her news when everyone was at tea together. Once they had all gathered and Mama and Aunt Agnes had poured out for them, she cleared her throat.

"I have a bit of news," she began. "I hope you don't think it presumptuous of me, Aunt Agnes, but I have invited someone to our picnic tomorrow."

Her aunt frowned slightly. "Who might that be, dear?"

"I met the new Lord Cressley and his niece while I was taking a walk around the lake earlier today."

Before she could continue, everyone began peppering her with questions.

"Wait," Mama said, causing everyone to go silent. "Let Cornelia continue uninterrupted." Her mother looked expectantly at her. "Please, continue."

"Aunt Agnes was correct in thinking that he had gone into the military. Lord Cressley attended Cambridge and then entered the army, working his way up to the rank of major. He sold out when he received word of his brother's grave illness and returned home." She paused. "He will be raising his niece, Miss Celia Cummings, as well."

"Oh, Lord Cressley wed?" Aunt Agnes assumed, and Lia did not correct her. "It does not surprise me, though. He was getting on up in years.

"The niece has recently turned five, and her nursery governess is not qualified to teach her. Viscount Cressley will be looking for a governess for Celia," Lia explained. "I asked him to tomorrow's picnic not only to meet his neighbors but also to talk with Mama and Aunt Agnes about how to go about finding a governess. I even mentioned to him that Verina and Justina also needed a new governess to take Eden's place."

"That is splendid," Aun Agnes. "Alice and I will be more than happy to guide Lord Cressley through this process."

"I am looking forward to meeting a fellow peer," Tray added. "It will be good to make Cressley's acquaintance. Thank you for facilitating a meeting between us, Cousin."

The rest of tea was spent talking about the menu Verina and Justina had created for the picnic.

"We tried to include favorites of Tray's, along with introducing our cousins to foods peculiar to Cumberland," Verina shared.

"You are going to love the damson tarts best," Justina predicted. "They are small and dainty, filled with custard and damson, which is a type of plum."

"I love anything sweet," Tia said. "What else might we be having?"

"Cook will include the usual ham and roasted beef sandwiches," Verina said. "But she will also include Cumberland sausage. It comes from selected parts of pork. The difference is that it is chopped instead of minced, so the texture is different from most sausages."

"It is also very long," Tray added. "Thicker than a regular sausage. It comes in a flat, circular coil instead of in links. The seasoning is what makes it shine, though."

"It sounds delicious," Lia said. "My mouth is already watering."

"Cook will also have some cheeses and apples for us," Justina told the group.

"You mentioned my favorites," Tray said. "I hope Cumberland Rum Nicky will be found in the baskets."

"What on earth is that?" Mama asked.

"A bit of heaven, Aunt Alice," Tray replied. "It starts with a shortcrust pastry. Cook will fill it with dried dates and other fruits which have been soaked in a blend of rum and spices before she bakes it. Last century, our own port of Whitehaven became part of the sailing route which brought ginger, sugar, spices, and even tobacco to Cumberland. Everyone who lives in this area eats Rum Nicky."

"Well, I look forward to everything we will have," Aunt Agnes proclaimed. "I only hope our weather will cooperate."

Unfortunately, the next morning the heavens opened up, and the rains came pouring down, canceling the picnic. Lia asked her aunt if she might be the one to write the note to Lord Cressley, telling him that the picnic had been postponed but would hopefully occur the following afternoon. Her aunt agreed, and she used her best penmanship as she penned the note to the viscount. She told him they would try again the next day if the weather cleared up.

An hour after a footman was sent to deliver the note, the servant returned with a message for Lia. She opened it, pleased to see that Lord Cressley had replied.

Dear Lady Leah—

I am sorry the weather has run afoul of our plans and postponed the picnic which Celia and I were to attend today with your family. My niece is most disappointed, but I have assured her that the plans are to aim for the next dry day. Hopefully, that will be tomorrow.

Thank you for notifying us. If I do not hear from you again, I will assume the picnic will happen tomorrow as planned.

My best to Lady Traywick, as well as Lord Traywick and the rest of your family. Celia and I look forward to making everyone's acquaintance.

By the way, my niece cannot stop talking of you. You made quite the impression upon her.

Sincerely,
Rupert Cummings, Viscount Cressley

Lia could not help but smile to herself, thinking how much she was looking forward to seeing Celia again.

And Lord Cressley.

She would also have to share the correct spelling of her name with the viscount and perhaps even tell him the origin of her name and that of her siblings and cousins. He would probably find it amusing. Something inside her wanted to make him smile. She believed he had lived a lonely life, perhaps not as lonely as that of his niece's, but a difficult one, all the same. He'd had no mother and never saw his father. His brother was years older, and she understood they had never been close.

From the stories he had shared with her about the army, he seemed to have found a home amongst his fellow officers and soldiers, but even that had been taken from him once he'd received word to return home. She hoped he would settle into the neighborhood and make some good friends. With the Season now over, his peers and their wives would have returned from town. Lia also hoped Aunt Agnes might help smooth the way for Lord Cressley. She decided to broach that topic with her aunt now.

She found Mama and Aunt Agnes in a small parlor. Both women had needlework in their laps, but Lia didn't think much embroidery had taken place. Even after all these years, the longtime friends could talk the day away.

"Am I interrupting anything?" she asked, standing in the doorway.

"Not at all, Lia, dear," Aunt Agnes said. "Do come in."

She took a seat and said, "I received word back from Lord Cressley, so he knows the picnic for today has been cancelled. He said Celia was disappointed, but he was trying to keep her in good spirts."

"It is good he replied to your note," Mama said. "That is the mark of a gentleman."

"Lord Cressley and I talked for over an hour yesterday while he and his niece were fishing," she told the pair. "I think he is sad to have left his army days behind."

"What, with all that killing and marching about?" Mama said. "He should be grateful he now has a title and that it gave him the opportunity to leave."

"He has not been in the area for many years," Lia said. Looking hopefully at her aunt, she added, "While it is good that the viscount and Tray meet before he returns to university, Lord Cressley will also need to get to know others. You had mentioned having him to dinner, Aunt Agnes. I hope you would still do so. You could even invite a few others from the surrounding area."

"That is an excellent idea, Lia," Aunt Agnes said. "I will set a date for next week, before Traywick leaves, and host a dinner party. Lord Cressley does need to get to know others. I hope he wants to be a more active part of the neighborhood than his brother ever was."

"From what he indicated yesterday during our conversation, he will reside at Crestbrook and only go to town for the Season."

"Good," her aunt said. "He can find a bride and become more of a leader here in our community. I look forward to making his acquaintance." She paused. "Of course, he will need to be careful when selecting his viscountess."

"Why is that, Aunt?" she asked.

"Because of the child," Mama said. "Not every young lady would wish to have an instant family. Cressley is the guardian of his niece now. The girl will be a part of the viscount's life and that of his chosen bride. The girl might not be accepted well by the new wife."

"You think the viscountess would draw a distinction between her children and Celia?" Lia asked, upset by that thought. "She is a lovely child."

"Be that as it may, most women would differentiate between

children they gave birth to and other ones in the household."

"Well, that is simply wrong," she declared. "I would never do such a thing."

Aunt Agnes said, "Of course, you wouldn't, Lia, dear. You are such a thoughtful young lady."

She felt Mama's eyes upon her and met her gaze.

"Are you interested in the viscount, Cornelia?"

Her face flamed. "No, Mama. I barely know him. This is most embarrassing."

"You are a duke's daughter. While I am certain Lord Cressley is a lovely man, you might wish to set your sights . . . higher."

"Mama!" she objected. "How can you say that?"

"Ariadne wed a marquess. You are just as beautiful as your older sister."

"But Ariadne was in love with Julian," she pointed out.

Mama frowned. "Do you seek a love match, Cornelia?"

She swallowed. "I have thought of it. But I know they are not very common amongst the members of Polite Society. I do want a man who will be kind and respectful to me." She hesitated and then spoke her mind. "You have taken to Eden, Mama. *She* is a viscount's daughter. A former governess who wed a duke."

Mama looked offended. "I do like Eden. You know that. She is beautiful and intelligent and will do well as Valentinian's duchess. Besides, a woman always tries to marry up—not down. I respect the fact Eden did so."

"But you do not wish for me to even think of wedding a viscount," she argued.

"*Are* you interested in Lord Cressley, Cornelia?" her mother pressed.

"I like him," she admitted. "He was very attentive and thoughtful to his niece. I do not really know much of him, though."

But she did. He had been open with his affection for Celia, and he had only met his niece the previous week. Already, Lord Cressley was loving and protective toward Celia. It would be a privilege if a man such as the viscount was interested in her.

"You may be polite to Cressley," Mama said. "Even a bit friendly. But remember that you are to make your come-out next April. If I were you, I would rid myself of these romantic notions of love. You will meet many gentlemen next Season. They will court you. Millbrooke and I will assist you in making the decision as to which one should become your husband."

Her mother's answer irritated Lia to no end. Not that she was daydreaming about Viscount Cressley, but if something developed between them, Lia would certainly be open to it. A friendship.

Or even more . . .

She rose. "I will leave the two of you to your needlework. I only wished to inform Aunt Agnes that Lord Cressley had sent word. I will see you both at tea."

Lia left the parlor, closing the door behind her. Then she did something awful. Something Tia would do without a second thought.

She left the door slightly open. Just enough so she could hear what her mother and aunt might say. It was wrong to eavesdrop—but she was curious as to what their conversation might be after she left. Would they discuss Lord Cressley? Or her? Might they totally change the subject?

Standing next to the door, holding her breath, she listened.

"She is becoming almost as willful as Thermantia," Mama remarked.

"And what is wrong with that, Alice? Where do you think Tia—and perhaps Lia—got such stubbornness from?"

"You are saying that *I* am the stubborn one?"

"All I am saying is that your daughters are grown women, Alice. They are thoughtful young ladies and have minds of their own. If Millvale had not passed so suddenly, both of them might already be wed and increasing, ready to become mothers of their own. My advice to you?"

"Do I have to listen to it?" Mama asked drolly.

"Let them be. You should let your daughters decide whom they are interested in without paying attention to rank. Let them make their own mistakes. Only if you see they are headed for disaster or disappointment should you intervene. Lia is a sensitive thing. She has always been wise beyond her years. She may—or may not—be interested in Viscount Cressley. You badgering her will only push her into his arms. Give her a chance to sort out her own feelings."

Mama snorted. "Just because you caught one look at George and fell madly in love does not mean my Cornelia will do the same."

"No, but the possibility is there. She has already spent time in Viscount Cressley's company, chaperoned by a five-year-old. Lia has always had a tender heart when it comes to children."

"I do not want my daughter to wed simply because she likes a man's niece."

"She would not do so. Lia is discerning. She would have to like—if not love—the man himself. She is far too wise simply to wed Cressley because of his niece. The child might be a small, but significant, detail that merely enhances the situation."

Her mother sighed. "You are right, Agnes. As always. The more I protest, the more I will push Cornelia toward this viscount."

"He might be a lovely person, Alice."

"True," her mother agreed begrudgingly. "I will keep quiet and keep the peace. Either my daughter will have a passing fancy for Cressley, which will soon be over, or she might be on the verge of falling in love with him. It is her life. Not mine."

Lia quietly closed the door completely and slowly walked away.

Was she interested in Lord Cressley as a man? A potential suitor? Or was she merely taken by the sweetness he had shown toward his niece?

She decided that she would let things unfold between them. Perhaps they would form a friendship. It might possibly even become something more, an attachment which could even lead to a betrothal.

But whatever came to pass between her and the viscount, Lia knew it would be on her terms—and no one else's.

CHAPTER EIGHT

RUPERT FELT SOMETHING touch his face and awoke with a start. A silhouette stood next to the bed.

"Celia, what are you doing here? It is the middle of the night."

He could not see her face in the dark, but she seemed to grow smaller, reacting to his sharp tone. He reached from the bed and cupped her cheek.

"What is it, little love? Why are you here?"

"I went outside, Uncle Rupert. It's not raining! We can go on the picnic today with Lady Lia."

He could not believe that she had already been outside. Then again, she moved about the house like a wraith. He supposed all the servants were still abed. Not wanting to climb all the way to the top of the house to put her back in bed, he lifted the bedclothes.

"Come. Get in bed with me. There is still sleep to be had."

She scrambled up, snuggling against him as he lowered the bedclothes.

"You're warm, Uncle Rupert."

"Close your eyes, Celia. Go back to sleep."

Within a minute, he heard her soft, even breathing. Thank goodness he still wore his trousers to bed. It was an old habit from his spy days, which he had yet to break. Sleeping in his clothes had allowed him to escape on more than one occasion from a tricky situation without getting caught.

He lay in the dark for several minutes, struggling to go fall asleep again. He would need to talk to his niece about wandering outside without a chaperone present. Rupert only hoped Lady Traywick would be able to give him some good advice on hiring a governess.

As he hoped sleep would come soon, his thoughts turned to Lady Lia Worthington. She was as kind as she was beautiful, and Celia had taken to her. Then a thought struck him.

What if he wed Lady Lia?

True, she had yet to make her come-out, but she certainly was of age to wed. In fact, if she had made her debut when she was supposed to, she very well might be a married woman now.

She had told him, however, that her brother and sister had both made love matches. He had seen the stars in her eyes when she mentioned that, and he would not be able to help her there. Yes, he had loved Celia almost instantly, but it was a protective, familial love. An adult who wished to care for a child. Rupert did not believe in romantic love. At least for himself. It would be a disservice to wed the sweet, gentle Lady Lia or to offer for her. Better that she make her come-out as planned next Season. Hopefully, she would find a gentleman worthy of her, one who would bring love into her life.

The next time he awoke, morning had come. Celia slept on beside him, and he rose and rang for Damsley.

When the valet appeared, pitcher of hot water in hand, Rupert motioned to the bed, indicating the sleeping child, and then followed the valet into his dressing room.

Damsley poured hot water from the jug he had brought into the basin, and Rupert sat, allowing himself to be shaved. Then the servant dressed him for the day.

"What is the weather like this morning?" he asked.

"A bit cloudy, my lord, but the rain has cleared up. It looks as if the rest of today will be a nice one."

"Good. Miss Celia and I are to attend a picnic today at Traywick Manor. Lord Traywick is returning to university soon, and his sisters are holding a picnic as a send-off for him."

"The little one will like that, my lord," Damsley replied.

"She most certainly will."

The valet left, and Rupert returned to the bed, sitting on it. Celia yawned and rubbed her eyes, opening them.

"Good morning, Celia."

"Good morning, Uncle Rupert. You're dressed."

"I am. We need to take you upstairs so you, too, might dress for the day. Damsley tells me the rain has stopped, so we should be able to go to the picnic this afternoon."

That news got his niece moving. He pulled back the bedclothes and lifted her from the bed, carrying her to the nursery. Once there, he dressed her in the gown which fit her the best and knew it was time to take her into the village for new clothes. Perhaps Lady Lia might accompany them and provide guidance.

Rupert brushed and then combed Celia's black hair before braiding it in one, long plait. He had seen one of the maids who wore her hair in a similar fashion and asked her to show him how to create one. She had been nervous, but her hands were gentle, and he quickly learned how to separate Celia's hair into separate sections and weave the tresses together.

"Shall we go down to breakfast?" he asked.

Rupert scooped Celia into his arms again and made his way downstairs. While he knew small children usually took their meals in the schoolroom, he did not want his niece to do so alone. Once he had hired a governess, they would get into better habits.

She sat in his lap as he asked for breakfast to be brought for the both of them. As they ate, Celia chattered away like a magpie.

When they finished their meal, he said, "We should go to the gardens now and work on your colors."

She scrambled from his lap and held out her hand. It touched him that she already trusted him so much.

Taking it, he led her outside, where they strolled the gardens. Newton had done nothing to educate the girl, and so Rupert was teaching her all about the small things in life, from numbers to colors to letters. Celia soaked up whatever he told her, and he believed she would thrive once a governess had been engaged for her and gave her proper lessons.

"Today, we will work not only on our colors, but also talk about the kind of flowers we see."

Rupert showed Celia everything from purple crocus to yellow autumn daffodils. She favored the pink dahlias and blazing orange chrysanthemums. Eventually, they traced their way back the way they had come, with Celia repeating colors and the varieties of flowers. A couple of times, she asked what a flower was again. Overall, she had learned the names quickly, though, far better than he had at her same age.

He decided when they went into town to get her something new to wear, he would also buy her some toys and books. He should have thought to do so sooner, but he had been too busy learning about his estate and how to manage it. Celia, naturally, had been with him each step of the way, already comfortable riding atop a horse with him, as he made his way around Crestbrook.

His niece now accompanied him to a meeting with his steward. Williamson was kind enough to provide the girl with pencil and paper, and she sat on the floor, drawing pictures for him while he and Williamson discussed estate business.

Celia presented him with her picture when they left the steward's office. She had drawn a picture of the two of them, along with some of the flowers they had seen earlier.

"You did such a nice job with your art," he told her.

She flipped the paper over. "I also worked on my letters, too," she said brightly.

"Say the alphabet to me, and point to each letter as you do so."

Celia complied with his request. Rupert saw that she had drawn the *P* backward, and so he told her it needed to be flipped around. Other than that, she had mastered her letters with ease.

Soon, she would be reading. Hopefully, Celia would not be too far behind by the time the governess arrived.

"We need to leave now for our picnic," he said.

"I liked Lia. She's very nice."

"Lady Lia," he corrected. "You must always use someone's title when addressing them. If they have one, that is."

Celia thought on that a moment. "The servants all call you 'my lord'."

"They do. It is a sign of respect shown to me. When I am with others of my rank or higher, they will call me Lord Cressley or my lord. Some might even say Viscount Cressley."

"But I get to call you Uncle Rupert."

He grinned. "Only you may do so."

"The servants call me Miss Celia," she said proudly. He did not tell her he had met with them and told the staff they would do so going forward.

"That is because you are the daughter of a viscount, my brother's child. When you get older, they will address you as Miss Cummings because that is your surname. For now, though, Miss Celia will do."

As they left the house, he lifted his niece and set her atop his shoulders. She giggled gleefully.

"I can see everything up here!"

"It is a long walk to the lake. I did not want you to tire by the time we reached our destination and sleep through the picnic."

"What *is* a picnic?" she asked, causing him to burst out laughing. Of course, she would have had no experience of picnics under Newton's care—or lack of.

"A picnic is when you eat a meal outdoors. Sometimes, a blanket is placed on the ground, and you sit atop it. Food seems to taste better when you eat it outside."

"What will we eat?" she asked eagerly.

"Usually, it is something easy to hold. A sandwich. A biscuit or tarts."

"Who will be at the picnic, Uncle Rupert?"

"Some of Lady Lia's family," he shared. "She has a sister named Lady Tia who will be there. Her mama, the Dowager Duchess of Millvale, will also come. You will call her mother Your Grace. That is how you address a duke or a duchess."

"Why?"

He shrugged. "That is just the way it is done, Celia. Say the names with me again."

He repeated Lady Tia and Your Grace, satisfied that she knew how to address Lady Lia's immediate family.

"Lady Lia is visiting with others in her family. They, too, will be at our picnic. One is Lord Traywick."

"Oh, he's a lord like you, Uncle Rupert."

"He is, but Traywick is also an earl. An earl outranks a viscount, which is what I am." Rupert decided that was too much information to go into, and so he said, "Just call him my lord. That will be good enough. Lord Traywick's mama will be there. She is Lady Traywick. You may call her my lady. So, that will be Lord and Lady Traywick."

He could sense Celia nodding. "My lord and my lady."

"Lady Lia also has two cousins. They are sisters to Lord Traywick." He thought a moment, trying to recall their names. "Lady Verina and Lady Justina. If you call them by name, you must always say the word lady in front of their names, because they are the daughters of an earl."

"What are their names again?"

"Repeat after me. Lady Verina. Lady Justina."

Celia practiced the names several times until she seemed satisfied.

"That's a lot of people at the picnic."

"It is. They are our nearest neighbors, though." Thinking he should clarify that term for her, Rupert added, "A neighbor is someone who lives nearby. Lord Traywick lives at Traywick Manor. It is the estate beside Crestbrook. That means Lord Traywick and his family are our closest neighbors."

"Do we have other neighbors?"

He liked how curious she was. "We do. You and I will meet them now that I have to come to Crestbrook. I went to be measured for some new clothes when I arrived here, and they will be ready soon. The two of us will go into the village for those. You also need new gowns and some toys and books, so we will do some shopping for you, as well. In the meantime, today, I will ask Lady Lia whom we should see in the village for your clothes."

"I like Lady Lia. Could she come with us?"

"Why, that is a brilliant idea, Celia Cummings. We shall ask Lady Lia today if she might do so."

The lake came into sight, but they still had a way to go. He knew where the Traywick boathouse was since he had passed it many times as a child.

They walked several more minutes, and then Celia cried, "I see Lady Lia!"

Celia began waving and must have caught the young woman's attention, because she began waving in return.

"She sees me, Uncle Rupert!"

"Yes, she does. Because you are so high up."

He counted the people he saw and decided he'd named everyone who would be at the picnic. Lady Lia had separated from the group and came toward them.

When she reached them, she turned her gaze upward, shading her eyes. "My, Celia. You have grown so tall since the last time I saw you."

Her words caused Celia to giggle. "I'm not tall, Lady Lia. I'm riding on Uncle Rupert's shoulders."

He reached above his head and lifted her to the ground. Celia immediately wrapped her arms about Lady Lia, saying, "I missed you."

Embracing the child, she said, "I missed you, as well, Celia." Still holding her arms about the girl, her gaze met his. "Good afternoon, my lord. I am so happy you were able to bring Celia to our picnic today."

"She was eager to come. Even though she did not know what a picnic was," he added, smiling at her, taking in how the sun caused her auburn hair to gleam brilliant shades of red. The light also caused her eyes to seem even a richer, deeper blue than he had remembered from before.

"Come and meet my family," she said, taking Celia by the hand and leading them back to the others. He watched the gentle sway of her hips as she moved, sparking something in him that he quickly tamped down.

Rupert saw that servants had brought chairs and two tables. A couple of blankets were also spread on the ground for those who preferred to eat in a more relaxed fashion.

The two older ladies, who had been seated, came to their feet. Lady Lia introduced them first.

"This is my mother, the Dowager Duchess of Millbrooke, and my aunt, Lady Traywick. May I introduce you to Lord Cressley."

He took the duchess' hand first since she outranked her sister-in-law. "The pleasure is all mine, Your Grace." He then greeted the countess. "Thank you for extending the invitation today, Lady Traywick. My niece was thrilled about coming to her first picnic."

He indicated Celia, who still held Lady Lia's hand. "This is my niece, Miss Celia Cummings."

Then Rupert realized he should have taught Celia how to curtsey.

The two older women did not seem to mind, however, with Lady Traywick saying, "Miss Celia, it is good to get to know a new neighbor."

"Neighbors live close to you," Celia said eagerly, showing off her new knowledge.

"They most certainly do," Lady Traywick agreed. "Her Grace, however, lives quite far away. You must ride in a carriage for many days before you reach where she lives."

Celia's eyes grew wide. "That is a long time. I never ride in a carriage."

He looked at the women apologetically, choosing his words carefully. "My niece's mother was lost in childbirth. My brother, the previous viscount, had Celia brought to Crestbrook, feeling it more appropriate for her to be raised in the country."

Left unsaid was how father had never visited daughter.

"Come meet the others," Lady Lia encouraged, leading him to the younger people present.

"This is my cousin, Lord Traywick."

The earl extended his hand, and Rupert took it. "It is delightful to meet you, my lord. I hear you are a student at Cambridge."

"At least for one more year, Lord Cressley, and then I will return to Cumberland for good."

"I would be interested to hear about your studies. I have fond memories of my own university days. Perhaps we might talk later. I also know that your steward and mine have developed a close friendship, despite being decades apart in age."

"Yes, Hillman is always talking about Williamson and his vast experience. The four of us should meet before I depart next week."

"I would enjoy doing so, my lord," Rupert said. He read others well, and he had a good feeling about this young earl.

"Come meet my sisters and cousin, my lord," Traywick said.

Lady Verina and Lady Justina were introduced to him, as well as Lady Tia. The latter bore a strong resemblance to her twin in the face, but Lady Tia was taller and had strawberry blond hair. In turn, he introduced his niece to them.

"It is so good to meet you, Lord Cressley. Celia, too," Lady Verina said. "Your brother was absent from Crestbrook for many years. It is good the house will be occupied again."

Lady Tia asked, "Will you be attending the Season next season, Lord Cressley?"

"Yes, my lady, I do plan to do so. I hear that you and your sister will make your come-outs next spring."

"We will. It will be nice to have a friendly face amongst a sea of new ones."

Traywick said, "It looks as if Larsen is signaling that it is time for us to eat. Shall we?"

Celia jumped up and down, her excitement apparent, and the earl, seeing that his cousin still held the young girl's hand, said, "Why don't you take Miss Celia through the queue first, Lia?"

"I would be happy to," she replied. "Come, Celia. We have so many good things to choose from. Let us see what you might like."

The two went to where the food was, and he held back, allowing the ladies to go first as he stood talking with the earl about Cambridge. He explained that he was an Oxford man, but he had served with several officers who had attended Cambridge.

"I envy you a bit, my lord," Traywick said. "As the only boy in the family, my destiny was set in stone. I claimed my title at only ten years of age. Up until then, I had played tin soldiers with my brother and had dreams of going off to war."

"An heir apparent rarely joins the military," Rupert said. "I can only think of one lieutenant I served under who was the heir to his father's viscountcy."

"I gather your brother was a good deal older than you. You must have thought you would make a career of the army instead of coming home to Cumberland as the viscount."

"I will admit it was a surprise, but I find I am happy being back in the country. Since I was not raised to be the heir, I am having to learn as much as I can about the estate and its management."

"And caring for your niece," Traywick pointed out.

He smiled. "Celia has been the best part of coming home. We have taken quickly to one another."

"Come sit with us, Uncle Rupert," his niece called, and he saw she and Lady Lia had taken a spot on one of the blankets.

"I will be right there," he called, accepting a plate from the butler and finding Cumberland sausage, his favorite, along with several cheeses and fruits and sweets.

He joined them and Lady Tia, who had also taken a place on

the same blanket, lowering himself to the ground.

"Do you have everything you need, Celia?" he asked.

She nodded. "And I save the sweets for last."

"Yes, that is correct."

She had wanted to eat sweets first at tea each day, and he had told her they were a treat and must come at the end of any meal.

"When you are older, Celia, you may eat sweets first," Lady Tia said, a mischievous glint in her eyes.

"Really?" asked his niece.

"Really," Lady Tia said solemnly.

"How old?"

They all burst out laughing, and Rupert said, "Eat your cheese and fruit first. Then you may have whatever you wish."

"Can I ask Lady Lia about going with us to the village?" Celia asked.

"What is this?" Lady Lia said.

"Celia is in need of new clothing," he explained. "I told her we would go into Kidsgrove to purchase what she needs."

"And some toys," Celia reminded him, causing them to laugh again.

"Yes, my lord. I would be happy to accompany you and your niece." Looking to Celia, she said, "I know far more about what a little girl should wear than your uncle does."

"But I think he will pick out good toys," Celia said.

Clearly biting her lip to hide her smile, Lady Lia said, "I agree. Lord Cressley does know how to choose a toy, but I will help find you a doll."

Celia clapped her hands, smiling widely. Her look of happiness warmed him, and he turned to Lady Lia as his niece began chatting with Lady Tia.

"Thank you for agreeing to go with us, my lady. Celia has taken to you."

"I do love children. Celia is a darling girl. I am happy to help the two of you with this errand."

She smiled at him, a genuine one which caused her face to

light up and his insides to melt. Rupert felt a sudden rush of desire pour through him. Not because of how she responded to Celia.

Instead, he acknowledged to himself the growing attraction he felt for Lady Lia Worthington.

CHAPTER NINE

L IA HAD NEVER felt so free as she did in Lord Cressley's company. He was quick-witted, yet never mean-spirited, in his comments, and he was absolutely in his element with Celia. Why, the man was born to be a father. He would no doubt be a wonderful one to his own children, seeing how comfortable he was in the presence of his niece.

She reflected on the conversation she had overheard between her mother and aunt yesterday, wondering what they now thought of Lord Cressley having met him. Lia decided she would seek out their opinion of the viscount after the picnic. For now, however, she would focus on Lord Cressley and Celia.

"What do you think of the damson tarts?" she asked the pair.

He grinned. "I have always had a fondness for custards."

"I like sweets," declared Celia.

"It looks as if you have finished eating, Celia," Tia said. "Would you like to go walk with me down to the boathouse? We can look at the rowboats. Perhaps your uncle might even take you out on the water in one of them."

The girl shot to her feet. "Let's go, my lady!"

Tia took Celia's hand, and they departed, leaving her alone with Lord Cressley.

"You and your sister favor one another," he remarked. "But your hair color is very different."

"Each of my siblings has a different shade of red. Val's is a deep chestnut, with mostly brown. You can only tell it is red if he is out in sunlight. Ariadne's hair is copper, a mix of red and bronze shades, and quite pretty. And you have met Tia now and see that hers is strawberry blond. Our father had red hair, and so we four children inherited that from him. No one I know has red in their hair but us Worthingtons."

"Your hair is a beautiful shade, my lady," he said, causing her scalp to tingle with the compliment.

"Thank you." She paused, deciding to share some about her name and that of others in her family. "I am afraid I must correct your spelling, my lord."

"What?" he asked, looking perplexed.

"The note you wrote to me misspelled my name. L-E-A-H is a common spelling, but my name—rather, my nickname—is L-I-A. You see, my given name is Cornelia."

"Ah, Cornelia Worthington sounds like a formidable dowager in her sixties or seventies," he teased. He thought a moment. "I suppose your twin is T-I-A."

She laughed. "Yes, Tia is the diminutive form of Thermantia."

He laughed along with her. "I can see why Lady Tia changed her name. It, too, sounds like a stern dowager."

"All ten cousins are named after various Roman and Byzantine emperors and empresses," she explained. "Papa, my aunt Charlotte, and my uncle George were all passionate about ancient history. They made a pact, deciding to name any children they had after historical figures they had studied and admired."

"You have mentioned your siblings, Ariadne and Val."

"Ariadne kept her name, but Val is actually Valentinian." Lia smiled. "I so rarely think of him that way. It was a surprise to hear his full name used when he wed."

"I assume Lady Verina and Lady Justina have kept their Christian names."

"They have. Traywick's given name is Hadrian, something he despised as a boy. His father and Lucius, his brother, perished in a carriage accident years ago. When he assumed the title, he asked that he be called Tray, and Aunt Agnes agreed."

"Do you have other cousins with fanciful names?"

"Three more. They are my aunt Charlotte and my uncle Arthur's children. Constantine, who is Viscount Dyer, goes by Con. Lucy, who just wed the Marquess of Huntsberry, is originally Lucilla. And Drusilla, the youngest Alington, became Dru."

"It is nice you have these things in common. I am a bit jealous of your large, loving family."

"Have you no cousins or other relatives?"

"None. Celia is my only living relative. I hope to fill Crestbrook with half a dozen children or more. I think having a large family would make me very happy." He gazed intently at her. "Do you hope for many children, my lady?"

"Yes," she said softly. "I do hope to have several."

The air between them grew charged as he held her gaze. Then Celia appeared, dashing up and falling to the blanket between them.

"I want to go in the boat, Uncle Rupert. Please, can we?"

"Let us ask Lord Traywick."

"I want to ask," Celia begged, running off to where Tray was eating. "My lord, can we take a boat out? Please?"

Tray beamed at her. "Of course, Miss Celia. That is what a pleasant day like today is for. The rains are gone. The early morning clouds have lifted. The water is calm, and sunshine is abundant. Would you like to go with me?"

"Oh, yes!" cried Celia, bobbing up and down in her excitement.

Tray called, "Do you trust me to take your niece with me, Cressley?"

"Yes, my lord," the viscount replied.

"I will go with the two of you," Verina said. She offered her hand to Celia, who took it. "Let us go see which boat you wish Traywick to row. He will be doing all the work, while we ladies sit back and enjoy the water."

Lord Cressley looked to her. "Would you care to go out on the water, Lady Lia?"

"Yes. Very much so. We have no lake at Millvale. I have never been out in a rowboat."

"You will enjoy it," he told her.

Lord Cressley rose and offered his hand to her. Lia took it, and he brought her to her feet. Touching him caused her cheeks to burn and her belly to turn twice over. When he released her hand, she had to fight to keep from grabbing hold of it again. Her hand in his, even for a brief moment, had felt absolutely right.

"The boathouse is this way," she said, trying to cover the rush of emotion going through her.

He fell into step beside her, and they saw Tray handing Verina into a boat. She settled herself, and he lifted Celia into it. The girl settled in Verina's lap, a huge smile on her face.

"Look at me, Uncle Rupert. I am in a boat."

"Listen to everything Lord Traywick and Lady Verina say, Celia."

"I will," she promised.

Tray pushed the boat farther into the water and then jumped into it, taking up the oars and rowing from the shore. Celia waved madly at them for a moment, and then she became distracted.

"She is having a fun time today," Lord Cressley said. "Again, I thank you for inviting us."

He entered the boathouse and brought out another rowboat, returning to fetch a pair of oars. Lia offered to take them, and the viscount easily lifted the boat, taking it down to the water's edge. He righted it and held it steady, helping her inside before nudging it and jumping in himself. She handed him the oars, and he inserted them into a slot, then began to row, causing them to glide effortlessly across the calm water.

Grinning, Lia said, "I feel a bit as Celia does, my first time in a rowboat. You look very comfortable, however."

"Remember, I grew up here. Crestbrook used to have our own boathouse. I am not certain what happened to it, but many a time, I took a boat out onto this lake. Sometimes, to fish. Other times, simply to float. I would lie down and stare up at the sky, watching the clouds pass by."

"Do you ever look at clouds and see if you can see something in their shapes?" she asked.

"No," he said, laughing as he pulled again at the oars, taking them farther to the lake's center.

She looked up, frowning a moment, then said, "There. I see a man with a beard."

"Where?"

"Right there." She pointed and looked at him as he gazed up.

Then he smiled. "Yes. I do see him. Why, he looks as old as Methuselah." He scanned the sky. "I spy a horse."

He told her where to look, and Lia bit her lip, concentrating. "Oh, wait! Is that his tail? Now, I see his body. My, he is leaping."

They looked at the skies for a few more minutes, having fun spotting various shapes.

"My neck is aching," he admitted. "I am looking down from now on. At you."

Her gaze met his. For a long moment, she was lost in his eyes. A deep yearning filled her.

Then he tugged at the oars again, propelling them across the lake several more feet. They continued to talk. About books they had both read. A little about the war. He seemed surprised that she read the newspapers and kept up with the war and politics.

"I know I am a woman and should not show an interest in such matters, but I like to know what is going on about me."

"You are well-informed, Lady Lia. In fact, I think you have a better grasp on economics than I do."

She felt the blush heat her neck and face and turned to see where Celia was.

"Would you be free tomorrow morning to accompany us into Kidsgrove?" he asked, forcing her attention back to him.

"Celia is in desperate need of new gowns. I also want to buy her a few things to play with, as she already told you."

"Yes, tomorrow morning would be convenient, my lord."

"We shall pick you up in my carriage at ten o'clock then," he declared. "Celia will be most pleased."

Boldly, Lia asked, "And what of you, Lord Cressley? Are you also pleased?"

She could not believe she had been so brazen. Lia had never done anything so out of character.

He held her gaze. "Yes, my lady. I am most pleased."

She wet her lips nervously. Tried to reply and simply couldn't. They continued to stare at one another, him looking as if he might gobble her up in a single bite. It caused her heartbeat to quicken. Her insides to race.

Then Tray's boat bumped theirs, breaking the spell. Lia looked up, shading her eyes with a hand. "Was that on purpose, Traywick?"

"Celia dared me," her cousin retorted.

"I did not!' the little girl said indignantly. "But . . . can we race?"

"We most certainly can," Lord Cressley agreed. "And I shall claim victory."

"I want to ride with you, Uncle Rupert," Celia whined.

"What? You are deserting me, Miss Celia?" Tray asked, a hand to his heart, looking wounded. "Oh, betrayal at the worst level."

Lia and Verina laughed, as the viscount said, "Bring your boat next to mine, Traywick. There. Good." He rested his oars and held out his hands. "Come to me, Celia."

Tray lifted Celia by her waist, placing her in their boat. Lord Cressley secured his niece, kissing her on both cheeks.

"Are you having fun, little love?"

"Picnics are very fun," she proclaimed.

Tray and the viscount agreed to race from the middle of the lake to the shore where the others still gathered. They lined up their boats, side-by-side, close but not so close that they couldn't row properly.

Celia shouted, "Go!" and they took off.

Lia held tightly to the girl as their boat cut quickly through the water. Both Tray and Lord Cressley had shed their coats, and she could see how broad the viscount's shoulders were. How large his biceps were. How he rowed with strength and ease.

They reached the finish line first, followed immediately by Tray and Verina. Celia crowed her delight.

"We won! We won!" She leaped from Lia's lap and threw her arms about her uncle.

"We did," he agreed, kissing the top of her head. "But a good winner never gloats."

"What's gloats?"

"To brag about your triumph. Winning," he amended, when Celia looked confused.

"What do we do then?" Celia asked.

"We offer our hand and shake that of our opponent. Tell them that they ran a good race. And give them a very large smile."

"Let me," Celia insisted. She thrust out her hand, and Tray took it, looking solemn, but Lia saw the mirth in his eyes.

"It was a good race," she said, shaking Tray's hand. Then Celia beamed. "And we won!"

"You most certainly did," Tray agreed.

Everyone was laughing now, both in the boats and onshore.

"Let us put the boats back," the viscount said. "Would you like to get off here or stay?"

"Stay," Lia and Celia said without hesitation.

Lord Cressley picked up his oars and moved them through the water with barely a splash, heading back toward the boathouse. When they reached the shore, he got out first, then lifted Celia from the boat. She stood on the shore waving at Verina and Tray, who were fast approaching.

The viscount gave Lia his hand. The boat rocked slightly as

she moved and he released her hand, catching her by the waist, causing her heart to slam against her ribs. He picked her up with ease and set her on the shore. She was afraid if he spoke, she wouldn't hear him because the blood pounded so fiercely in her ears.

"Thank you," Lia managed, taking Celia's hand and leading them in the direction back to the others. All the way, her pulse beat rapidly, as if she had run a long race.

What was happening to her?

Tia had traveled along the path next to the shore, coming to meet her. She slipped her hand through Lia's arm, and Lia released her grasp on Celia's hand. The child ran ahead of them.

"Are you all right?" Tia asked, looking concerned.

"Yes," she said, sounding strangled and anything but all right.

Tia halted them. "You *like* him. Lord Cressley."

She looked at her twin helplessly.

"You do," Tia whispered. "I thought you did. You seemed so at ease with him. That is why I took Celia away, so that the two of you might have a few minutes alone to yourselves." Tia snorted. "Well, as alone as you can get at a picnic, with Mama and Aunt Agnes looking on."

Her sister started moving again, and somehow, Lia managed to pick up her feet.

"He is quite handsome. And charming," Tia said. "Do you think you will wed him?"

"I have only met him," she said, shaking her head. "How do I know something such as that?"

"Aunt Agnes knew right away when she met Uncle George," Tia insisted. "Do you love him?"

"I do not know. I do not think so. Or . . . perhaps . . . oh, I cannot say. Please, do not mention any of this to anyone."

Tia looked offended. "I never tell anyone what the two of us talk about."

They were coming close to the others now. Celia had already arrived. She glanced over her shoulder and saw Tray and Lord

Cressley fast approaching behind them, Verina with them.

"He wants me to go with Celia and him to Kidsgrove tomorrow. To look for toys and clothes."

Tia frowned. "I doubt Mama would let you go alone with them. I will volunteer to come along. Verina and Justina would also go. I can steer them away. We could run our errands separately, then we could all meet up for tea and a scone."

"You are brilliant," Lia said.

Her twin smiled widely. "Perhaps I will become a matchmaker in London and put couples together during the Season. I will experiment on you and Lord Cressley first."

Laughing, Tia released her and picked up her skirts to run. Lia did the same, and they ran the short distance to the others. Her sister collapsed onto the empty blanket they had eaten their picnic on, while Lia went straight to her mother and aunt.

"Remember, Lord Cressley wishes to speak to the both of you about Celia and how to go about employing a governess for her," she said, out of breath.

"Have him join us," Mama said.

But Aunt Agnes looked at Lia a long moment, as if she knew something was afoot. "Yes, have Cressley come and sit with us, my dear."

She turned and met Tray and the viscount. "Mama and Aunt Agnes wish to speak with you, my lord," she told Lord Cressley. "About engaging a governess for Celia."

"Thank you," he said, striding off.

Tray looked at Lia. "Thank you for inviting Lord Cressley today. I hope we will strike up a friendship, especially after I complete university. In the meantime, I asked him to ride with us the day after tomorrow. Remember, we are going to tour some of the Lake District on horseback."

"That was a lovely gesture, Tray. Thank you for inviting him. I believe Lord Cressley is in need of a few friends. He was reluctant to leave his fellow officers behind when he sold out."

"Cressley will be a wonderful addition to the neighborhood," her cousin proclaimed. "Come, Lia. I have worked up a thirst with all that rowing."

"And I worked one up watching the two of you row," she teased.

Larsen poured them both some lemonade, and they joined Verina and Justina.

Lia would see the viscount tomorrow in the village and again while they rode about the area. That would make for four days in a row. Something told her that she would know where her heart stood at the end of that time.

CHAPTER TEN

RUPERT HEADED TOWARD the two older women, still seated at a table. He was a bit intimidated by the haughty gaze the Duchess of Millbrooke cast upon him, but he put on his most charming smile.

"Might I join you ladies?"

"Please do so, Lord Cressley," Lady Traywick said, her manner friendly. "We are delighted that you were able to join us for today's picnic."

"I appreciate the invitation more than you know, my lady. Since I have only recently arrived at Crestbrook, I have yet to meet any of my neighbors. This was a wonderful way to begin."

"It will be good for Traywick," his mother said. "My son took his title at a tender age and has had to grow up faster than his friends. Most of the peers in the area are a good two decades older than he is, so I hope the two of you will come to know one another and get along well."

"The earl is an impressive young man," he said. "Based upon what my steward has shared with me, Lord Traywick has been involved in the management of his estate for a good many years now. I will be the one who will need to learn from him."

"Cornelia tells me that you are in need of engaging a governess for your niece," the duchess commented, apparently ready to steer the conversation to its intended purpose.

"Yes, Your Grace. It is one of the reasons I accepted today's invitation, so that I might speak with you and Lady Traywick regarding this matter. I have no experience with children and am not certain how to go about the process of finding the right woman to guide Celia."

The duchess' gaze turned to Celia and then back to him. "Tell me about yourself—and your niece."

"You do realize you are as intimidating as any general in His Majesty's army, Your Grace."

That brought a smile to her lips. "Good."

"As Lady Traywick may have mentioned to you, I was in the military. My commission was purchased for me by my brother, the previous Viscount Cressley. He was many years older than I was, and I can only recall seeing him a handful of times. My father enjoyed life in town, as my brother did, so he was rarely at Crestbrook. I learned from an early age to be independent and find my own way."

"Did you attend university?" the duchess inquired.

"I graduated from Oxford. Once I finished my studies, I entered the military and served these past eight years."

The duchess' gaze met his. "And what do you think of Bonaparte, my lord?"

"I believe he is the greatest threat Europe has seen since Alexander the Great. Except the Little Corporal has none of Alexander's finesse or sophistication. England is in for a long war, Your Grace. Long—and bloody."

She nodded approvingly at him. "You do not mince words, Cressley. That is in your favor. Tell me about your niece. You seem very close to her for having only arrived at Crestbrook a short while ago."

He shrugged. "It is not something I believe I can put into words, Your Grace. There has been an affinity between Celia and me since the moment we met. A trust that is natural and real. I will be honest and share with you that her previous nursemaid left much to be desired. I doubt my brother cared one whit for his daughter, most likely because she was a girl. My guess is the nursemaid was illiterate, and so Celia has not been taught as she should have. I found this nursemaid to be . . . negligent in her duties. Because of that, I dismissed her. That is why I seek to employ someone kind and gentle to guide Celia, hopefully for many years to come."

"A good governess is difficult to come by," Lady Traywick said. "It is possible you might find one in the surrounding area, but my advice would be to write off to town for one. That is what I am having to do now that Miss Snow wed my nephew recently. Miss Snow was recommended to me by a friend, which is how one usually finds the best servants and governesses or tutors. This time, however, I plan to write to an employment agency I have used in the past."

Lady Traywick paused. "If you would like, my lord, you may include your own letter with mine. I would be happy to add a postscript to my own request, recommending you."

"If you would do so, my lady, I would most grateful. I want the best for Celia. She has been dealt a harsh hand in her five years of existence. I am quite fond of her and plan to treat her not as a ward, but as a daughter."

"Do you plan to attend the upcoming Season, Cressley?" the duchess asked.

"Yes, Your Grace. I am well aware of the fact that I am only Viscount Cressley because my brother did not provide an heir for his title. I will not let that happen on my watch. I intend to take a bride as soon as possible."

The duchess looked at him pointedly. "Will you tell your prospective bride of this close bond you and your niece share?"

He nodded solemnly. "I consider us a family. Any lady I am interested in making my viscountess must understand that she is not only to become my wife—but also a mother to Celia."

"That might eliminate a great number of candidates on the Marriage Mart," the duchess informed him. "Are you in financial straits, or will you be able to wed a woman of your choice?"

Rupert thought her question impertinent, asking him about

his financial situation, but he gathered dukes made their own rules, and that might well include their duchesses.

Without giving anything away, he said, "I will be able to select a bride with no extenuating circumstances. And yes, Your Grace, I will make it perfectly clear from the start that I am almost as a widower, bringing a child into whatever union I seek. I will inform both the young lady and her family. No surprises."

The duchess pursed her lips a moment and then nodded to him. "Good for you, Cressley. You seem to be a forthright gentleman, one filled with integrity and aware of duty to your family. I admire that."

Lady Traywick cleared her throat. "Are there any specific qualities you are looking for in your governess, Lord Cressley?"

"I do not want a woman who is a harsh disciplinarian," he began. "Celia was left unsupervised on too many occasions in the past. Because of it, she has developed a bit of an independent streak. While I do wish for her to learn to discipline herself, she needs a gentle, guiding hand to help her learn how to do so, not someone who is a strict authoritarian.

"Other than that, I would hope the governess would be genteel enough to teach Celia not only academic subjects, but also of Polite Society itself. I want my niece to grow up comporting herself as a young lady should. So, to answer your question, my lady, I seek someone who would commit to the post for a good number of years, hopefully a dozen or more. If I am pleased, I would expect this governess to remain with Celia until she makes her come-out."

"That is a very long time for someone to devote to a child," Lady Traywick said. "Then again, many women do look for a long-term position as you are offering. I shall write my own letter requesting a governess when I return to the house this afternoon. If you will do the same, my lord, we can send both off in tomorrow's post."

He thought of the plans he had made to go into town. "Celia is in need of new gowns, as well as some toys and books. Lady Lia has agreed to accompany us into Kidsgrove tomorrow to assist with these purchases. I fear I know nothing about the type of clothing my niece requires. Celia has also taken to Lady Lia. I can pick her up in my coach tomorrow and post our letters in the village tomorrow, Lady Traywick."

"That will not do," the duchess said emphatically.

"I am unclear, Your Grace, as to your objection."

"Cornelia is not out in Polite Society, my lord. She will not be going anywhere with you alone, despite the fact your niece would be present. A five-year-old is not a suitable chaperone."

"Alice," Lady Traywick said gently, "we are in Cumberland and not town. Why don't we have the other three girls accompany Lia on this errand?" She looked to Rupert. "If you would not mind escorting both my daughters and nieces, I believe that would be just the compromise necessary, my lord."

He realized he had much to learn about the ways of the *ton*. "Yes, my lady, I would be happy to take all four young ladies to the village. I am certain Celia would be delighted to have so much company. More opinions would also be advantageous as we select a new wardrobe for her."

Rupert paused, waiting for a sign from the duchess.

Finally, she nodded curtly. "All right, I shall agree to this outing."

"If I may say so, Your Grace, I believe we may be in the village several hours. I am to have a final fitting on clothes for myself at Mr. Burrows' shop. I had planned to drop Lady Lia and Celia at the dressmaker's, joining them once my fitting concluded. I think it will take a good while for the four young ladies to talk with the dressmaker and choose materials for the gowns to be made up for Celia. Then, as I mentioned, I wish to buy my niece some toys and books."

"Oh, you can do so at Mr. Shaft's store. He carries all kinds of wonderful things," Lady Traywick enthused. "I have bought many a thing from Mr. Shaft. Because you will in the village so long, my lord, perhaps you might treat everyone to sweets at

Mrs. Shaft's teashop and bakery."

"I would be happy to do so in order to repay the kindness they are doing for me," he replied. Looking to the duchess, he asked, "Is that to your liking, Your Grace?"

"I would prefer Traywick accompany your group, but I know my nephew is trying to finish up projects on the estate before he leaves for university next week." She looked to Lady Traywick. "If you are agreeable, Agnes, then so am I."

He breathed a silent sigh of relief, glad that he would have the advice of several young ladies, including Lady Lia's opinion.

Rising, Rupert said, "Thank you for your time this afternoon, Your Grace, my lady. I will see the letter is written and include it with yours. If you will excuse me, I will let the others know about tomorrow's plans and then return to Crestbrook."

He went to where Celia was tossing a ball to Lady Lia and Lady Tia.

"Oh, what have we here?" he asked.

"His lordship found a ball in the boathouse," Celia told him. "I like playing with a ball."

"Then I hope we will find one on our trip into the village tomorrow."

Celia looked at him, wide-eyed. "We are going to the village?"

He nodded. "Lady Lia and Lady Tia are to accompany us, along with Lady Verina and Lady Justina. That is, if it is convenient for them to do so."

Lady Justina said, "Good. I have needed to look at some new ribbons. And Verina, you mentioned needing new embroidery thread yesterday."

"An outing to Kidsgrove sounds wonderful, my lord," Lady Tia said.

He looked to Lady Lia, since she was the only one yet to comment. "Are you agreeable to this trip, my lady?"

"I would enjoy going into Kidsgrove with you and Celia, my lord," she said demurely.

Celia yawned, and Rupert said, "It is time we head back home."

"Do we have to?" Celia whined.

"Yes. A guest should never overstay their welcome. Let us go thank our hostess for inviting us."

He took his niece's hand, and they went to the two older women, where Rupert said, "Thank you for a lovely afternoon, Lady Traywick. Celia and I enjoyed ourselves immensely."

His niece smiled brightly. "Thank you, my lady. I never went on a picnic before. I had so much fun." Celia then handed the ball to Lady Traywick. "This is yours. Uncle Rupert might buy me one tomorrow."

The countess returned it to Celia. "I think you should keep this one until you have one of your own, Miss Celia."

She beamed at the older woman. "Thank you, my lady."

He went and bid farewell to the others, arranging to pick them up tomorrow morning at ten o'clock, and Celia said, "Can Lady Lia walk with us?"

His gaze met hers, and she said, "I would be happy to accompany you part of the way to Crestbrook, Celia."

"Goodbye!" Celia called, skipping ahead.

Rupert and Lady Lia fell into step beside one another and followed.

"Celia had the most marvelous time today, my lady. I cannot tell you how much I appreciate the invitation to the picnic."

"Celia was a pleasure to watch. It is nice to view the world through a child's eyes. To me, the idea of a picnic was fun. Watching Celia experience her first picnic, though, made it quite special for me."

She stumbled over a rock in the path, and he caught her elbow. "Here, take my arm."

Lady Lia slipped her hand through the crook of his arm, and Rupert felt suddenly at peace. He told himself not to develop feelings for her. That only a love match would make her happy.

And yet everything inside him yearned to stop and kiss her.

Celia turned and ran back to them, and he was glad he had not acted upon that impulse. She asked if she could ride atop his shoulders again, and Lady Lia released his arm. Losing her touch felt as if he had been cut adrift at sea. Rupert swallowed the lump in his throat and picked up Celia, bringing her to rest upon his shoulders.

"I like being high," she declared.

"You can see so much from your perch," Lady Lia said.

"Maybe you can ride on Uncle Rupert's shoulders, Lady Lia."

The thought of her legs wrapped around him, his hands holding her calves, caused him to shudder.

"Are you cold?" Celia asked him.

"Not a bit," he said breezily.

"I think I should turn back now," Lady Lia said.

Their gazes met. Rupert thought he could lose himself in those deep blue eyes forever.

"Until tomorrow, my lady."

He turned, Celia waving, and strode off.

"Too fast," his niece complained, and so he slowed a bit.

Celia jabbered the entire way home, talking about the boat ride and the food and the ball she had been given. Rupert grunted every now and then, which satisfied her.

His thoughts lingered on Lady Lia Worthington, though. Worry filled him because while he knew he should put her from his mind, he neither wanted to—nor could he seem to. She was as a beacon of light, shining into his thoughts. He had no defense against it.

Rupert vowed he would allow her to assist him tomorrow. For Celia. Then he must fix his focus on Crestbrook.

And not a lovely, auburn-haired beauty who was charming her way into his heart.

CHAPTER ELEVEN

T HE TALK AT breakfast centered on their outing to Kidsgrove that morning. She was surprised that Mama and Aunt Agnes had come down for the morning meal since they usually breakfasted in their rooms.

"I apologize that I cannot accompany you ladies," Tray said. "Remember, though, that we are to take our ride on horseback around the area tomorrow. Be sure to remind Lord Cressley about it. I think he would enjoy going with us, but he did not commit yesterday."

Having thought about Tray's invitation to the viscount, Lia now said, "I am not certain Lord Cressley would wish to leave Celia by herself all day, especially since she has no governess. He has been keeping her with him during most of the day. If he does go, he would most likely wish to bring her along."

"Nonsense," Mama said. "As long as you will be gone, that is too long for a child. If Cressley does not trust his niece with his servants, then he may leave her with Agnes and me. We will see to her care."

She exchanged a look with Tia, who rolled her eyes. Mama had little to do with any of them while they were growing up. She doubted that her mother knew the first thing to do with a child. On the other hand, Aunt Agnes had been much more involved with her children, possibly because they had lost their father at such a young age. Aunt Agnes was a favorite amongst all the cousins, and she likely would know how to keep Celia entertained.

"If you do not mind, Aunt Agnes, I will tell Lord Cressley that he could bring Celia here for the day."

"Please do so, Lia. That boy needs a bit of fun. I cannot imagine being at war for years, only to come home and have an estate to worry about and a child to deal with." Her aunt's face softened. "Lord Cressley does seem quite fond of his niece, though."

"I still think the child will be a drawback as Cressley hunts for a bride next Season," Mama said. "Though he is quite good-looking and seems to have his financial affairs in order, he will certainly find someone to wed him. Whether she accepts the child as hers remains to be seen."

Lia felt her face grow warm at that thought and turned her attention to her eggs as Verina and Justina began telling them a bit about the village.

"It is not as large as Willowshire," Verina said. "You and Tia have been fortunate to have such a large village near you. We do have a wonderful dressmaker, however. Mrs. Penny will be the ideal person to see today regarding clothes for Celia."

"And Mr. Penny is a shoemaker and bootmaker," Justina added. "He shares the shop's space with his wife, so if either of you need any new footwear, I can highly recommend Mr. Penny."

"I could stand to have some new riding boots made up," Tia commented. "Perhaps I will be allowing this Mr. Penny to fit me for a pair."

They returned to their rooms to fetch bonnets. Lia decided to slip into her spencer. The weather was certainly cooler in the Lake District this time of year than it was in Kent. They met downstairs, and Larsen told them that a footman had just spied Lord Cressley's carriage coming up the lane. They went outside to wait for him.

Lord Cressley exited the carriage, greeting Mama and Aunt

Agnes, who had come to see them off.

"Thank you for entrusting me with the care of your daughters today," he told the two older women.

"Here is the letter for you to post, my lord," Aunt Agnes said, handing it to him.

"I shall have my coachman post both our letters once we arrive in Kidsgrove, my lady."

They moved toward the carriage, and the viscount handed up each of them into the carriage. Lia went last, and as she boarded the vehicle, Celia said, "Sit with me, Lady Lia."

She sat on the cushion beside the girl, who sat by a window. That meant the only remaining spot for Lord Cressley to sit in was next to her since her sister and cousins already sat opposite her.

He seated himself beside her, and their bodies were pressed together from their shoulders to hips. She had never sat in such close proximity to a man and found that odd sensation running through her again, the one she experienced whenever he was near.

As the carriage set out, Celia crawled into Lia's lap. Though there was now more space available on the cushion, she thought it would seem odd if she scooted away from the viscount, and so she remained where she was. Celia began talking about how she was going to have new things to wear and that her uncle had also promised her new shoes, too.

"Since Celia enjoys being outside, you might consider having a pair of sturdy boots made up for her, my lord," Lia suggested. "My cousins tell me that the shoemaker is husband to the dressmaker, and they share shop space. We could manage both errands at the same time."

"I recall Mr. and Mrs. Penny, if they are the couple you speak of. Mr. Penny used to make all my footwear for me. I do like that idea, my lady. Celia does enjoy roaming my estate. I know you ladies will know exactly what my niece's needs are. Feel free to order whatever you wish for her."

"Do not forget about tomorrow's ride," Tia prodded, and Lia added, "Tray is taking all of us on a ride for several hours about the area. He expressly wished that you join us. You would be able to see places from your youth and if anything has changed since you were last in the area."

He frowned slightly. "I gave it some thought. Normally, I would be happy to accompany you, but I am afraid that would be too long in the saddle for Celia. She does not ride yet, and so I would have her with me."

Justina spoke up quickly. "Mama and Aunt Alice have said that you should leave Celia with them. They will make certain she is well cared for while we are gone."

"I hate to impose," the viscount said.

"It would not be imposing at all, my lord," Verina told him. "Mama loves children. She has even told me that she wished she could go back in time to when we were Celia's age and do things all over again."

"Let us ask Celia." Lord Cressley turned to his niece. "Would you like to go stay with Her Grace and Lady Traywick tomorrow while I attend to some business?"

"Can I bring my ball? They can toss it with me."

Both Lia and Tia burst into laughter, thinking of Mama tossing a ball back and forth with the little girl.

"You may take whatever you wish. Would you mind staying at Traywick Manor while I am gone for the day?"

Celia nodded, and Tia said, "Then it is settled. Celia will be cared for while we see the surrounding countryside."

They reached Kidsgrove, and the carriage stopped. The viscount said, "I asked to be dropped at Mr. Burrows' shop. I will meet you at the dressmaker's soon."

He looked to Celia. "Be a good girl and do as Lady Lia says."

Celia said, "I will, Uncle Rupert."

The viscount kissed her brow and then left the carriage.

The vehicle started up again but slowed after only a minute, and Verina said, "We are here."

A footman handed down each of them, and Celia took Lia's hand. She was glad the girl trusted her, and a warm feeling spread through her as they entered Mrs. Penny's dress shop.

"Lady Verina, Lady Justina, it is so good to see you again," said a spry woman with kind eyes and gray curls piled high atop her head. "How was your visit to your cousins' home?"

"We had a wonderful time in Kent, Mrs. Penny. In fact, here are two of our cousins. They came home with us for a visit. This is Lady Lia and Lady Tia Worthington. But our true reason for visiting you today is Miss Celia Cummings. She is Viscount Cressley's niece and in need of a new wardrobe."

Mrs. Penny smiled at the child. "Well, Miss Celia, let's measure you first. Then we can talk about all the pretty new things you will have to wear."

As the dressmaker took Celia's measurements, she caught them up on the local gossip. Then they began talking about all Celia would need, including shoes and boots. That drew Mr. Penny's attention, and he stopped cutting the leather he worked with and came to visit for a few minutes before returning to his workbench.

Mrs. Penny had them gather around a table. Celia crawled into Lia's lap after she sat. They had only looked at bolts of material for a few minutes when Lord Cressley entered the shop and came toward them.

"Good day, Mrs. Penny. I hear you will make up some clothes for my niece. Spare no expense."

Lia decided to intervene. "While I know you wish for Celia to have an abundant wardrobe, my lord, children grow quickly at this age. I think you should limit the number of gowns made up for Celia. We could ask for Mrs. Penny to make five or six gowns, and then she could also make up a few more which are slightly larger. That way, when Celia begins a growth spurt, she would have something to transition into while new clothes are made up for her."

"That is very practical, my lady," Lord Cressley said. He

looked to the dressmaker. "Do as Lady Lia asks." Then turning back to her, he asked, "Might I seem you in private for a moment, my lady?"

"Yes, my lord," she responded, lifting Celia and placing her upon Tia's lap. The girl did not protest, for which Lia was grateful.

Lord Cressley led them to a corner of the store, and she asked, "What is it?"

"I would like you to accompany me now to Mr. Shaft's shop. I want your advice in selecting toys and books for Celia without her being there. She might be overwhelmed seeing so many items, especially after having had next to nothing up until now."

"I would be happy to help you in choosing these items. Let me claim my reticule and tell Tia where I am off to. The others can meet us at Mr. Shaft's when they finish. I know my cousins have shopping to do there, as well."

She returned to the table and leaned down, whispering to Tia where she would be. Her twin nodded. Celia was enthralled looking at different bolts of material, and Lia doubted she would be missed.

Claiming her reticule, she stepped outside the shop, where Lord Cressley waited for her.

"I used to frequent Mr. Shaft's store when I was not much older than Celia. His shop is just a stone's throw from here."

He offered his arm to her, and she took it, trying to ignore the physical feelings stirring within her.

When they entered the shop, they were greeted in a friendly fashion by Mr. Shaft. Lord Cressley introduced the two of them, and the older man broke out in a wide smile.

"I recall you coming to see me when you were a boy, my lord. It is good to have you back in Kidsgrove. The previous viscount never came around. We are happy you are in residence at Crestbrook"

"I plan to remain in the country, only going to town for the Season each spring," the viscount replied. "I have inherited a niece, along with my title, Mr. Shaft, and she is in need of entertainment. Would you please show us some toys and books? She is five years of age."

The shopkeeper took them to a section with some toys.

"I will defer to you, my lady, in what we should select," Lord Cressley said.

Mr. Shaft fetched a basket. For the next few minutes, Lia studied the toys for sale, thinking which ones would be appropriate for Celia. She chose a doll, a ball, and a few other small items that she thought would please the girl.

After those items had been placed in the basket, she looked at the small selection of books and chose three.

"Oh, I wish you carried one which was read to me when I was Celia's age. It was full of fables, and the illustrations were magical."

"I know the one you speak of, my lady," Mr. Shaft said. "I could order it for you if you'd like."

"That would be wonderful, Mr. Shaft. Miss Celia would enjoy it quite a bit."

"Would you have these items sent to Crestbrook, Mr. Shaft?" Lord Cressley asked. "I want to surprise my niece with what we have chosen today."

As the shopkeeper took the basket to the counter, she said, "My advice, my lord, is to not give all these to her at the same time. It might be too much, too soon," Lia explained. "You know she already enjoys playing with a ball. I would let her have that and perhaps the doll. Not only will she enjoy playing with the doll, but she also most likely will sleep with it."

"Excellent idea, my lady."

They started to leave the shop, but the rest of their party entered. Mr. Shaft quickly set the basket on the counter behind it so that Celia would not see what was inside it.

"We finished at Mrs. Penny's, "Tia shared. "Celia was also fitted for a pair of slippers and some boots by Mr. Penny."

"You will need to bring her back to Kidsgrove in a week, my

lord," Verina said. "A few of her gowns will be ready by then, along with both pairs of shoes."

The viscount looked to the three and said, "Thank you for handling this matter. You have my gratitude."

"We have shopping of our own to do at Mr. Shaft's," Justina said.

Tia asked, "Did you finish getting what you needed here, Lia?"

She nodded.

By now, Celia had found the toy section, which was depleted after their visit. "Look at this," the girl said.

She and Lord Cressley moved toward her, seeing a single tin soldier in her hand.

"What is this?"

"It is a soldier, Celia," her uncle explained.

The child studied the small figure and said, "He looks a little like you, Uncle Rupert."

Everyone laughed at her remark, and Celia asked, "Can I have him?"

"Of course. Would you like a few more soldiers to accompany him? He might be lonely by himself."

"Yes, please." Looking on the shelf, she said, "But I don't see anymore."

Mr. Shaft stepped up. "I have no more now, Miss Celia, but I can order some if his lordship agrees."

"How many soldiers would you like to have?" the viscount asked.

Celia thought a moment. "Five."

"Then order four more soldiers if you would, Mr. Shaft. Send word when they come in, and Celia and I will come and claim them."

Tia said, "I know you have completed your shopping, my lord. Why don't you and Lia go to Mrs. Shaft's tearoom and wait for us there? We will be along shortly."

Lia didn't have to wonder why Tia had suggested this, knowing her twin was trying to give her time alone with the viscount. Then she watched as Tia took Celia's hand and said, "Come look at the ribbons with Lady Justina and me. We might find a pretty one to buy for you to wear in your hair."

Her sister led the girl away, and Lord Cressley chuckled. "I suppose we are no longer needed here. If you would like, we could stroll for a few minutes and allow you to see what else is in Kidsgrove."

They left the shop and went down what was not only the main street—but the only street of the village. Shops lined both sides. At one end was the church. At the other was an inn on one side and Mrs. Shaft's tearoom and bakery opposite it. They entered, and Lia saw that it was empty of customers at the moment.

A short, stout woman with lively blue eyes greeted them. "How might I help you today?" she asked.

"It is Rupert Cummings, Mrs. Shaft. Now, Lord Cressley. And this is Lady Lia Worthington, cousin to Lord Traywick. Lady Lia's sister and cousins are at Mr. Shaft's shop as we speak, along with my niece. We have come ahead of them to find a table for our party and look at your heavenly baked goods."

She beamed at him. "It is wonderful to have you at Crestbrook again, my lord. We are not used to the viscount being in residence. My condolences on the loss of your brother."

"Thank you, Mrs. Shaft. It is good to be home again after so many years."

"I recall you came in often as a young boy, my lord. You were particularly fond of the toffee buns."

"You have an excellent memory," he praised. "I still have a fondness for a sticky bun, especially toffee. You also baked the best bread I have ever eaten. I was disappointed that Crestbrook no longer purchases it."

"They stopped ordering from my bakery many years ago, my lord. It was after you left for university."

"Then I will have them start again at once."

She brightened. "That would be much appreciated."

"I have a large household. Send ten loaves a day to Crestbrook. Rather, I shall have a footman come into town each morning to pick them up from you."

Her eyes widened. "That is most generous of you, my lord."

"Yours is the best bread to be found, Mrs. Shaft. It will also save my cook hours of time." He smiled. "Then everyone at Crestbrook can reap the benefits of eating your loaves of tasty bread."

"How many will be in your party, my lord?"

"Counting Lady Lia and myself, four more, Mrs. Shaft. We will need tea and sweets."

"I will put on water to boil now, my lord. Have a seat."

The viscount led Lia to a table and seated her, saying, "All the tables in here are small. I will push a few together in order to seat all of us."

He spent a moment moving the furniture about and then took a seat next to her. Their thighs brushed together, and she caught the intoxicating scent of bergamot again, which she had smelled in the carriage earlier.

"Thank you for agreeing to join us on tomorrow's ride," she said. "I know it is hard for you to leave Celia behind. You will have to think of temporary care for her, however. It will take time for your inquiry to reach town, much less for a governess to be found and sent to Cumberland."

Then an idea struck her. "I would be happy to care for Celia until her governess arrives."

He looked startled. "You do not have to volunteer to do so, my lady. I will keep Celia with me when I can. At other times, I will ask a maid to watch her for me."

"I am going to be here until mid-November, my lord, and I adore children. You see how much she and I enjoy one another's company. Let me help you until you have a more permanent arrangement in place."

The viscount studied her a long moment, his eyes seeming to

penetrate to her soul.

"If you do not believe I would be taking advantage of you, Lady Lia, then I would be happy for you to help with the care of my niece."

CHAPTER TWELVE

L IA DECIDED TO wait and share her news about looking after Celia until she and her family sat down to tea in the drawing room. She went straight to the pianoforte in the music room and practiced for an hour after they returned home from Kidsgrove. She had always found comfort in playing, and today was no exception.

Steeling herself, she made her way to the drawing room, knowing Mama would be the biggest obstacle to her plans. She found everyone had already arrived and slipped into a seat next to Tray as the teacart was rolled into the room. She had a feeling if Tray came to her defense, Mama might not object.

"So, how did you find Kidsgrove?" Tray asked, placing a sandwich and two tarts on his plate.

"It is certainly smaller than our local village," Tia said. "I liked it, though. Everyone was quite friendly. And Mrs. Shaft's cake was outstanding."

"What kind did you try?" Aunt Agnes asked.

"I had lemon crème," Tia said. "But I took a bite of Verina's baked apple pudding and also one of Justina's mince pie. All were delicious."

"I had a slice of pound cake," Lia shared. "It was so rich and buttery. In fact, I may only drink tea now since I am still full."

"What of Celia's gowns?" Mama asked. "Tell us what you chose."

Her mother was interested in fashion and had spent hours with Tia and her as they looked at designs for gowns and various materials for their come-out gowns. Lia only hoped the wardrobes they'd had made up for their debuts could be worn, even if they were a year old.

They took turns discussing what Mrs. Penny would create for Celia, and Justina told them about the girl's boots and slippers.

"Lord Cressley is supposed to return with Celia in a week," Justina concluded. "I think one of us should go with him to make certain things fit Celia properly."

"I would be happy to do so," she said, ready to lead into her new duties. "I have volunteered to help Lord Cressley look after Celia until her governess arrives."

Immediately, she felt Mama's gaze upon her. "Why on earth would you do something like that, Cornelia? You are here to visit your cousins, not play nursemaid to some child."

"You know I am terribly fond of children, Mama. Lord Cressley is in a bit of a pickle, having dismissed Celia's worthless nursemaid. We have compromised regarding her care. Celia will come to Traywick Manor every Monday, Wednesday, and Friday, while I will go to Crestbrook on Tuesday, Thursday, and Saturday. I will still get to see my cousins plenty, and I know they, too, will enjoy being around Celia."

As she had expected, Tia leaped to her defense. "Yes, Mama. We all adore Celia. It will be good to have her around. She has had no guidance in her life. It will be good for her to be in the company of us all. The viscount has worried about her manners, and we can all take time to help teach her the things a young girl her age needs to know."

Before Mama could complain further, Verina and Justina also echoed the same sentiments, assuring their aunt of how much they like Celia.

"It will be good practice for all of us when we have children of our own," Lia concluded. "If we had made our come-outs as planned, Tia and I both might already be wed—and with child.

Having the four of us watch over Celia a few days a week will give us a better idea about how to raise a child."

"And what of you going to Crestbrook?" Mama asked. "You are an unwed lady, Cornelia. It is not the done thing for someone in your position to traipse about a viscount's house."

Lia stifled a giggle. "The only traipsing might be about the country, Mama. It is only for a few weeks, until a governess arrives at Crestbrook. I will spend a good portion of the day with Celia in the schoolroom. We can also enjoy playing outside. She enjoys the gardens, so we can stroll through them. And I asked Lord Cressley if I might teach her how to ride, as well. Tia and I sat our first ponies when we were only three or four. As a viscount's daughter being raised in the country, riding is definitely a skill Celia should master. I would love to get her started on that path."

"It sounds as if Lia will not even encounter Lord Cressley during her days at Crestbrook, Aunt Alice," Tray said, contributing to the conversation. "As a man in a similar position, I can tell you he will be busy and away from the house much of the day."

She flashed Tray a grateful smile.

Mama sighed. "It seems your mind is already made up, Cornelia. You would think you might have discussed the matter with me beforehand. But what do I know? I am only your mother."

Aunt Agnes chuckled. "Oh, Alice, do not be so put out. I think it is lovely that Lia has been kind enough to offer to help our neighbor. And you admitted to me that Celia is an enchanting child."

"True," Mama said grudgingly. "I suppose we shall see since the two of us are supposed to watch over her tomorrow." She looked to Tray. "How long will you be out riding, Traywick?"

"Most of the day, Aunt Alice. There is much to see. I wish I had more time at home. I would take you all down to Grasmere. That is where Wordsworth lived and wrote about."

"Is it too far to ride to tomorrow?" Lia asked. "I so enjoy Mr.

Wordsworth's poems."

"I am keeping us closer to home," he replied. "I planned for us to see Derwentwater, which is a beautiful lake, and have us walk a bit around Buttermere. That valley is surrounded by mountains, and the views are stunning. And I know Mama would be up to taking you by carriage to Kenwick. It is the most northern town in the Lake District. It is but five miles from Traywick Manor."

"It does sound exciting. Perhaps we can see Grasmere at another time," she said, trying to hide her disappointment, knowing her cousin was already taking valuable time to take them out tomorrow when he was so close to leaving for his final year of study.

"Mama, you could take everyone to Grasmere while I am gone," Tray suggested. "You are familiar with the area."

"Not as much as you, Traywick," her aunt said. "But it is a thought. We could go down by carriage early one morning and see the sights along the way. It's a lovely town, and I know exactly where we could stay overnight."

"We could even rent horses to ride and see Mr. Wordsworth's former cottage," Justina said with enthusiasm.

"Under no circumstances will I allow my daughters to roam the wilds of northern England without proper supervision," Mama said, dampening the spirits of everyone in the room.

"What if Lord Cressley went with you?" Tray mused. "He could help in hiring the horses and ride out with all the young ladies. They would be safe in his care."

Mama harumphed. "That would be quite a bit to ask of someone we barely know."

Tray smiled at Mama, and Lia knew just how susceptible her mother was to male charm. "But he is our neighbor, Aunt Alice. Yes, he has been gone a good while, but he will be next door to us for decades to come. He might enjoy such an outing, and I know my sisters and cousins would, too. And Mama would also be going."

"Would you go with them, Agnes?" Mama said.

"In the carriage," Aunt Agnes said. "I would be happy to take you all about the shops in Keswick. Riding is not for me, however. Alice, you and I could stay at the inn while the young people had a bit of fun on their own."

Before Mama agreed, Tray said, "I will tell Cressley about this future outing to Grasmere tomorrow during our ride. See if he would be amenable to accompanying all of you in my absence."

The matter seemed settled, and Lia was grateful her mother did not turn the conversation back to Lia keeping Celia for the next several weeks.

Because she was determined to do what she wished to do, and that meant spending more time with Celia—and her uncle.

WHY ON EARTH had he agreed to allow Lady Lia to watch over Celia?

Rupert and his niece now rode in his carriage toward Tray-wick Manor. He looked at the small girl sitting next to him, her hand in his. A new burst of love for this child filled him. She was the reason he had agreed to Lady Lia's generous proposal.

His growing attraction to her would only spell disaster for the two of them, and he vowed to keep his distance from her. His days would be tied up on his estate anyway, while she would be spending hers with Celia.

Rupert leaned down and kissed the top of his niece's head.

She glanced up. "Why did you kiss me?"

"Because I love you," he declared, causing her to say, "I love you, too, Uncle Rupert."

He had sent a message to Lord Traywick when he realized he had no horse to ride on today's tour. Because his brother never came to Crestbrook, the only horse in the stables beyond the carriage horses Rupert had brought was the one his steward used. Williamson had graciously given the horse over to Rupert to use the times he had ridden out on the property. He had taken Celia with him, and his niece seemed to enjoy riding. Now that he would live in the country a majority of the time, he would need to add a few riding horses to the Crestbrook stables.

In the meantime, the earl had returned his message, saying that he had a good mount which Rupert could borrow.

He looked forward to today's outing. It had been so many years since he had taken in the beauty of the surrounding area. He knew he would not only enjoy seeing it—but seeing it through Lady Lia's eyes, as she was exposed to the true beauty of Cumberland.

They arrived at Traywick Manor, and he dismissed his coachman, telling him to return by six o'clock that evening, the time the earl had previously recommended.

Rupert took Celia to the door and was greeted by the butler before he even knocked.

"Good morning, Lord Cressley, Miss Celia," Larsen said. "Lady Traywick and Her Grace have just gone to the parlor if you will allow me to escort you to them."

He followed the butler, Celia carrying her new doll in one arm and the borrowed ball under her arm. The two women were chatting and rose to greet their guests.

"The others have just gone down to the stables, my lord," the countess informed him. "You may join them there." She looked to his niece. "It is so good to see you again, Celia. I see you brought back the ball. Is that a new doll? My, she looks very pretty. Would you mind showing her to me and Her Grace?"

Celia looked at him, and Rupert bent to one knee. Clasping her by the shoulders, he said, "Remember that you are to stay with Lady Traywick and Her Grace today while I am off on business."

"Will you be gone long?"

"All day, but tomorrow will be a special day. Lady Lia will come to Crestbrook to spend the entire day with you."

That caused her to brighten considerably.

"Be a good girl, Celia. I will see you tonight."

"And Lally, too?"

He smiled. "Lally, too." He then kissed the doll's brow and Celia's before taking his leave.

As Rupert made his way to the stables, he was happy Celia liked the doll he had purchased for her. She had named it immediately, and Lally was already her constant companion. As Lady Lia had predicted, Lally had slept nestled against Celia last night. He had told her to bring the borrowed ball back to Traywick Manor because he showed her the new ball he had bought at Mr. Shaft's shop yesterday. Rupert had taken Lady Lia's advice and not showered her with all the toys he had bought, thinking he could bring them out one at a time over the next several weeks, giving her something new to play with until her governess arrived.

The stables came into view, and he saw everyone gathered outside the structure. He strode toward them, seeing two grooms bringing out the first pair of horses to be ridden.

"Cressley!" Traywick called. "I am glad you could join us for our tour today."

"Where might we ride today, my lord?" Rupert asked.

"Throughout the area the poet Thomas Gray wrote about fifty years ago."

"I have read some of Gray's poems," Lady Lia said. "He was very fond of Cumberland. His poems are so descriptive. Tia and I look forward to seeing more of the area."

Traywick continued, telling Rupert, "We will ride south toward Derwentwater, the lake closest to us. I have already told my cousins it is the most beautiful they will ever see. From there, we will head southwest to Buttermere."

The earl looked to his cousins. "Buttermere is a small hamlet, and we can stable our horses and walk along the path that encircles Buttermere Lake. You will enjoy seeing the fells along the way."

"What are fells?" Lady Tia asked, frowning.

Lady Verina said, "It usually means hills, but in our area, it can encompass the moors and high barren fields, as well."

"After our lengthy walk around the lake, we can eat at the local pub," Lady Justina said. "We have done so in the past. The food is quite good, and we will have worked up an appetite after our long walk."

"We can reclaim our horses after that and head back toward Keswick," the earl said. To Rupert, he added, "I have told everyone we will not have time to visit Keswick, but it is a bustling town with plenty of shops to enjoy. Sometime soon, Mama will take my cousins to Keswick."

"It sounds like a very full day," Lady Lia said. "I am eager to start."

The earl looked to Rupert. "My cousins have assured me they are comfortable being in the saddle all day and are competent riders, able to ride over some of the rocky terrain we will encounter. I am assuming the same for you, my lord, since you grew up here."

"I am happy to ride all day through Cumberland," he said. "I am passionate about the beauty of the area. It is the chief reason I will choose to remain in the country most of my time. Even when I was a soldier, far from here, my heart always belonged to Cumberland."

By now, the grooms had brought out horses for their entire riding party. He asked Lady Tia if she needed help mounting, and she accepted his assistance. He moved on to her twin.

"Might I help you into the saddle, Lady Lia?"

"Yes, please."

His hands spanned her waist as he lifted her into the saddle. Once again, he asked himself why he felt nothing when assisting her twin, and yet his insides seemed to turn to marmalade simply touching Lady Lia briefly.

Rupert headed to where Lord Traywick stood with the last two horses, and the earl said, "This is the mount I chose for you, Cressley. Ajax is a fine horse. Since you have no riding horses in your stables, I am happy to give you use of Ajax as long as you have need of him."

"That is very generous offer, my lord. Yes, I do need to purchase a few new horses for my stables. Carriage horses cannot be ridden about the estate, and being in the country, you know as well as I do that having horses to get around is essential."

"I hope you will get along with Ajax."

He stepped toward the horse and patted his flank. "I believe Ajax and I will do just fine together."

The two men swung into the saddle, and their party began to canter. Conversation would be impossible as they rode at this pace, which Rupert was grateful for, simply because he suddenly found himself tongue-tied in Lady Lia's presence. What was it about her that made him feel like an awkward schoolboy?

Even worse, he knew she hadn't a clue as to how he felt about her. Rupert reminded himself of her wish to wed for love, as her two siblings had. He was afraid his time in the miliary had wrung all emotion from him, officers having to be stoic no matter what the circumstances. It had surprised him how quickly he had come to love Celia, but he thought any tender feelings left within him would be used up on his niece.

He promised himself to keep his distance from Lady Lia in the coming weeks. To focus on learning more about his responsibilities at Crestbrook. Then when the Season did arrive next spring, he would go to town and find someone he believed would be a good viscountess and mother to his niece. That he would make a suitable match—not one based upon love.

And Rupert told himself that he would learn to be happy with that match.

CHAPTER THIRTEEN

L IA WAS ENTHRALLED by the passing scenery.

Almost as enthralled as she was with Viscount Cressley.

She could not seem to stop thinking about the man, no matter how hard she tried. Tia had cornered her last night when they went to their shared bedchamber, asking Lia again about her feelings regarding Lord Cressley. Being twins, they had never bothered to hide anything from one another. Oftentimes, they knew how the other one felt without asking, and this was the case with Lord Cressley.

Tia had told her that she knew the viscount stirred something within her twin, and that is why she had encouraged them to go off on their own to Mrs. Shaft's tearoom yesterday, asking if the time alone together had helped anything to blossom between them. Lia admitted she had feelings for the viscount but could not say if they were returned, citing how stoic he appeared at all times. Tia had mentioned the viscount turned tender whenever he looked at his niece, and she told Lia she had caught Lord Cressley looking at Lia in a similar fashion.

That had given Lia hope.

Suddenly, making her come-out seemed incredibly unimportant. Yes, she would enjoy the balls because she adored dancing, but she was not as outgoing as her twin. Lia had always done better in conversations with one or two people, and the thought of having to make small talk with an entire ballroom of guests caused her heart to race. She was fast coming to love Cumberland and could see herself living here.

With Lord Cressley and Celia.

In their conversations, she had told the viscount of how Ariadne and Val had made love matches and how she was eager to do so for herself. She feared now that might have frightened him off. Lia realized he was a man whose life was in tremendous transition. Lord Cressley had been a second son, knowing his destiny lay in the military. Suddenly, he was yanked from the only life he had known and thrust into a new one. Not only did he have new duties in being Viscount Cressley, but he also had Celia placed under his care. Lia could tell how close the pair had become in the short time they had known one another, each clinging to the other.

Would there be room for her—and would Lord Cressley be able to open his heart further to Lia—and love?

She would be in Cumberland about another two months. Hopefully, that would give her time to decide if she truly wished for a marriage and life with Lord Cressley. In return, he would have the same amount of time to see if she might be the one who could bring him lasting happiness. Lia thought they already had a strong foundation of friendship. Perhaps that might be a pathway to love. Most *ton* marriages were made in order to strengthen a family's social status within Polite Society and many couples lived separate lives from one another. In fact, if she had made her come-out last spring, Mama had explained that Lia might only speak to a gentleman a handful of times before a betrothal was announced.

Having these two months in Cumberland to get to know Lord Cressley would be a vast improvement over having danced with a gentleman two or three times and then becoming engaged to a stranger. She could not force the issue, however. For now, Lia would settle for a budding friendship with Lord Cressley and enjoy the time she was able to spend with Celia. If she returned to Kent without an offer of marriage from the viscount, she would have to accept that they were not right for one another.

They slowed their horses to a walk several times, simply to enjoy the beauty of Derwentwater Lake and the surrounding mountains. They passed through Watendlath, a small hamlet surrounded by rugged beauty, and then they reached Honister Pass. Sheep grazed on the hills of both sides of the pass, and Tray pointed out the local slate mine.

"They produce what is called Westmoorland slate, which is a striking green in color. You will see it used throughout London and beyond."

"This landscape is breathtaking," she said.

Lord Cressley, who had stopped his horse next to hers, said, "I could not agree with you more, my lady. I have seen more than most, thanks to my travels in the army, and I can tell you there is no place on earth quite like Cumberland."

They reached Buttermere, a tiny hamlet, and stopped at the pub. While they stayed with the horses, Tray went inside to speak with the owner. He came out a few minutes later.

"I have arranged for our horses to be kept in a stable next to this pub."

Each rider dismounted, and they led the mounts to the stable, where a boy of about ten and five would water and feed their horses.

As they emerged, Tray said, "We will now walk about Buttermere Lake's footpath. It is a leisurely footpath, not challenging in the least. You will enjoy seeing the High Stile range to the south and Dale Head range to the north."

"I like the view from Cat Bells," Verina said. "From there, we will be able to see the western side of Derwentwater."

"How long will it take to walk about the lake?" she asked.

"Usually two to three hours," Justina said. "It will depend on how often we stop to admire the views."

"I told the pub owner we would be back in about two and a half hours," Tray said. "I requested that he have a meal ready for us at that time."

"The path is this way," Justina said, linking her arm through her sister's and leading the way.

Tray offered his arm to Tia. "Come, Cousin. Walk with me. I will probably bore you with talk of birds, so kindly tell me to be quiet when you tire of me."

Tia laughed and slipped her arm through Tray's.

That left Lia with Lord Cressley, who smiled at her, offering his arm. She placed her hand through the crook of it, inhaling the scent of bergamot as she did so.

They followed the others and reached Buttermere Lake quickly. For a few minutes, they strolled quietly, and then Lia asked, "Are you settling in at Crestbrook?"

"Actually, I feel I already have. I had not been to my family's estate since my first year in university. I had forgotten how beautiful it is. I am beginning to know my tenants, and Celia and I have walked every inch of the grounds. At five years of age, she knows Crestbrook better than I ever did, and I always roamed the land as a child."

"Were you lonely growing up?" she asked.

He thought a moment before responding to her question. "Yes—and no. Yes, in the sense that I did not ever feel I had a family. With my mother dying in childbirth and my father staying in town most of the year, I had no parents in my life, to speak of. Perceval was years older than I was, away at school or university much of the year. Then later, he always stayed in town. I rarely saw him and really never spoke with him. The servants were the ones who looked after me, especially the butler and housekeeper. From what I gather, the couple retired five years ago and moved to Grasmere, where they now live with their daughter and her family. I did have a tutor before going away to school, but for the most part? I think I raised myself."

They walked on in silence again, looking over the lake, which appeared as glass on this windless day. It reflected the mountains surrounding it, giving her pause as she absorbed the stunning beauty of the landscape.

Then Lord Cressley broke the silence. "I suppose that is why I want much more for Celia and any children I might sire. While my childhood and lack of upbringing led me to be incredibly independent and self-reliant, it was a lonely existence. I want Celia to feel a sense of family. I hope I will have several children so that she will have many cousins to grow up with."

"My sister Ariadne has a unique philosophy. We Worthington siblings felt abandoned each year when Mama and Papa went to town for the Season. Instead of leaving Penelope behind, Ariadne took her babe to town when she and Julian attended this past Season. She believes the season is more than attending social events. She and Julian will bring their children to town each year, so they will never be apart from them. Ariadne has asked her siblings and cousins to do the same. I have told you there are ten cousins in our families, and we only saw one another on one occasion when we were children. If we all bring our own children to town each year, we can meet up frequently with one another, and all the cousins will have a strong sense of family."

"That is a very different way of doing things, totally unlike what is practiced now by the *ton*. I admire your sister's perseverance in this endeavor."

"Val and Eden have agreed to do so. Tia and I will also abide by this and bring our children to town. I know Ariadne has already asked the same of our cousins Con and Lucy. Lucy is supposed to talk to her sister Dru about it, as well. I have yet to mention this to Tray, Verina, or Justina, but I think they will be amenable to the arrangement."

He halted. "I think I must do the same. I cannot imagine Celia alone here at Crestbrook when I go to town for the Season next spring and hunt for a bride. Why, I could be gone several months. It would break her heart to be separated from me for so long. Mine, as well."

Lia thought her own heart would break with his words. Obviously, the attraction she felt toward him was one-sided since he was talking about finding a bride next Season. Hurt filled her, a physical pain, and she pulled her hand from his arm. She crossed her arms and paused to look out over the lake, tears brimming in her eyes. Above all, she could not let him see her shed a single tear over him. Blinking rapidly several times, she hoped they dissipated.

She told herself that he wouldn't be a good husband to her. That he would always put Celia above his wife. While she thought it admirable that he thought so much of his niece and was protective of her, Lia believed a marriage should be sacred, and the love of husband and wife should outshine everything, even the children they had. Yes, children were important and deserved to be loved for who they were, but not if it sacrificed the relationship between their parents. Despite her tender feelings toward the viscount, she saw now that he could never return the same to her. Celia would always be between them.

Much as Lia liked the little girl, she would never play second fiddle to anyone.

Marching ahead, Viscount Cressley caught up to her. "You took off without me."

Tamping down the strong emotions still running through her, and not wanting to embroil him in her personal turmoil, which he was totally unaware of, she apologized.

"I am sorry, my lord. I got caught up in my own thoughts and the beauty of the land." She gazed ahead. "We should catch up to the others."

Lia hurried off, not waiting to take his arm. She did not think she could stand to have him touch her again and would do whatever it took to avoid his touch. She would not be able to avoid seeing him, however, especially since she had agreed to help him in supervising Celia. Then again, while Celia was in her care, it would free Lord Cressley so that he could attend to his duties. If she were lucky, she would only see him sporadically.

They continued their walk around Buttermere Lake. Lia made certain from that point on, they were close to the others, enough so that she could converse with her sister and cousins.

Every now and then they would stop and point out something of interest. She had a fondness for birds and spotted a white-throated dipper and a peregrine, while Tia saw a red kite and Tray identified a raven. She also enjoyed seeing the numerous red squirrels in the area, so very different from the squirrels running about Kent.

"The area is frequented by those wishing to see its beauty during the summer months," Tray said. "A travel guide was written last century, describing the area, and the name Lake District took hold. In late spring and throughout the summer months, the surrounding region has hordes of visitors descend upon it, wishing to tour from Keswick to Grasmere."

"I am glad we are seeing it at this time of year," Lia said. "I am not particularly fond of crowds."

They arrived back in Buttermere close to two and a half hours after they had set out. The pub owner greeted them, saying he had an upper room where they could dine in a bit of privacy. The ladies excused themselves to take advantage of using the facilities, and when they returned, cold ale was set out on the table. Lia drank half her mug in one swallow, parched after their long trek.

The food brought to them was tasty, a hearty stew, filled with chunks of meat, potatoes, and vegetables. Fresh, hot bread and crocks of butter were also brought.

When Tray asked if dessert was available, the pub owner said to leave it to him. Minutes later, bowls of baked apples sprinkled with cinnamon arrived, with scoops of apricot ice cream atop them.

"I have never tasted anything so good," she declared.

Then her gaze met Lord Cressley's. He sat opposite her, and she had avoided looking at him, talking to everyone but him as they ate. He held it, and she sensed a deep yearning, something which confused her to no end.

Tia tapped her arm, breaking the spell, and Lia turned to her twin, who asked her a question. By the time she had answered and looked back, Lord Cressley was speaking with Justina.

"Is everyone finished?" Tray asked. "We should claim our horses and make our way back. We will go home a different way than the way we came. Newlands Valley will be a large part of the scenery and something different for us to enjoy."

"Can we stop at the waterfall?" Justina asked. "It is only about a quarter-hour walk from the road we will be on."

"No, I think not," Tray said. "We have no one to tend to our horses. Most likely, there is no place we could tie them up. And the path is too narrow and rocky to ride them to the waterfall. Perhaps another time, Justina."

Tray settled their bill with the pub owner, and they claimed their horses again. She made certain her cousin helped seat her upon her horse, and she chose to ride close to Tray on their way back. He told her about some of the mining in the area.

"Cumberland is full of other mines beyond slate. Copper. Lead. Even graphite, which is used in pencils."

"I am keeping a journal of what I have seen on my travels from Kent to Cumberland," she told him. "I will certainly rave in my writings about what we have seen today. The cloud-capped fells. The clear blue of Derwentwater. The rugged beauty of the fields. I am glad we made the circuit about Buttermere Lake. It was idyllic being surrounded by mountains and such breathtaking views"

They cantered on and off the rest of the way home, and Lia was pleased that she did not have to speak once to Lord Cressley.

When they arrived at Traywick Manor, she was glad to finally be home again. It would take time to nurse her bruised heart, but now that she knew Viscount Cressley held no interest in her, Lia could push aside the foolish notions she had held about him and merely enjoy her visit to Cumberland.

She dropped to the ground from her horse and took the reins, leading it inside the stables and handing a groom the reins before exiting the structure. They walked as a group up to the house. She couldn't help but be aware that the viscount walked with

Tray, and she thought it a good thing. Lord Cressley might not be interested in her as a wife, but he would be a good friend to Tray, especially once Tray completed his studies and returned to Traywick Manor for good.

They were met by Larsen, who said Cook had anticipated they would be hungry after the long day and that a buffet would be set up in the breakfast room for them.

"I should be off," Lord Cressley said. "Where might my niece be?"

"Last I knew, she was in the schoolroom having milk and bread with Lady Traywick, my lord," the butler replied.

Lia saw the others had headed toward the breakfast room, so she said, "I can take you to Celia, my lord. We should discuss what time you need me to arrive at Crestbrook tomorrow."

She went to the staircase and climbed the stairs without his assistance. They reached the top, and she turned to her right.

"The schoolroom is this way, my lord," she said, hoping he would follow her.

Suddenly, his hand took her elbow, preventing her from moving. "My lord?" she asked, frowning at him.

His gaze burned in to her, boring to the depths of her soul.

"You said you had never tasted anything as good as those baked apples," he said, his voice low and rough. "Since that moment, all I have wanted to taste . . . is you."

His words hung in the air. Lia shook her head, utterly confused. Then he took a few steps into the nearest room, a small bedchamber, bringing her along with him. His fingers still held her elbow, the heat of them scalding her. With his other hand, he cradled her nape.

"I may regret this, but I am going to kiss you, Lady Lia. The way I have wanted to ever since we met."

She stilled. She had never been kissed. It was a moment she had not thought much about, simply because Mama had harped upon the fact that she was never to be alone with a gentleman. That if she were found that way, especially if in an embrace, she would be ruined.

The viscount's head bent, his mouth touching hers almost reverently. He pressed his lips against hers softly, breaking the kiss, then kissing her again. And again. His bergamot scent swirled about her, intoxicating her, even as his lips danced against hers. Lia reached up and linked her fingers behind his nape, pulling him closer to her.

His arm went about her, pinning her to him, their bodies flush against one another. Heat sparked within her, rushing through her limbs. His kisses grew more demanding, lasting longer each time. Then he shocked her, slowly running his tongue along the seam of her mouth, causing her to gasp. Quickly, his tongue slipped inside her mouth, gliding along, caressing her tongue, bringing about the most incredible sensations. She tasted him, even as he tasted her, and he was far more divine than any baked apple could ever be.

They continued kissing, her tongue now warring with his as she quickly learned the art of kissing from him. The blood pumped loudly in her ears, roaring so that if he had spoken to her, she would not have heard a word. The place between her legs came to life, aching, then throbbing, wanting something she did not understand.

Then as quickly as it began, he broke the kiss, his hands lightly clasping her wrists, bringing them back to her side. She stared up at him in wonder.

"You tasted of those baked apples and cinnamon," he said softly, his thumb sliding along her bottom lip. "But also of so much more."

Then his hand fell away. He stepped back, leaving her perplexed.

"I thought . . . you did not like me," she told him.

A gleam came into his eyes. "I find that I like you too much, Lia." He cleared his throat. "We must go to Celia."

He returned to the corridor, and she joined him, her legs shaky. They continued down the hall, and she showed him the door, incapable of words.

Opening it, he exclaimed, "There is my girl!"

Celia ran to him, standing on tiptoe and throwing her arms about his waist. He scooped her up.

"How was your day with Lady Traywick and Her Grace?"

"Fun," she said. "We played with dolls. Her Grace took me to the music room. I got to touch the . . ." She looked back at Aunt Agnes, who smiled and said, "The pianoforte."

"That's it. I played music, Uncle Rupert! And we went to the stables and petted the horses. I got to play with a cat."

"It sounds like a wonderful day, Celia." He turned to face Lia. "Might you be at Crestbrook by nine o'clock tomorrow morning, my lady?"

"Of course, my lord," she said demurely, her heart still beating far too quickly. "I can stay as long as you need me to do so."

"I should return every day by teatime. In fact, I will try to do so before then so that you might be back at Traywick Manor to take your own tea with your cousins."

Disappointment flooded her. He had just given her a magical, enchanting kiss, one which made her feel womanly and desired— and now he was acting as if nothing out of the ordinary had occurred.

Raising her chin a notch, she said, "That would be most acceptable, my lord."

"Then I will be back by half-past three tomorrow." He looked to her aunt. "Lady Traywick, I am forever in your debt and that of Her Grace's for watching over Celia today."

"She is a good girl. We had a marvelous time." Aunt Agnes looked to Lia. "How was your tour?"

"Very good. I have never been swept away by such incredible scenery." Lia was proud she was able to put a full sentence together and grateful that her words actually made sense. "Larsen said Cook has prepared a buffet for us. Come and join us, Aunt Agnes."

"Might you stay, Lord Cressley?" her aunt asked.

"I fear I need to get this little one to bed, my lady, but thank you for your kind offer."

He left with Celia still in his arms. Lia and her aunt followed him downstairs, where he told her he would send his carriage for her.

"That is not necessary, Lord Cressley. I will ride over. It is more convenient."

"Then we will see you tomorrow."

"See you tomorrow, Lady Lia," Celia cried gleefully, and Larsen let them out the front door.

Lia turned and headed toward the breakfast room with her aunt, who caught her arm just before they entered.

"Do you have anything you wish to share with me?" Aunt Agnes asked, a knowing look in her eyes.

"No. Not at this time. Maybe after I reflect upon things I will come to you."

"Then I shall say nothing to Alice."

She hugged her aunt. "Thank you."

They entered the breakfast room and as Lia fixed herself a plate, she tried to push the kiss from her mind. It was definitely something she must think on at length. Alone.

She and Aunt Agnes took a seat, and they began reliving their day, talking about what they saw. She made certain to join in so that her mother would not suspect anything was amiss. Lia did not want Mama to forbid her from going to Crestbrook tomor-row.

When they finished eating, Lia said, "I need to go practice since I missed doing so this morning."

"You are so dedicated to your music," Justina said.

"It soothes me," she said, excusing herself and heading to the music room, knowing if she went anywhere else, someone would be around, and she would not have the time alone she needed.

Closing the door, Lia played for a few minutes, and then she stopped. She needed to consider what Lord Cressley's kiss had meant.

And how it had now changed things between them.

CHAPTER FOURTEEN

RUPERT ROSE AFTER a sleepless night. He poured water into the basin and then plunged his face into it, hoping the cold water would act to jolt him.

Not just physically—but emotionally.

He had done something extremely careless yesterday. Acted upon an impulse. He prided himself on being a disciplined man, a gentleman who would never take advantage of anyone, much less an inexperienced young miss such as Lady Lia Worthington. Yet that is exactly what he had done. Given in to his base desires. He had kissed her in a most ungentlemanly manner.

It was obvious she had never been kissed. The way she held her mouth. Her body. And oh, what a body it was. She was petite, just a couple of inches over five feet, but her bosom was more than ample. As it pressed against his chest, he wanted to tear his mouth from hers and greedily suck hard upon her breasts until she cried out his name.

He had only meant to kiss her for a moment. But one moment turned into several. One kiss had become many. And Lady Lia was a quick learner when it came to kissing. Before he knew it, she was kissing him back, stoking the fires buried deep inside him, causing him to want her more than he thought wanting a woman was possible.

Then he had dipped into the nectar of her mouth. The sweetness of her. The goodness. It was as tangible a taste as he had ever sampled. And now having tasted her, it only made him hunger for more. Her tongue had been like velvet, first as he grazed against it, then even more so as she glided it across his own. The little vixen had caught on to kissing so quickly, she almost began dominating the kiss.

That was when he'd had to end things between them. Before he took things even further. Before *she* took it further. If left to her own devices, Rupert wasn't sure what Lady Lia might have done. Just the thought of her slowly lowering her gown, releasing her breasts from their stays, had him almost panting. Or she might have raised her skirts, allowing him to view trim ankles and sleek calves.

"Stop!" he commanded harshly. "You cannot think of her as some wanton."

He scooped up water into his hands and splashed it against his face, letting it run down his neck and bare chest. He'd had to remove his trousers in the middle of the night, recalling guiltily how he had taken his cock in hand, all the while thinking of Lady Lia.

This was insanity. She was not for him. Lady Lia Worthington was the daughter of a duke and the sister to another one. Having already met her mother, he knew Her Grace would set her sights high for both her daughters, wishing for them to wed wealthy men with lofty titles who came from some of the most important families in all of England. He was but a lowly viscount from the northern regions. Wealthy, yes, but possessing no social connections. His only family was his niece, a by-blow who would not be accepted into Polite Society if they learned of her origins. Lady Lia had given Rupert several good pieces of advice, but the best was for him to keep Celia's illegitimacy to himself. Perceval, the only one who knew the whole truth, was dead. While a few servants knew about Celia's background, they were buried in the country with him and would remain loyal—and quiet—if they wished to maintain their positions in his household.

By the time Celia made her come-out more than a dozen

years from now, she would be accepted as his niece and be able to wed a gentleman. She would have had years of grooming and would know everything from how to curtsey and address those titles to everything involved in the womanly arts.

Rupert collapsed into a chair, his thoughts turning back to Lady Lia. He didn't know how he was going to face her again. He wondered if Lady Traywick suspected anything had passed between them before they had entered the schoolroom. The countess had looked at him oddly. He hoped she had not pressed her niece.

He was going to have to forget that the incident ever occurred. Never speak of it again. If he apologized, Lady Lia might be embarrassed. He also feared if he brought it up, she might assign more importance to the kiss than it should hold. In the grand scheme of things, it had merely been a kiss. A powerful, all-consuming kiss, but a kiss, all the same. No one had witnessed it, which protected her reputation. Neither he nor Lady Lia should be obligated to make a commitment to one another, based upon a single kiss. Not only was he not an ideal candidate which the dowager duchess would consider for her daughter, he was not in love with Lady Lia. That alone should keep her from thinking of him as her future husband.

Telling himself that he had satisfied his curiosity by kissing her, he thrust all thoughts of her—and the kiss—from his mind.

That lasted all of five seconds.

"Bollocks!" he proclaimed.

The kiss had been the best of his life. That still did not mean anything needed to come from it. He had satisfied his curiosity. Lady Lia was physically appealing to him. In a way, he was a bit proud to have given her the first kiss of her life. Now, she would have a barometer in which to compare other kisses she received as next Season unfolded.

Then why did the thought of another man kissing her seem to drive him to the point of madness?

"Bloody hell," he muttered, ringing for Damsley.

His valet arrived several minutes later, carrying hot water. Rupert sat still as Damsley shaved him, his thoughts drifting again and again to the kiss. This time, he allowed them to do so. He told himself there was no harm in thinking about it. It was a very pleasant memory, not something to be banished. He simply could not, at any future time and under any circumstances, act upon impulse and kiss her again. It would be wrong to do so. It would convince her he was interested in her. It might even cause him to offer for her, which was the last thing he might intend.

No. She was a friend, if men and women could *be* friends, that is. Lady Lia was doing him a favor. Helping him care for Celia while he awaited the arrival of a London governess. He would keep their conversations light. Only speak of his niece or something as inane as the weather.

Damsley assisted him in dressing, and Rupert went to Celia's bedchamber. She still lay sleeping, Lally held close. In sleep, his niece looked much younger than her five years. He leaned over, kissing her brow. She stretched, slowly opening her eyes.

"Good morning, my little love."

Immediately, she asked, "Is Lady Lia here?"

Even hearing the name caused his heart to shrivel. "No, not yet. You must rise and dress and be ready for her when she comes to spend today with you."

He helped her to get ready for the day, braiding her hair carefully, wanting Celia to look perfect for Lady Lia.

They went down to breakfast together. His appetite, usually robust, seemed to vanish.

Then a footman came in the breakfast room, whispering to Prater. His butler immediately came to him.

"Lady Lia Worthington has arrived, my lord."

She was early.

His heart racing, Rupert said, "Please show her to the breakfast room, Prater."

Moments later, Lady Lia appeared. Celia scrambled from his lap, running across the room to greet her.

"Come see Lally, Lady Lia. She's my doll. Uncle Rupert got her for me."

With a glint of mischief in her eyes, Lady Lia said, "I will wager Lally will become your best friend, Celia."

She came to the table, Celia holding her hand. He rose. "Have a seat, my lady. Would you care for a cup of tea?"

"No, thank you." She glanced at the table. "Celia, you must finish your breakfast before we are off."

"Where?" his niece asked.

"Oh, we have lots of things we will do today while your uncle works about his estate."

He seated himself again, picking up Celia and returning her to his lap. "Eat, little love."

"I hope you do not mind that I am a bit early," Lady Lia said. "I thought the sooner I arrived, the sooner you could get started on what you needed to do for the day."

"I am meeting with a few tenants who say they need new roofs," he told her. "Fortunately, with the loan of Ajax, I can reach them sooner."

"I will have Celia in the drawing room at half-past three today and every day after that, my lord. At least the days I will be here. Are you still willing to have her come to Traywick Manor on the other days?"

"Yes. I will either bring her myself or have Mrs. Prater ride with her in my carriage and deliver her to Traywick Manor."

"That would be inconvenient for you. Why don't you allow me to fetch her? I have quite taken to Orion in my cousin's stables. The horse would not mind the addition of another rider who is so light."

"That would be going out of your way, my lady."

"Nonsense," she said, waving her hand in the air. "I shall come for Celia at the same time each day and then bring her back to Crestbrook on the days she visits with us at Traywick Manor."

He finally allowed his gaze to meet hers. "If you are certain."

"I am, my lord."

Rupert suddenly wondered why she wasn't mentioning the kiss. Then again, they were in a room with his butler, two footmen, and a five-year-old. Besides, he had already decided to act as if it had not occurred. Apparently, Lady Lia had come to the same conclusion.

"I'm through," announced Lia, climbing from his lap. She reached for Lally, who had been sitting on the table.

Lady Lia rose. Holding out her hand, she said, "The first place we will go will be the gardens. I love the smell of fresh flowers in a garden, especially early in the day."

"Lally likes flowers," Celia said.

"Then it seems as if we all have much in common." She led the girl from the room, pausing at the door and glancing over her shoulder. "Good day, my lord."

Before he could reply, she was gone.

Rupert stood, placing his napkin in the chair. He drained the rest of the coffee from his cup and left the breakfast room, heading toward his study. For an hour, he tried to review a report Williamson had compiled of the autumn harvest, comparing it to harvests from the previous five years. It proved to be impossible. He set the report aside and made his way to the stables, asking for Ajax to be saddled for him. He rode the estate for a bit before heading toward the area where his tenants had their cottages. He met with three of them, using a ladder to climb up and inspect the roofs himself. Williamson had admitted to Rupert that those days were behind him, hinting again that he would be retiring soon.

Once he was on the ground again, he said, "I agree. All three roofs need to be replaced. I will speak to Mr. Williamson and see that the supplies are purchased. As soon as we have them in hand, we will place new roofs on these cottages."

"You might want to look at all the roofs, my lord," one of the men said. "It has been a while since any tenant received a new roof. Our three were simply in the worst shape."

Returning to the ladder, he lifted it and said, "Where to next?"

Two hours later, he had examined each roof in the grouping of cottages. Fortunately, he had brought a small notebook with him, and he drew a map of the area, drawing squares for each cottage, then marking the ones needing immediate replacements of their roofs. He then used a numbered scale with one being the lowest need and five indicating the highest need of replacement.

"I will draw up a more concrete plan at home," he told his tenants. "We will start replacing roofs on a rotating basis. I will keep accurate records of when we do so, and then we can rotate our schedule in the future so that a few at a time are replaced or repaired."

As he rode back to the house, ready to visit with Williamson in his office, he decided he needed to confront the longtime estate manager and think about replacing him.

When he arrived, Williamson was hard at work, as always.

"I hate to interrupt you, but I would like to talk about new roofs."

The steward set down his pencil. "Ah, yes. Thank you for climbing up there, Lord Cressley. My old, creaky bones are no longer fit to do so. Not that I ever enjoyed heights anyway."

Not wanting to hurt the older man's feelings, he said, "You have dropped hints to me that you are thinking of retirement. Is that what you wish to do, Williamson?"

Relief swept across the steward's face. "Indeed, it is, my lord. I have been at Crestbrook since your father's time, when you were a small boy. My eyesight isn't what it used to be. Steward-ship is a game for a younger man. I was ready to write to Lord Cressley in London and tell him it was time to look for my replacement—but he died—and you came. I could not simply walk away and leave you in a bind, my lord."

"That was most thoughtful of you, Williamson."

"You are good man, Lord Cressley. You will make for a won-derful viscount. Already, you have a solid grasp on your duties. With an efficient steward, you will be set."

"Do you have any recommendations for me? I know oftentimes positions such as these are filled by word of mouth," he said, recalling that Lady Traywick had mentioned it to him earlier.

"As a matter of fact, my cousin's boy is an assistant steward on an estate near Eskdale. He is nearing thirty years of age and itching to manage his own estate."

"You believe he would be the best candidate to replace you?" he asked.

"I do, my lord. His name is Adam Holson. He is thoughtful. Dedicated. And what he doesn't know, he learns how to do."

"Write to him, Williamson. Say that I am interested in hiring him. If he agrees to come, have him turn in his notice to his current employer."

The steward looked surprised. "You do not wish to interview him, my lord?"

"You have put heart and soul into Crestbrook all these years. You would not willingly turn it over to someone who is unworthy. Yes, I will meet with him—and you—when Holson arrives. I would hope you would stay on a bit to help him get his bearings." Rupert paused. "But if you believe he is the man for this post, then I simply agree with you."

Williamson's smile was wide. "Thank you, Lord Cressley. I promise that you will not be disappointed."

He left, his step lighter, and returned to his study for a bit. When it was a quarter after three, he went to the drawing room, surprised to see Lady Lia and Celia already there.

His niece caught sight of him. "Uncle Rupert! We're looking at the globe."

Coming toward them, he smiled. "Celia is fascinated with the globe."

Lady Lia nodded. "She most certainly is. We have spent the better part of an hour finding places on it and talking about them."

Celia tugged on his hand. "I'll show you. This is England. We live here. And this is France, where a bad man lives. He is mean and wants to take land that isn't his."

"Yes, Bonaparte. He is a mean man," Rupert agreed, keeping a straight face.

His niece went on for several minutes, showing him places on the globe and naming them. China. Canada. Egypt. It surprised him one so young could remember so much.

"You have learned quite a bit today," he praised.

"Lady Lia says I am very smart. I also practiced my numbers and letters." She paused. "I can write my name!"

He turned to Lady Lia. "You have worked a small miracle with her today, my lady."

"She is like an empty vessel, waiting to be filled. I knew children learned quickly, but Celia surpassed my expectations."

"May I walk you to the stables and your horse?" he asked.

Her chin went up a notch. "That is not necessary, my lord."

"I insist."

She nodded. "Celia, you can stay here for a few minutes and look at the atlas. Your uncle will be back soon, and then you can have tea together."

His niece nodded happily, heading toward the atlas. Rupert escorted Lady Lia from the drawing room. He did not say anything while they were inside the house. Only when they were outside and could not be overheard did he speak.

"I wanted to talk to you about our kiss," he began, not certain where to go from there, especially because he had told himself this was the last thing he planned to do.

"I suppose we should clear the air between us regarding the kiss," she agreed. When he said nothing, she took up the reins. "I think it only natural that sometimes there is a brief attraction between a man and a woman. You gave me my first kiss, Lord Cressley, and it was quite a good one. One which I will always treasure. But we both know that we are not meant for one another. I have shared with you that I seek a love match. You have told me that you plan to look for a bride come the spring Season. While the kiss was a pleasant experience, I do not believe either of us should make too much of it."

Her words made sense, but they also cut him to the quick. He had been afraid he would hurt her.

Instead, she was crippling him.

"I hope that we can remain friendly," she continued. "For Celia's sake and the fact that I believe you will become close friends with Tray. But I would prefer that we spend no time alone together, my lord. After all, we really shouldn't have done so in the first place. I have yet to make my come-out, and there are certain rules in Polite Society that we both should be adhering to."

They reached the stables, and a groom said, "I'll fetch Orion for you, my lady."

"Thank you." To Rupert, she added, "I hope with my taking on Celia, it frees you up to devote time to your new duties. In the future, I can make my own way to the stables, and you must remain with your niece in the drawing room. I do not plan to come inside Crestbrook tomorrow. I will call for Celia on Orion. A footman can let you know I am here and send Celia out to me."

She paused. "Do you have any questions for me, Lord Cressley?"

Deflated, he said, "Not a one, Lady Lia. You seem to have covered everything thoroughly."

"Well, I am known for my practical nature. Ah, here is Orion."

She stepped away from him and to the horse, allowing the groom to toss her into the saddle.

"I wish you a good day, Lord Cressley."

"And I wish you the same, Lady Lia," he replied, his words like dust in his mouth.

Nudging her horse, she took off at a brisk canter. Rupert watched her riding away, feeling as if he had lost all hope for his future.

CHAPTER FIFTEEN

As Lia rode from Traywick Manor to Crestbrook the next morning, she finally admitted to herself that she had hoped yesterday's conversation with Lord Cressley had gone much different than it had. When she had told the viscount that they needed to limit the contact between them and brushed aside the kiss, she had secretly wished he would declare that he had feelings for her. Not that she thought he was in love with her—and she still wasn't certain if she was in love with him—but she had wanted him to protest what she had said. Instead, he had acquiesced to her wishes, and now she would not see much of him at all.

That thought threatened to send her into a deep melancholy.

Lia knew she must rally from this setback. She had an obligation to be happy around Celia as she cared for the child. Just because her relationship with Celia's uncle now proved to be almost nonexistent, she could not blame an innocent child for the mess two adults had made. In fact, she suspected that helping to care for Celia would become the bright spot of her day.

She rode around the lake, which was the shortest way to reach Lord Cressley's house, and came to a stop outside it in the circular drive. Almost immediately, the door opened, and a footman called, "I will fetch Miss Celia for you now, my lady."

He closed the door, and she sat atop Orion, composing herself in case Lord Cressley did accompany his niece outside. Lia had told him it would not be necessary, but she needed to prepare herself, all the same.

Both relief—and disappointment—flooded her when the door opened again, and Celia was escorted out by the housekeeper.

"Good morning, Mrs. Prater," she called, swallowing the lump in her throat. "And good morning to you, too, Celia."

"Thank you for taking on the child until a governess comes, my lady," Mrs. Prater said as she lifted Celia up to Lia. "None of us really know what to do with a small girl. You are a blessing in disguise."

As she settled Celia in front of her, she told the housekeeper, "It is a delight to have Miss Celia's company. I will bring her home by half-past three today, Mrs. Prater."

Turning Orion, she began walking the horse, allowing Celia time to get used to being on Orion with her.

"Go faster," Celia demanded.

Laughing, Lia complied, nudging the horse into a brisk canter.

They reached the lake and rode along the path until they were on Traywick lands. After they left the lake behind, Celia asked if they could go even faster.

"Hold on tight," she told the girl, bringing Orion into a full gallop for a few minutes.

She slowed the horse as the stables came into view, and Celia laughed in delight.

"Do you like being atop a horse?" she asked.

"I want to ride a horse like you and Uncle Rupert."

"Then that shall be the first thing we do today. I know of just the horse for you. It is a pony named Posey."

"Posey, Posey," Celia said in a sing-song voice.

They reached the stables, and she saw Tray standing in front. He took Celia from her, lowering the girl to the ground, and then helped Lia from the saddle.

"I get to ride today, my lord," Celia said happily. Lady Lia said so."

"That sounds quite fun, Celia," Tray said jovially.

A groom appeared with Tray's horse saddled, and her cousin took the reins in hand. Lia handed her reins to the same groom, and he led the horse into the stables.

"Are you riding out for a final time today?" she asked.

"Yes. I will miss being at Traywick Manor. I am thankful I was still here when you and Tia arrived. It has been so enjoyable connecting with you again, Cousin. Since tonight is my last night at home, Mama has promised me a dinner with all my favorite foods. She invited several neighbors to this dinner, but it struck me that Lord Cressley arrived after the invitations went out. Would you do me a favor and ask him if he would come and join us this evening?"

"I can do so when I return Celia to Crestbrook this afternoon," Lia said, not in favor of having to spend time in the viscount's company without Celia as a buffer.

"I think Cressley is going to be a wonderful addition to the neighborhood. He seems a decent fellow."

"Yes, I am certain the two of you will grow quite close over the years." Celia had been moving toward the stables and now entered, so Lia added, "I need to make certain my charge is all right. I hope you do not mind if I use Posey to teach her how to sit a horse. Celia is of an age where she needs to learn the basics of riding."

"Posey is perfect for a child's riding lessons. I will leave you to it, Lia."

Tray mounted his horse and gave a wave before riding away. She went inside the stables, catching up to Celia. They stopped in front of a stall where a horse leaned out, and Celia gazed up.

"He's so tall."

She picked up the girl and said, "Horses like to be scratched between their ears. Like this."

Lia demonstrated and then Celia did the same, causing a contented look to cross the animal's face.

"He's happy," Celia said.

"It does not take much to make a horse happy. Here, stroke his nose, like this."

She took Celia's hand in hers and had the girl pet the horse's nose and then the side of his neck.

"I like horses," the child declared.

"I learned to ride when I was a little girl. I have enjoyed doing so my entire life. Hopefully, you will take to it and feel the same way."

They continued down the row of stalls, talking to and petting several of the horses, finally coming to Posey.

She signaled a groom and said, "Please saddle Posey and put a leading rein on her."

"Right away, my lady."

Lia placed Celia on her feet again and took the girl's hand, leading her outside once more. After Posey appeared, ready for them, she told Celia a little about horses. Then she placed the child atop Posey's back, seeing Celia beam with joy.

For the next half-hour, she led the horse about, allowing Celia to grow comfortable at such a great height by herself. Being that far from the ground didn't seem to bother the girl in the least, and as Lia guided the horse, Celia called out to the head groom, who had come to watch the lesson.

"I'm riding!"

"I think that will be the end of today's lesson."

She motioned to the groom who had been standing nearby in case he was needed and gave him the leading rein. "Thank you," she said, pulling Celia from the saddle and placing her on the ground.

Celia slipped her hand into Lia's and said, "Can I ride again later?"

"Not today. The next time you come to Traywick Manor, though, we will have another lesson. You will be coming here every other day until your governess arrives."

As they began walking back toward the house, Celia asked, "What's a governess?"

It surprised her that Lord Cressley had not informed his niece of the person coming soon.

"She will be a very nice lady who will come to Crestbrook and teach you all kinds of things. She will also care for you. Bathe and dress you. See your hair is combed and braided. You will learn so much from her, such as how to read a book and do maths."

"I want *you* to be my governess," Celia said stubbornly, her bottom lip thrusting out in a pout.

"I am helping out your uncle for a couple of weeks until your governess arrives. I do not live here, though, Celia. Traywick Manor is the home of my cousins. Lady Tia and I live far away from here. You have to get into a carriage and ride for many days before you would reach Millvale, my home."

Tears welled in the girl's eyes. "Can't you stay here, Lady Lia? I want you to. Uncle Rupert does, too."

Her throat grew thick with unshed tears. Lia swallowed hard, forcing down the emotions. "I must go home to where my family lives, Celia. I miss them. Then I plan to go to the biggest city in England. It is called London. I will show you where it is in the atlas. There, I will find a nice man whom I wish to wed, and I will become his wife. We will have children together."

"You could be Uncle Rupert's wife," Celia suggested, not realizing how her words hurt Lia.

"Your uncle Rupert is also going to London next spring when I do. We call London town. He will also find a nice lady to wed. He will bring her home to Crestbrook, and she will be your aunt. The children your uncle Rupert and his wife have will be your cousins, just like my cousins are Lady Verina, Lady Justina, and Lord Traywick."

Celia looked up at her. "Why can't you wed each other?"

Lia could see how that would make perfect sense to a child. She would try to explain it the best she could.

"Because we do not suit one another," she said firmly. "I am looking for certain things in my husband, just as your uncle is looking for certain things in his wife." She paused. "We are just looking for different things, that's all. We are friends, but we will never be husband and wife."

She had them cut through the kitchens, hoping that would distract the girl from further talk of marriage between her and the viscount. As she suspected, Cook was thrilled to see the little girl.

"Miss Celia, isn't it? I'm so glad you came to see us. I am baking a special cake today. I hope you'll want to try some of it and let me know how it tastes."

The girl's eyes lit up at the mention of cake. "I like cake," she proclaimed. "Could I help?"

Cook looked taken aback at the request, but Lia nodded encouragingly, saying, "I think it would be a wonderful lesson for Miss Celia to see how a cake is created. Would you mind if we stay in the kitchens and watch you do so, Cook?"

"Why, I suppose so," the old woman said. "Let me get what I need, and you can help mix the ingredients, Miss Celia."

Cook brought a bowl to mix the cake in, along with such items as butter and eggs. She showed Celia how to crack an egg and then asked the girl to beat it. Cook cracked several more eggs into the bowl, with Celia stirring furiously. Then Cook used a different bowl, adding in flour, sugar, baking powder, and cream. Celia got to blend all the ingredients together, and then Cook added the eggs to the batter, giving it several good stirs to make certain it was properly blended.

"Now, we pour what you've mixed into cake pans," Cook explained, picking up the bowl and dishing the batter into three different pans a scullery maid had brought over.

The pans were placed into the oven to bake, and Cook allowed Celia to help her create an icing for the cake.

The three of them sat at a table, Celia in Lia's lap, as Cook entertained them with different stories about mishaps in the kitchen at other households she had worked at. Cook had Celia help her check several times until the cakes were a golden brown, then Cook removed them from the oven.

"These have to cool a bit. If not, any icing put on a warm cake just runs something terrible. We don't want a messy cake now, do we, Miss Celia?"

"No," Celia said, her eyes round and wide.

"Tell you what. Come back in an hour with Lady Lia, and I'll let you watch me ice the cake. If Lady Lia says you may lick the bowl, you can do so."

Celia clapped her hands as Lia said, "Thank you, Cook. We shall return in an hour."

"What are we going to do now?" the girl asked.

"Remember how you and Her Grace played some notes on the pianoforte? I thought you might like to do that again."

Lai took Celia to the music room, and they spent an hour there. She taught the girl the names of the different notes, and then Lia played *Hot Cross Buns*, a simple song.

"Now, you are going to learn the song."

At first, Celia played the short song with the tip of one finger. The Lia showed her how she could use three different fingers, one for each note. Celia played it several times, and the two of them sang together.

"I know a song now!" she cried in delight. "I'm going to play this for Uncle Rupert."

"I am certain your uncle will be most impressed with your musical skills. For now, though, we must head back to the kitchens."

Cook had removed the cakes from the three pans and put them on a rack to cool. She explained what she did as she iced the first layer of cake and set a second cake on top of the first. She iced that layer and then the final one, finishing by smoothing the icing.

Looking to Lia, she nodded in approval, so Cook offered the bowl to Celia.

"Here's a spoon, Miss Celia. Scrape up as much of the icing as you can. This is a special treat, though," Cook warned.

"Thank you, Cook," Celia said, dipping her spoon into the bowl.

Lia smiled at the older woman. "Thank you for allowing us to spend time in the kitchens with you today. Also, Lord Traywick asked if I would see if Lord Cressley might be able to come to dinner this evening, so an additional place will need to be set."

"I'll let Larsen know, my lady. Don't worry. I am making plenty of food as it is."

By now, Celia had finished what remained of the icing and gave the bowl and spoon back to Cook. Lia took her up to the schoolroom, having Celia practice writing her letters again. She also had the girl practice writing her first name. Since Celia was doing so well, she added Cummings to the slate.

"This is your last name. Cummings. Your first name and last name together make up your whole name."

Celia frowned. "That's long," she complained.

"Not as long as my last name," Lia said, chuckling.

She retrieved a second slate and wrote *Cornelia Worthington* across it. Slowly, she guided Celia's finger along each syllable, helping her sound it out.

"I thought your name was Lia."

"My given name is Cornelia. I use a shortened form of it. And just look how long my last name is. Worthington. It took me forever to learn how to spell and write it. You will have no trouble with Cummings."

The rest of the day passed quickly, and Lia took Celia back to the stables. Orion had already been saddled since she had let the head groom know the times she would need the horse ready each day.

As they trotted back toward Crestbrook, Celia told her, "When I'm bigger, I'm going to ride a horse all by myself. I'll hold the reins."

"You most certainly will, and you will do a good job of it. You will make your uncle proud."

She rode directly to the house, where a footman stood outside waiting for them. Then the door opened, and Viscount Cressley strode out.

"Uncle Rupert! I rode a horse today," Celia shared.

He came toward them and raised his arms, taking Celia into them.

"Thank you, my lady, for looking after my niece today."

"It was a pleasure, my lord. Now that I have you here, I am passing along an invitation from my cousin. It is Tray's last night at home, and Aunt Agnes is having all his favorite foods prepared. Tray asked that you be present at dinner this evening. I know the invitation is being issued rather late and you might have other plans, but—"

"I would be happy to come and see Lord Traywick off. What time should I arrive?"

Her aunt usually had them gather in the drawing room at half-past six, and so Lia gave him that time.

"I will see you in a few hours then, my lady." He then whispered something in Celia's ear.

Immediately, she said, "Thank you, Lady Lia. I had a nice day with you."

"As I did with you," she replied, nodding, and then turning Orion and trotting away.

Lia hoped she could avoid speaking to Lord Cressley tonight since many others would be present. She doubted there would be a reason to invite him again for dinner once Tray was gone. Already, it was hard enough to see him on a limited basis. She hoped the governess from town would arrive soon so that she would never have to see Viscount Cressley again before they returned to Millvale.

CHAPTER SIXTEEN

ESTHER WAS HELPING Lia and Tia to dress for tonight's dinner. Usually, Aunt Agnes kept a relaxed dinner table in the country, and they never changed gowns for dinner. Tonight, though, with it being a dinner in honor of Tray—as well as one serving as an introduction of Lord Cressley to the neighborhood—they were donning the best gowns they had brought with them.

After Esther finished dressing Tia's hair and left the bedchamber, Lia said, "I want to talk to you about Lord Cressley," deliberately keeping her tone neutral.

Her sister, however beamed at her. "Oh, this sounds as if the relationship is progressing. Has the viscount kissed you yet?"

Tia's eyes held such hope for Lia, and she found her spirits flagging. The mask she had been wearing now slipped, and she finally let her twin see her misery.

"Wait. What is wrong?" Tia asked. "If you need me to knock sense into him, I will."

"Everything is wrong," she responded. "Even worse than I imagined."

Tia took her hand and led her to the bed. They sat huddled together, her twin's supportive arm around Lia.

"He did kiss me. My feelings for him have been growing, and I thought the kiss enchanting. It caused my body to respond in ways unfamiliar. I cannot explain it. You will simply have to experience a kiss yourself to understand what I am saying."

She paused, collecting her thoughts a moment. "But he does not love me, Tia. Yes, he is—or was—attracted to me. I think he might have been curious about what a kiss between us would be like. Now he knows, but he has brushed it off."

"But he *kissed* you, Lia. Surely, he must offer for you now," Tia insisted.

"No one witnessed the kiss." She swallowed painfully. "Lord Cressley knows I seek a love match. He informed me that he plans to go to town next spring and peruse the Marriage Mart for a bride."

"That blighter!"

"No, really, it is good I know now. I do not think Lord Cressley is capable of love. I think because of the way he was raised and his experiences in the war, he may not have the capacity to love. Or if he does, he is using up all he has on Celia."

She took Tia's hands. "I adore that little girl, but I cannot play second fiddle to her. The man I wed must always put me first, even ahead of our children. If we have a strong marriage, full of love, then our children will also be taken care of and be loved by us. But I must be first in my husband's heart—and Lord Cressley cannot seem to put me in that position."

Tears formed in her twin's eyes. "I am so sorry, Lia. I had such high hopes. I have observed the viscount gaze upon you with tenderness. I thought perhaps he did love you."

She shrugged. "I think he is like most men in Polite Society. His marriage will be more of a business arrangement. I do think he will be kind to his wife, but I believe I deserve more than kindness. I will not settle for anything less than love."

Tia hugged her tightly, saying, "I know it hurts now, Lia, but we have the Season to look forward to. We will meet all manner of gentlemen in town during the many social events. With Ariadne and Val already married, they will be able to help guide us to find our soulmates."

Lia did not know if she believed in the idea of a soulmate

anymore. She wasn't even certain she believed in love. Despite being deliberately vague about her feelings for Lord Cressley with her twin, Lia realized she had loved Lord Cressley. That she still loved him. The only thing that would mend her broken heart would be time and distance. Fortunately, they would return to Kent, so being in close proximity with him would soon end. Then it would be another five months after they were home before the Season would begin. Yes, she would certainly encounter the viscount at social affairs, but she hoped by then her heart would have healed, and she could smile politely and greet him without her heart feeling as if it were being torn in two.

"You are right," she said, not totally convinced but needing to keep this to herself. "For now, I simply wanted you to know the state of everything."

"I can help you avoid Lord Cressley this evening," Tia promised. "Either I will talk with him and keep him busy and away from you, or I will intervene if I see the two of you have been inadvertently thrown together."

"With so many guests, I believe I can remain away from him, at least before dinner, when everyone will be meeting him. I only worry about after dinner, when the guests will go to the drawing room. You know Aunt Agnes will want us to play for the guests. I do not think I am up to it. If I plead a megrim, though, I am afraid Mama will figure out what is going on. She has already asked me about the viscount and if I had feelings for him. I do not want her to know we have kissed, much less that Lord Cressley has no interest in me."

"Aunt Agnes and Mama will expect us to play," her twin agreed. She thought a moment. "What if *I* were the one to come down with a megrim? Naturally, you would be the one to care for me. Mama could not object to that. And Verina and Justina can entertain the guests."

They agreed that Tia would be her usual self until the final course and then become withdrawn. While the gentlemen stayed at the table for their port and after dinner cigars and the ladies adjourned to the drawing room, Tia would tell Mama of the megrim, asking for Lia to come with her to their bedchamber.

Their plan settled now, they went downstairs. Mama and Aunt Agnes were talking about who would be in attendance this evening. Verina and Justina stood talking with their brother. Lia thought now would be the perfect time to address Ariadne's proposal with their cousins, especially since Tray would be gone early tomorrow.

They joined their cousins, and Lia asked, "Did it ever feel odd to you when your parents left for the Season and were gone for months?"

"I never really thought much about it," Justina said. "Miss Snow—Eden—usually made things fun for Verina and me. I did not mind staying behind at Traywick Manor."

"It was hard on me," Tray said. "I have always felt something was missing in my life. I chalked it up to losing Lucius and Papa at such a young age. I will admit that I was terrified those first few years when Mama left for the Season. I feared we would get word that she, too, had been taken from us in a carriage accident."

Verina touched her brother's sleeve. "You should have said something to us, Tray."

"I did not think I should confide in you," her brother admitted. "I was the man of the family. I wanted to be strong for my sisters."

"Tia and I, along with Val and Ariadne, came to resent Mama and Papa leaving," Lia continued. "Not that we were ever as close to them as you were to your parents, but we felt neglected being left in the country." She paused. "Ariadne wishes to change that."

She explained how her older sister had taken Penelope with her to town this past Season.

"Not simply because she was only a few weeks old, but because Ariadne wanted to have her daughter with her. It is something she and Julian have agreed to. They always intend to bring their children to town for the Season, unless they are away at school. They intend to spend more time with their children, and they also would like it if their siblings and cousins also brought their children to town each year."

"Why, it would be like when the ten of us came together in London all those years ago," Verina said, excitement in her voice. "Not only could we cousins see one another, but our children could also see each other frequently."

"Exactly," Tia seconded. "Ariadne has spoken of how the bonds between siblings and cousins would grow under these circumstances."

"Ariadne has discussed this arrangement with Val, Con, and Lucy. They have all agreed to this plan."

"Count me in," Tray said. "Not that I will have children for many years, but once I finish my studies, I will be attending the Season each year. I will need to help my sisters find their husbands before I consider taking on a bride myself, but I think it would be wonderful to bring all our children together and let them get to know one another."

"Verina and I agree," Justina said for herself and her sister. "I think it a marvelous idea."

"Then it is only Dru who will need to agree to Ariadne's proposal. She went to visit Lucy and Judson, so I am certain Lucy has already told her sister about it," Lia shared. "Oh, this will be so much fun. It will make the Season even more special. It will be about family, as well as our social obligations."

Larsen announced the first guests, and Tia stayed by Lia's side as they were introduced to various neighbors from in and around Kidsgrove. She was actually enjoying herself until she felt someone's gaze upon her. Turning, she saw Lord Cressley had entered the drawing room, and he looked as if he were headed straight for her.

Thankfully, Tray caught his arm, greeting him and keeping Lord Cressley by his side, moving about the room to introduce him to all those present whom he had not met. That kept the viscount busy until the butler came in and announced that dinner was served.

As they began moving toward the dining room, Tia caught up with her.

"Where did you go?" Lia asked as her sister slipped an arm through hers.

"With Tray keeping Lord Cressley occupied, I went to the dining room and changed a few of the seating cards," Tia replied. "You were to sit next to Lord Cressley. I switched our name cards, and now I will be the one who will sit next to him. You will be on the opposite side of the table, about eight spots away from him, too far for him to engage you in conversation."

"Won't Aunt Agnes notice?"

"If she does, she will not say anything. With our names being only one letter apart, she might even think Larsen placed one seating card in the wrong place."

"Thank you."

"Do not thank me yet," Tia warned. "I still wish to throttle Lord Cressley for toying with your heart. It is disappointing because I thought him more a gentleman than that."

"I still think he is a gentleman. Just not the gentleman for me," Lia said softly.

Lia tried not to be distracted at dinner, giving her full attention to those seated on each side of her, as well as those across the table. Every now and then, however, she glanced up the table in Tia's direction. Once, she saw Lord Cressley turn his gaze on her, and Lia quickly averted her eyes.

Her twin was her usual, lively self, but as they had discussed, Tia became less animated near the end of dinner. Lia even saw Mama look upon Tia with concern.

As they rose to leave the men for half an hour, Lia went and linked arms with Tia.

"You should be on the stage," she whispered. "Even I think something is wrong with you."

They left the dining room, where Mama awaited them.

"Are you all right, Thermantia?"

Tia winced. "Not really, Mama. My head started throbbing

suddenly a few minutes ago. It never pains me."

Mama frowned. "It could be a megrim."

"I think you are right, Mama," Tia said. "Perhaps if I go and lie down a bit, I might rejoin the guests later."

"No, that would not be wise." Mama looked to Lia. "Take your sister upstairs to your bedchamber. Ring for my maid. She can bring cold cloths. She also has a tisane you can drink. I have tried it before when a megrim has struck me, and it usually is effective."

"May I stay with Tia, Mama?" Lia asked. "If she is better, I can quietly rejoin the group in the drawing room."

"Yes, do so, Cornelia."

They left and made their way back to their bedchamber. Once inside, they hugged one another.

"Do not sound too gleeful," Lia warned. "We still must ring for Mama's maid. You are not done playacting just yet."

The maid brought cold compresses for Tia's head and returned a short time later with the tisane. Tia drank it and said she was going to lie down. Mama's maid insisted upon helping, and so Tia was prepared for bed.

"Ring if you need anything else, my lady."

"I will," Tia said, sounding quite puny.

Once the maid left, Lia said, "If you cannot find a husband to your liking, the London stage awaits you."

Tia grinned. "I was rather good, wasn't I? Stay with me a while, then I think you should go back downstairs. It will almost be time for everyone to leave by then, and it will be easy to avoid Lord Cressley."

Lia shared what she and Celia had done yesterday. Her sister and cousins had accompanied Mama and Aunt Agnes to a visit to the vicar's wife and had been gone much of the day.

"You are so good with children, Lia. I would not have thought to have Celia riding, much less take her to the kitchens to watch a cake being baked. You are going to be a wonderful mother."

She hoped she would be—but she would not be the mother of Lord Cressley's children as she had begun to hope.

"I should go downstairs," she finally said after they had talked for half an hour.

"Do not have any fun without me," Tia warned playfully.

Returning to the drawing room, Lia entered and found everyone listening to Verina play the pianoforte as Justina sang. She moved to stand next to Tray, who stood near the back.

When the song ended, everyone applauded. Her cousins returned to their seats and conversations picked up around the room. She stayed with Tray, who introduced her to the vicar and his wife, and they had a pleasant conversation about life in Cumberland.

Then an elderly earl announced it was time for him to go home, and the dinner party guests seemed to agree. She walked downstairs with Tray, helping to see the guests out. Mama joined them, while Aunt Agnes and her other cousins did the same.

Then Lord Cressley appeared, and Lia smiled politely. "Good evening, my lord."

"We did not have a chance to speak, my lady," he said.

She looked about. "Well, there were so many others present this evening. I do hope you enjoyed yourself. This party was as much for you as it was Tray."

"By the way," her cousin said. "I told Cressley how I had not had a chance to take you, Tia, and Aunt Alice into Grasmere. He agreed that it is a lovely spot and that you should not miss seeing it. Once the governess for Miss Celia arrives and Lord Cressley is comfortable in retaining her, he said he would be delighted to escort all of you to Grasmere."

"Yes," the viscount said. "We can take Traywick's carriage down. Once there, I can escort you ladies about if you wish to do some shopping. Traywick mentioned that you, in particular, are very fond of Wordsworth's poetry, Lady Lia. We can rent horses and a group of us can go past where the great poet's cottage stands."

The last thing Lia wanted to do was accompany him to Grasmere. Still, Tray had gone to the trouble of asking Lord Cressley to chaperone them. She did not want to appear churlish to her cousin.

"I will leave the planning up to Aunt Agnes and Mama," she said. "I know we are all eager to see Grasmere. Thank you for your kind offer to escort us there, my lord."

She smiled at the viscount as if everything were perfectly normal between them, listening as he wished Tray a good term at university, and they made plans to meet up once Tray had returned for the Christmas season.

After all the guests were out the door, Aunt Agnes said, "Well, I think that went rather well."

"It did, Mama," Tray said, going to his mother and kissing her cheek. "You are always an excellent hostess. It was good of you to include Lord Cressley. I think he met everyone present this evening."

"How is Tia's megrim?" Mama asked.

"I think much better. She drank the tisane and went straight to sleep. Hopefully, a good night's rest will make a difference."

They began climbing the stairs, and Lia found herself next to Aunt Agnes, following the others up the stairs.

"I hope you enjoyed tonight, Lia."

"I did. I am only sorry Tia felt poorly near the end."

Aunt Agnes paused on the landing and softly said, "And I am sorry that Tia switched the name cards. I had planned for you to sit next to Lord Cressley this evening. I thought something might be developing between the two of you, and I wanted to help things along if I could."

Deciding to admit to the ruse, she said, "I asked Tia to do so, Aunt Agnes. I am a bit uncomfortable in Lord Cressley's company."

Her aunt took Lia's wrist to halt her progress. "Has he done something to upset you? *Kiss* you?"

Lying, she said, "Nothing like that, Aunt. I merely thought we would suit, but I have come to the conclusion that we never would. While I am happy to help care for his niece for a short while, I have no wish to speak to the viscount. Tia switched the cards at my request."

Sympathy filled her aunt's eyes. "I am very sorry things did not work out as you might have liked, Lia. Better now than later, however."

"I agree," she said, a lump forming in her throat.

They continued up the stairs and parted to go to different wings. As Lia walked to her bedchamber, guilt flooded her. She had never knowingly lied to anyone, much less her beloved Aunt Agnes. She vowed to remain truthful from now on.

Once she arrived, she told Tia, who was still awake, about the trip to Grasmere.

"It is unavoidable. Tray asked Lord Cressley to escort us there. Aunt Agnes and Mama already know about it. I will simply have to make the best of the trip."

"At least it is not anytime soon," her twin replied. "The new governess will have to arrive and settle in before Lord Cressley will agree to this trip. Who knows? By then, it may be too late and time for us to return to Kent."

Lia thought her sister was being optimistic. She knew this outing would occur.

She would simply have to keep her contact with Lord Cressley to a minimum.

CHAPTER SEVENTEEN

TODAY WAS ONE of the days Celia spent at Traywick Manor, so Rupert was trying to get as much done as possible without his niece underfoot. Thank goodness he wasn't having to review any kind of reports with Williamson because his mind would have strayed.

To Lady Lia.

He had barely seen her since the dinner party Lady Traywick had given a few weeks ago. She spent her days with his niece, but he rarely came in contact with her, thanks to the arrangements they had made. He also had been invited to dinner by several of his new neighbors, as well as visiting three other estates in the area, discussing land management with the owners. He had attended the local church with Celia. It seemed Rupert was settling into the neighborhood with ease.

And yet he was bloody miserable.

Did he love Lia Worthington?

He didn't think he did. Yes, he was taken with her. Yes, he wanted to kiss her senseless and explore every sweet curve she possessed. But love for a woman seemed such a foreign concept to him. Gentlemen in the *ton* did not love their wives, and he was most certainly one of their number now. A man's role in Polite Society was to wed and sire heirs and spares, all while going along his merry way. Love wasn't a part of a gentleman's life. He simply chose the lady who would most benefit him, be it her generous dowry or social standing.

Rupert couldn't change himself or the society he lived in. Yes, there were exceptions, the love matches Lady Lia yearned for. Well, she would have to find one with someone else. If he were already so rattled by her that he could not think and handle his duties on his own estate, he did not need to let her in any further, much less weaken and love her.

As he was about to finish helping place the roof on a tenant's cottage, he saw Williamson riding on horseback. The steward reached him, calling up to him.

"My lord, the new estate manager has arrived."

Rupert was grateful for that. He'd already put on three roofs the past two days, and he could certainly stand to have a another strong back to assist him and the other tenants in this project.

"Where is he?"

"Headed this way, my lord. I decided to ride ahead and let you know he would be here soon."

He still hadn't had time to purchase a few horses for his stables, something he kept intending to do. Perhaps he could do so in Keswick. He would see if Holson knew anything of horses and if so, take the new steward into Keswick with him.

"Thank you, Williamson. I will be down shortly. You may return to the house."

Taking up his hammer again, Rupert finished his part of the roof and climbed down a ladder just as a man of about thirty entered the clearing. He met the new steward, offering him his hand. It was a test. Rupert wanted to see if the man would willingly shake his hand, with Rupert being filthy from head to toe.

Adam Holson passed with flying colors.

"Good morning, my lord. Or I should say good afternoon since it is past noon now." The steward shook hands eagerly with his new employer, despite the dirt. "May I say how grateful I am that you would hire me, sight unseen, not knowing a thing about me. Why, I believe that is unheard of."

"I only needed to know one thing about you, Mr. Holson, and that is Mr. Williamson thought you were the man to replace him. Williamson has served my family for decades. I knew he would not want to see his lifetime's work quickly crumble. He would want the best possible man he knew to replace him. The moment I had his recommendation, I had no doubt you would suffice. I know we still need to talk of such things as your salary and duties, but—"

"That can wait, Lord Cressley." Glancing about, Holson said, taking off his coat, "I see supplies out for at least one more roof. We should get started."

Yes, Williamson had been right. Rupert had a feeling they would get along well, and his newly hired steward would be with him for many years to come.

As Holson rolled up his sleeves, Rupert called over the others who had climbed from the roof, introducing the new estate manager to them. In turn, several of the tenants' wives came out, also greeting Holson. He learned names quickly, referring to others by their names. The women, who were preparing a meal for the men after they finished roofing, promised that Holson would be included, and they got back to work.

It was nice to see his new steward jump in and get his hands dirty. He obviously knew his way around a hammer and other tools, and the final roof went on speedily with an extra pair of hands involved. After they climbed down, they spent half an hour eating simple fare outdoors. Holson told Rupert a bit about the estate he had helped in managing, including some of the ideas he'd had.

"The steward was getting on up in years, and I had hoped to succeed him. He wasn't a man fond of change, however, and neither was the earl who owned the estate. I was ready to modernize several things, but the resistance was great. Because I did not believe I would be offered the chance to step into the role of that estate's steward, I was ready to look for new opportunities. When I received the letter about a guaranteed position at

Crestbrook, it was as if fate stepped in."

Holson paused, taking a swig of ale. "I cannot thank you enough, my lord, for valuing Mr. Williamson's opinion enough to hire me sight unseen."

"I will reach my thirtieth birthday next year, Mr. Holson, and you look to be of a similar age. I am hoping our partnership will last for many years to come."

Rupert tapped his mug against that of his new steward's, and both men downed the remainder of their ale.

"Let me take you to see where you will live. I have asked Williamson to stay on for a week or so, in order to help you transition into your new role here at Crestbrook, so you will share the cottage for a brief spell."

They thanked the ladies for the meal, and Rupert was pleased that Holson also spoke to each of the men by name, those who had helped with the roofing. By the time they were ready to leave, his gut told him he had made one of the best decisions of his life. He asked one of the men to ride Ajax back to the stables for him, and he walked with Holson about some of the property.

"Do you know much about horses?" he asked.

Holson chuckled. "I may have been a horse in another life, my lord. I have always had an affinity with them."

"Can you choose good horseflesh? I am in need of horses for my stables. I only recently took the title after my brother's passing. He preferred town and never came to Crestbrook, so I only have carriage horses in the stables now, along with the horse Mr. Williamson uses to get about the estate. I have borrowed a mount from my neighbor, Lord Traywick, but I need to return it soon."

"We aren't far from Keswick. You might be able to find what you need there. If not, we could try Penwith."

"Then that should be what we do tomorrow. Come up to the house and breakfast with me at eight o'clock. We can then ride in my carriage to Keswick, and Penwith, if necessary."

They reached the cottage where Williamson resided, and

Holson said, "It should be unlocked. Your butler said my bag would be brought here."

Entering the cottage and looking about, Holson said it looked as if he had everything he needed.

"Come to the house then," Rupert said. "I will show you your office."

They did so, finding Williamson working in it. The three took some time to talk about the estate in general, and Rupert shared their plans for buying some new horses tomorrow.

"I will let you and Mr. Williamson visit, Mr. Holson. He can begin to fill you in on what you need to know to help in managing Crestbrook. I will see you at breakfast tomorrow morning."

He rang for Prater, asking for bathwater to be sent to his chamber. Damsley was soon there, taking the filthy clothes away to be washed and ironed. Rupert sank into the tub, enjoying the feel of the hot water easing his already aching muscles. After soaking for several minutes, he began scrubbing the sweat and grime from him.

Damsley helped him to dress, and he headed downstairs to his study. Prater intercepted him before he reached it, however.

"My lord, Miss Wilson has arrived."

Puzzled, he asked, "And who might Miss Wilson be?"

"She is Miss Celia's new governess from London," his butler informed him.

Rupert's heart sank. While he had been eager to have someone permanently committed to look after Celia, it meant the end of Lady Lia coming to Crestbrook.

Of course, he could always invite his neighbors for dinner, to return the favor for introducing him to others in the neighborhood, but would Lady Lia even agree to come? She and her twin had vanished after dinner the night he was at Traywick Manor, and he suspected that he was the cause of that disappearing act. While Lady Lia had returned at the very end of the evening and they had briefly spoken, he had neither seen nor spoken to her since.

Then again, there still was the outing to Grasmere. Traywick had asked Rupert to accompany his female relatives to the picturesque town and show his cousins another beautiful part of the Lake District. With so many women in tow, he would never have a chance to be alone with Lady Lia.

And why would he even wish to be?

He'd vowed never to kiss her again, not wanting to confuse either her or him. She had already made it perfectly clear he did not suit her. Rupert couldn't see giving into her foolish notions of love. He told himself it was better the governess was now here so that Lady Lia could be out of sight.

And hopefully, out of his mind.

"Yes, thank you, Prater. I will meet with her now."

Rupert went to his study and entered, spying a rather plain-looking woman close to his age seated in the chair before the desk. Hearing him come in, she rose.

"Good afternoon, Lord Cressley. I am Miss Wilson."

"I am happy you have come to Crestbrook, Miss Wilson. Please, have a seat. I wish to tell you about my niece."

He went behind the desk and seated himself. "But first tell me something of you."

"I placed my references on your desk, my lord. If you would, please read through them first, and then I can answer any questions you might have."

He glanced down and saw several sheets of paper. "I will read them later, Miss Wilson. For now, humor me. Provide me with your background and share why you are qualified to be governess to my niece."

Without hesitation, she said, "Very well, my lord."

Rupert liked that. Most women would become flustered if things hadn't gone exactly to their plan. He liked Miss Wilson's flexibility and thought it would come in handy in teaching Celia.

"I am the daughter of Lieutenant-General Amos Wilson, who was the son of an earl. As a second son, my father first went to university and then into the army. My mother was a baron's only daughter." Miss Wilson paused. "She was lost in childbirth."

"Then we have that in common, Miss Wilson. My mother also gave her life in giving life to me. And I, too, am a second son. I was formerly Major Cummings."

"I see," she acknowledged. "I was raised by my great-aunt, who never wed. She was the earl's sister. When I completed my education, I knew there was no place for me in Polite Society. I was plain of face and possessed no dowry. My father, whom I have only seen a handful of times in my life, did not have funds to give me a dowry, so I always knew I would make my own way in the world."

He wanted to tell her that he, too, had rarely seen his own father and brother but kept silent. While they had much in common regarding their backgrounds, the fact that he was a man and she a woman had set them on far different courses in life. She had been left to fend for herself, while he had claimed a title and wealth.

"My great-aunt had always told me I could either become a companion or governess since I was of genteel birth and suitably educated. Since I like children and knew I would never have an opportunity to wed and have ones of my own, I decided governessing suited me best."

"What of the children you have taught?" he asked.

"My first charge was a boy six years of age. I spent three years with him before he went off to school. I next went to an earl's household, where I taught his only child. She had just turned ten years of age, and I remained with her for eight years, through her come-out Season this past spring. She made quite a good match."

"I recently claimed my title, Miss Wilson, after serving in His Majesty's army for the past eight years. My brother only had the one child, Celia, and I am now her guardian. To be frank, my brother had no interest in the girl. She was sent to live in the country, while my brother was fond of town."

"And her mother?" the governess inquired.

"Lost in childbirth. Celia did have a nursery governess, but the woman was not suitably trained. I had to dismiss her. I am afraid you will find my niece woefully behind other children her age, but I can tell you this—she is quite bright and soaks up everything she is exposed to as a sponge might. I believe once you start your lessons with her, you will understand what I mean."

"I will evaluate her, my lord, and start at an appropriate place for her learning."

"A family friend, Lady Lia Worthington, has been helping to care for Celia while I waited for your arrival. I would like the two of you to meet and talk about what Celia has been learning under Lady Lia's supervision."

"I would be happy to meet with Lady Lia, my lord."

"Then come to the drawing room now. Celia will be arriving for tea."

Rupert had deliberately not gone to the drawing room until the appointed time, wanting to abide by Lady Lia's wishes. Today, though, would be an exception. He took the new governess upstairs, telling Prater that both Miss Wilson and Lady Lia would be staying for tea this afternoon. He also asked that a messenger be sent to Traywick Manor to let Her Grace and Lady Traywick know that Lady Lia would be delayed in returning home today.

He ushered Miss Wilson into the drawing room, spying Celia and Lady Lia at the globe. Both looked up, a puzzled look on his niece's face, but Lady Lia seemed to understand exactly who Miss Wilson was. She took Celia's hand and brought her across the room.

"Lady Lia, Celia, I would like to introduce Miss Wilson. She will be serving as your governess, Celia."

Surprisingly, Celia dropped a curtsey, something Lady Lia must have taught the girl to do.

"It's nice to meet you, Miss Wilson," Celia said, making Rupert very proud at that moment.

"The pleasure is all mine, Miss Celia," the governess said, giving Celia a smile. "I hear you have been helping to care for

Miss Celia, my lady."

"I have, Miss Wilson. You are going to find Celia a delight."

Rupert said, "I know there are things you need to talk over with Miss Wilson. Would you please stay for tea so that you can discuss Celia with her?"

"Of course, my lord," she said graciously. "But I must let Mama and Aunt Agnes know I am to be delayed."

"That has already been taken care of."

Her brows arched. "I see." Then she said, "Come, Miss Wilson. I am eager to share with you about Celia and would enjoying hearing about you and your former charges."

They took a seat, and the teacart was rolled in. He asked Lady Lia to pour out, and she did so. Rupert sat quietly, listening to all she told the governess, with Celia interjecting every now and then, adding her own preferences. In turn, Miss Wilson talked at length about her last post and the many areas of study she could provide. He learned that she would be teaching Celia subjects such as French, geography, history, and maths. The governess would also work with Celia on reading and handwriting. As time passed, Miss Wilson would address various etiquette lessons, teaching Celia everything from how to address those with titles to how to pour out at teatime.

"I can also teach Miss Celia the pianoforte and give her dancing lessons, though my last employer eventually hired a dancing master for his daughter. Still, I can teach Miss Celia the basics of dance."

"It all sounds wonderful, Miss Wilson," Lady Lia said with enthusiasm. "I only have one question. I have begun to teach Celia to ride. Can you continue those lessons?"

He held his breath, hoping the competent Miss Wilson would not be an equestrian and give him an excuse to take Celia to Traywick Manor for riding lessons. Unfortunately, that wasn't the case.

"Oh, I adore horses," Miss Wilson assured them. "I would be happy to take over those lessons for Miss Celia."

"I do not know what horses Viscount Cressley has in his stables," Lady Lia said. "My aunt would be happy to lend Posey to you, my lord, while Celia continues learning."

"That would be excellent, my lady. My new steward just arrived today, and we are going to look at horses tomorrow. If we do not find a mount suitable for Celia, then I may discuss the loan of Posey with Lady Traywick."

Tea ended, and Miss Wilson said, "I think Miss Celia needs to show me the schoolroom and where her bedchamber and mine are. We have lots to talk about, don't we?" she asked the child.

"Will Lady Lia teach me anymore?" Celia asked, looking a bit put out.

"No, Miss Wilson is now your governess," Rupert reminded gently. "Lady Lia will be returning to Kent soon."

Celia grew teary-eyed, and Lady Lia took the girl's hands. "We have talked of this, Celia. You knew this time was coming. I think Miss Wilson is simply marvelous. Why, she will be with you for many years. One day, you will come to town to make your come-out, and Miss Wilson will come with you. I will be there. I will get to see you all grown up, wearing pretty gowns. You can meet my husband and children. We will have a lovely time."

He watched Celia, and she seemed to accept what Lady Lia told her.

"Go with Miss Wilson now," he told his niece. "I will come up later when you are having your milk and bread."

Miss Wilson smiled brightly. "Come along, Miss Celia. You will need to show me everything about Crestbrook."

"I know everywhere in the house. And Uncle Rupert and I go outside all the time. I have lots to show you," Celia said excitedly.

The pair left, and he turned to Lady Lia. "Do you approve of Miss Wilson?"

"I think she is exactly what Celia needs, my lord."

He hated how formal things sounded between them. "Since you are late returning to Traywick Manor, I will ride with you."

"It is not necessary."

"And yet I will do so anyway."

Rupert accompanied her to the stables and asked for Ajax to be readied for him. The groom left to do so, and he said, "I hope I will return Ajax soon since Mr. Holson and I intend to purchase a few horses in the next day or so."

"I hope you find what you are looking for, my lord," she said, turning away.

Nothing was spoken between them until the horses appeared. Not a word was said on the ride back to Traywick Manor. When they reached the stables, he remained atop Ajax, and she dismounted Orion.

"Thank you for seeing me home, my lord," she said, turning toward the house without a backward glance.

He rode home to Crestbrook, an ache in his heart.

CHAPTER EIGHTEEN

MISS WILSON HAD proven to be a godsend. Though Celia had not taken to her at first, Lady Lia had done as Rupert suggested and continued coming to Crestbrook for another week. She had also welcomed Celia and the new governess to Traywick Manor, as well. During that week of transition, his niece had begun to fall under Miss Wilson's spell. By the end of it, Celia told him she liked the governess—but she would miss Lady Lia terribly.

It was less than a week before the Worthington women left Cumberland for Kent. Since Miss Wilson had been there two weeks and seemed settled in, Rupert thought he could honor his promise to Lord Traywick and take the earl's relatives to Grasmere for their overnight excursion. Fortunately, he was more familiar with the town now since he and Adam Holson had bought one of his new horses in Grasmere. They had found none in Keswick to their liking, but two new additions to his stables had been found in Penrith. He had returned Ajax to Traywick Manor, and now Rupert alternated riding one of the three horses he now owned. Holson made use of the ones Rupert didn't, and so the new purchases were receiving ample exercise.

The only horse he hadn't found was one to continue teaching Celia on, and so Lady Traywick had graciously agreed to allow Posey to come stay at Crestbrook for as long as Celia needed. That had made Celia happy, and Miss Wilson had continued the girl's riding lessons.

Before he went to breakfast, he stopped in the schoolroom, where Celia and her governess were eating.

"I have come to say goodbye to you," Rupert told his niece. "Remember, I am taking those from Traywick Manor to Grasmere."

"You'll be gone tonight and come home tomorrow," Celia told him, echoing what he had told her numerous times.

"You are to stay here and make certain everything at Crestbrook is going well," he said with a straight face. "Miss Wilson will help you watch over things for me."

"And Prater and Mrs. Prater," the girl reminded him. "They can help, too."

"They most certainly can."

While he didn't like leaving Celia, it would only be for a brief period of time. He didn't want her lessons interrupted, especially since things seemed to be going so well. Miss Wilson had given him a report at the end of each of the past two weeks, and even the governess seemed a bit astounded at how fast her new charge learned.

Bending, he kissed Celia's brow. "Farewell, little love. I will see you sometime tomorrow."

She pecked him on the cheek, the first time she had done so, and it gave him a bit of a thrill. Celia had come a long way since Rupert had first met her. The bedraggled, wild child was now his greatest delight.

He breakfasted and then rode to Traywick Manor, leaving his horse with a groom. They would stable it overnight so that he would be able to ride the mount home tomorrow. Rupert went to the front of the house, where the earl's best coach sat, along with a second one which would convey servants and luggage. He would not be taking his valet with him, but Damsley had already packed a small valise and sent it to Traywick Manor.

The ladies began exiting the house, and he watched Lady Lia, a deep yearning filling him. They had not spoken since he had ridden back with her on the day Miss Wilson arrived at Crestbrook. He wondered if she would converse with him on this short trip or if she would keep to herself.

"Good morning, my lord," the women greeted, and his eyes went to the two older women.

"Your Grace. Lady Traywick. I hope you are ready for our outing."

"I do hope I can find a new pair of gloves," the duchess said.

"You will," Lady Traywick promised. "We will enjoy shopping for ourselves for once and not our daughters."

The plan was to arrive at the inn. The two mothers would shop, while he led the ladies on an excursion about Grasmere's countryside, including seeing where William Wordsworth lived.

"Then let us begin," he suggested, handing each of the six women into the carriage. He treated them all equally, and each one, including Lady Lia, murmured a thanks to him.

"Oh, the carriage is filled," the countess said, distress in her voice. "I had not realized we would take up all the room."

"I plan to ride atop with your coachman, my lady. If I took my own horse, he would be exhausted by the time we reached Grasmere, and I would have to rent another one. I will be fine—and it will leave the six of you to gossip to your hearts' delight."

Looking to the others, he said, "It is only a journey of about ten miles or so before we reach Grasmere. We will have plenty of time to tour the area."

Rupert mounted the coach, climbing next to the driver, and soon the vehicle rolled down the lane, heading south to Grasmere. The second coach followed them.

They reached the town, and he directed the coachman to the inn where he had reserved rooms for their party. Rupert went inside to let the innkeeper know they had arrived.

"Ah, good morning to you, Lord Cressley," the innkeeper greeted. "The rooms you requested are ready for you."

"My entire party is here, including a couple of servants to see to the ladies."

"Then have everyone come in, my lord. I will see the bags are brought in for you."

A quarter-hour later, all luggage had been taken to rooms upstairs, and the women had been shown to their rooms. He pulled the innkeeper aside.

"Remember that I would like a private supper for our group this evening."

"It will be ready at seven o'clock as you requested, my lord," the innkeeper assured him.

He returned to the group of ladies. "We can head to the stables now. Our rented horses should be ready for us. Is there anything you might need before I leave, Your Grace? Lady Traywick?"

"No, we are set, Lord Cressley," Her Grace said.

Rupert explained they would dine together in an upper room at seven that evening, and then he escorted the four young ladies the two blocks to where their horses were already saddled.

"Got word from the inn that said you were here," the owner of the stables told him.

"Thank you for having our mounts readied for us," he said, helping to assist each young woman into the saddle, ignoring the ripple of warmth that filled him when he assisted Lady Lia onto her horse.

"Follow me," Rupert called, and they cantered down the main thoroughfare of Grasmere.

He pointed out the river to them when they reached the edge of town, saying, "Grasmere is in the center of the Lake District. The town is on the Rothay River, which flows into Grasmere Lake, which we will see shortly."

Heading north, he took them to the rock hill of Helm Crag and pointed. "You can see the village is overlooked by Helm Crag. Many people enjoy hiking it to the top, but it is quite steep and would take us two-and-a-half or even three hours to do so. I would rather us ride and see more of the area. Look closely, though, for many people see a lion king standing over and looking down upon a small lamb."

They stared at it, and Lady Justina was the first to call out. "Oh, I see it!"

"Where?" Lady Tia asked, squinting. Then she, too, said, "I do see it!"

It took Lady Verina and Lady Lia longer, but once they made out the figures of lion and lamb, he turned their attention in the opposite direction.

"Look to the opposite end now, which is regarded as the true summit. You are supposed to see an old lady playing an organ."

Again, after studying the rock formation, each of the women agreed they could spy the old lady and her organ.

"This is marvelous," Lady Lia said. "We have nothing in Kent which compares to this."

"But our home is very beautiful," her twin said.

"Of course, it is," Lady Lia agreed. "But this is so different. A majestic kind of beauty."

They rode throughout the area, obviously charmed by the landscape. A deep pride filled Rupert, being from such a place of beauty.

As they studied Loughrigg Fell, Verina said wistfully, "I cannot believe you will be gone by this time next week. Justina and I have so enjoyed these past few months with you."

"You will see us sooner than you think," Lady Lia said. "Before you know it, you will be old enough to make your come-out, Verina. We will be at the Season together."

"Yes," her cousin agreed, "but you will already have done a Season. You will be an old married lady by then, Lia."

The others laughed, but Rupert felt a pang of jealousy grab hold of him.

"Do not worry," Lady Tia assured her cousins. "While Lia longs to wed and have babes, I plan to have fun."

"What do you mean?" Lady Justina asked. "Are you saying you will not wed?"

"Not immediately," Lady Tia said. "I plan to enjoy at least

two Seasons before I consider marriage. Possibly three."

"What does Cousin Val think of that?" Lady Verina asked.

"Val has told me I do not have to wed until I am ready to do so," Lady Tia shared. "Mama, now, will be another matter. She will be pressing me to wed from the opening night's ball. That is why I hope Mama will focus on Lia's wedding first and leave me alone."

Lady Verina turned to Lady Lia. "What do you want in a husband?"

Rupert held his breath as she said, "I wish for a kind, gentle man. One who values family and is respectful toward me." She hesitated. "I am hoping to find love."

"Love?" Lady Justina said, scoffingly. "I know Val and Eden love one another madly, and you said that Ariadne wed for love. But for it to occur three times in your family? That may not happen, Lia."

He saw determination fill the young lady. "Then perhaps Tia won't be the only Worthington who does not wed after her first Season. I am not willing to compromise, Justina. If I cannot have love, then I do not wish to wed."

"But what about babes?" Lady Verina asked quietly. "You say you want children. You cannot wait too long, or you could be left behind. You do not want to be placed on the shelf, Lia."

"I will know in my heart what to do," Lady Lia said, her tone resolute.

Rupert wished to squash all this talk of marriage and said, "We should ride to Dove Cottage now. It is where Wordsworth and his sister live."

They passed St. Oswald's Church on the way, and Lady Tia insisted they stop and look at the ruins. Their entire party dismounted and led the horses closer.

He shared, "The church is named after a seventh century Christian king of Northumberland. It is said he preached on this site where the church was eventually built."

As they walked around, Rupert pointed out the tower, porch,

and south wall, the only parts which remained of the church, which had been built in the fourteenth century.

They mounted up again and rode toward Dove Cottage, which lay on the edge of Grasmere. He had previously inquired where Wordsworth's rented cottage lay because of Lady Lia's interest in the poet.

As they drew near, he stopped his horse. "Wordsworth lives in Dove Cottage, which is just ahead. He moved there with Dorothy, his sister, and wed a woman named Mary five years ago. The innkeeper told me the Wordsworths have rapidly expanded their family, having three children in four years. He said rumors are circulating that the poet is ready to seek larger lodgings, due to how crowded Dove Cottage has become. If we see Mr. Wordsworth, we should quietly continue upon our way. Those who live in Grasmere say they give Wordsworth what he wants—peace."

They started up again, walking their horses, and Rupert gestured to a cottage, letting them know this was the one. A woman was seated on a bench just outside the dwelling, a small boy of about two next to her. A girl of about three and a boy a little older were running around the yard, entertaining the mother and child. Rupert assumed this was Mrs. Wordsworth and her three children. He tipped his hat to her as they passed.

Continuing on for a few minutes, he was about to stop when they came across a woman sitting on a rock. She held a pencil in her hand. A handsome man in his mid-to-late thirties wandered nearby, his hands behind his back. Then he started speaking, and the woman furiously scribbled what he said.

Rupert looked over his shoulder, seeing the four women had brought their horses to a halt. Lady Lia stared at the man as if he were a hero from a great battle. He stopped his own horse and listened, realizing they had stumbled across the great Lake poet himself, dictating lines to his sister.

For a moment, they listened, spellbound, and then Rupert motioned silently to them. They began to walk their horses again, moving away. Once out of sight, he stopped, the others following suit.

"It was him—Wordsworth!" Lady Lia cried. "Oh, I am trying to recall what he told his sister. She was writing down every word he uttered." She paused, a look of reverence on her face. "When the volume of poetry is published, I know I will recognize the lines we just heard."

She looked to him. "Thank you, Lord Cressley. I believe I have experienced something incredibly unique. To my dying day, I will recall my skin tingling as I heard the greatest living poet in all of England creating poetry aloud, his inspiration the surroundings about him."

They returned to the center of Grasmere, first returning their horses and then walking back to the inn together. As they entered, the innkeeper greeted them.

"Can I get you some ale, my lord? And perhaps lemonade for the ladies? You must be parched after your long ride."

"Yes, please," he said, indicating a table for them to sit.

The innkeeper's wife returned with a tray of drinks, and Lady Lia said, "We think we saw Wordsworth on our ride."

"If you did, he would be walking around, spouting poetry, while his sister records what he dictates."

"Yes, that is what we witnessed," Lady Justina said, barely containing her excitement.

"I've heard he likes to walk and think," the woman told them. "If anyone local comes across them, we leave them in peace."

"We did," Rupert assured her. "Not even one greeting was exchanged."

"It was as if they were in their own small world," Lady Lia continued. "They took no notice of us. In fact, I am not certain they truly saw us."

"It was as if we were not even there," Lady Tia said breathlessly. "It was genius in the making."

"Well, you'll have a story to tell your little ones," the innkeeper's wife said. "Let me know if you need anything else, my lord."

The duchess and countess entered the inn, and he stood, motioning them over. The two older women joined them, and the four young ladies excitedly told their mothers about their sighting of the great poet.

"And he did not even seem to see you?" Her Grace asked, puzzled.

"He was that focused on his art, Mama," Lady Lia said.

The duchess sniffed. "I think him merely rude. Let us tell you about our shopping expedition."

The women talked for several minutes, Rupert doing his best to glance at each one as they spoke, when all he wanted to do was focus his sole attention on Lady Lia.

They finished their lemonades and made plans to meet again when it was time for dinner. He returned to his room and sat on the bed, thinking of how next Season might play out. Him, dutifully looking for a bride who would care for Celia and provide him with an heir. Lady Lia, on her quest, searching for love.

Rupert lay on the bed, pillowing his hands behind his head, wishing he could have just one more kiss with her. Then he would let go of the sometimes foolish notions that played in his head about her, thoughts that came to him in the dead of night, when the house was still and he could not sleep.

Perhaps tonight might be the night. In fact, he realized this might be his only chance since he doubted he would see her before she left for Millvale. The question was where they could be alone without anyone seeing them.

And if Lady Lia would even permit a kiss from a man she did not love.

CHAPTER NINETEEN

L IA'S EUPHORIA FROM seeing the famous William Wordsworth slowly began to fade. To have seen him in his element, dictating lines of poetry to his sister, was something she could never have imagined. His concentration had been so great that he truly had not seen their riding party stop to watch him at work. And his sister had not even glanced up, so rushed by trying to get down every syllable uttered by her famous brother.

She wondered if all the Lake poets, as they were known, worked in a similar fashion. Lia had read all their works. Samuel Taylor Coleridge. Robert Southey. And naturally, Wordsworth himself. It had been wonderful not only seeing him at work in the place he wrote about but also seeing his family at Dove Cottage, the wife and three small children. Thinking of it caused sadness to well within her.

Soon, they would be leaving Traywick Manor. She would never see Celia Cummings again, or at least not for many years. While she knew it was wonderful that Miss Wilson had finally arrived and taken Celia's education in hand, Lia missed the days spent with the child. Celia was bright and optimistic and cared about everything around her. Being in the young girl's company made Lia certain she was meant to be a mother.

But who would become her husband?

She still loved Lord Cressley. She feared a part of her always would, despite the lack of reciprocation on his part. He had felt the same attraction she had, but he would not give into those deeper feelings. Why, she could not say. She supposed he thought himself incapable of love after having seen what he had during the war. Yet he did love his niece. Lia was certain of that. She only wished the viscount could open just a sliver of his heart to her. She would love him completely, with kindness and patience.

How would she bear to see him next Season, dancing with other women, even courting some? She already dreaded the day the newspapers announced his betrothal. Lia told herself she needed to wash her hands of the viscount and look to her own future.

But all she could think of was one more kiss. Just a final time. To be in his arms, their mouths pressed against one another, even as their bodies were, would be absolute heaven. And if it were to occur, it had to happen tonight. Once they returned to Traywick Manor tomorrow, she doubted she would even see Lord Cressley before they left for Millvale. How to grab a few precious moments alone now dominated her thoughts.

"Lia? Where are you?"

She looked up, seeing Tia hovering over her, concern written across her brow.

"I am sorry. What did you say?"

"What *haven't* I said?" her twin teased. "I have been talking to you forever, and I finally realized you were lost in your thoughts."

"I will admit I was woolgathering. Our time in Cumberland is coming to an end."

"Are you thinking about Lord Cressley?" Tia asked.

"A little. But also Celia. Being around her has convinced me even more than before that I am ready to have babes."

"You certainly were good with her," her sister agreed. "Why, if you were poor and had to earn your living, you would be highly in demand as a governess."

"I would, wouldn't I?" she said, then giggled. "I think I would prefer having children of my own and not having to go from post to post."

"We should let Esther know that we need hot water to wash with from our long ride. I also want to change gowns," Tia said.

They prepared themselves for dinner and went to the upper room where Lord Cressley had told them they would share a meal together. Mama and Aunt Agnes were already present. Verina and Justina joined them soon after, while Lord Cressley was the last to arrive.

"I just checked with the innkeeper. Dinner is on its way," he told them.

He helped seat each of them, and Lia found herself on the viscount's left. They were served an onion and leek soup with crusty bread, followed by venison and vegetables. When it came time for something sweet, they all decided to pass, feeling too full of all they had eaten. Instead, they asked for tea to be served.

"Why is the bread at an inn so good?" Justina mused. "I have eaten numerous slices slathered in butter. In fact, if all I had eaten tonight was the bread and butter, I would be more than satisfied."

"What are our plans tomorrow, Mama?" Verina asked.

"I was hoping we could take all you girls shopping in the morning, then we could return home in the afternoon."

They agreed this was a good plan. Lord Cressley said they could meet here for breakfast.

"I will arrange for it to be delivered to us."

"Shall we say breakfast at nine?" Mama said. "Then by the time we finish eating, the shops will be open."

They all agreed nine would be perfect. Mama and Aunt Agnes excused themselves, and those remaining talked another hour. Then Verina yawned.

"All that riding has exhausted me," she said. "Come, Justina. We should retire for the evening."

"I will go with you," Tia said. "Lia, stay and finish your tea. I know you would not want it to go to waste. Lord Cressley, please stay with Lia until she finishes. I do not want her left alone."

Lia knew her twin was trying to throw the two of them together a final time, hoping something might come of it. In this instance, Lia hoped she would be able to finagle a kiss from the viscount.

⋙⋘

THE OTHERS DEPARTED, and Lady Lia turned to him. Rupert could not have asked for a more perfect end to the evening. The innkeeper had checked on them a final time and should not be back. The mothers had retired, as had now the other young ladies. It left only the two of them together.

He turned to her and felt speechless as both her palms cupped his cheeks. Their gazes met, and he saw something burning in her eyes.

Could it be desire?

"I want to kiss you," she boldly told him.

"I would like that very much."

She pulled him toward her, and he did not resist. Their lips touched, and hunger for this woman filled him. His hands went to her waist, and he pulled them both to their feet. As he held her, they kissed, again and again. He felt the fire light within him, the white-hot fire of desire. Rupert pulled her closer, until their bodies brushed against one another. He heard her sigh, and she opened to him.

He took advantage of this, slipping his tongue inside her mouth, tasting the unique sweetness that was Lia Worthington. Their kisses grew bolder. More frantic, as tongues warred with one another. He began to feel lightheaded and wrapped his arms around her, holding her tightly to him, not ever wanting to let her go.

Abruptly, she broke the kiss, gazing up at him, her eyes searching his face silently.

"Do you love me?"

Her question shouldn't have caught him by surprise—but it did. And the answer that came to him surprised him even more.

He thought he might.

But to vocalize that would commit him for all time to this one woman, and Rupert didn't know if he could say the words. Even for Lia Worthington.

"No," he said huskily. "But I do care for you a great deal."

She stared at him a long moment, a knowing sadness filling those deep blue eyes. "I suspected as much."

Then she shocked him by kissing him again. It was a tender, loving kiss. It also tasted of goodbye. He knew it. And she certainly knew it. But he drank in the bittersweetness of it, knowing it was the last kiss they would ever share.

She was the one to break it. Tears misted her eyes. She gazed at him for a long moment.

"I hope you find happiness, Lord Cressley. It will be nice to see you in town at the Season next spring." She hesitated a moment and then added, "Goodnight."

But they both knew this was goodbye.

"Goodnight, my lady," he said, his voice breaking. "I hope you find the love you are looking for, Lia."

It was the first time he had addressed her by her given name. The first—and last.

She nudged him back, and he let her pass, his heart a raw, bloody mess. He asked himself why he couldn't give more of himself to her. Was it because he had never known love himself?

He hadn't enjoyed the familial love Lia had experienced within her tightknit group of siblings. He had never let himself get close to any of the boys at school, feeling something was wrong with him. That he was so unlovable that even his own family couldn't love him, much less want to be around him.

At war, he knew he chose not to get close to his men because he was the one who guided them onto the battlefield, toward death. That had been gut-wrenching. It was the chief reason he had volunteered for spy work when the call had come. He liked working alone, moving from place to place. For so long, he had only trusted himself and no one else.

But Rupert felt in his gut that he trusted Lia. That he truly might even love her. That they could have something special together. That she could be the answer he was searching for, even though he had not known he did so.

But would she believe him if he did tell her that he loved her? She had just tested him now. Asked point blank if he loved her.

And he had failed that test miserably.

He decided he needed to win her heart next Season. The Season would give them a fresh start. For now, he would let her go, and they could reacquaint themselves come next spring. Lia could meet other gentlemen. Compare them to him. Rupert would stay within her orbit. Ask her to dance. Call upon her. Even woo her. And when the time was right, he would confess his feelings to her.

Satisfied he now had a plan of action, Rupert returned to his rented room. And for once, he didn't mind that he dreamed of Lia Worthington.

CHAPTER TWENTY

L IA AWOKE, DREAD filling her. Tomorrow they would leave Traywick Manor. She was torn, having been taken with Cumberland ever since they arrived, but knowing it would be much easier for her heart to heal if she were home in Kent in familiar surroundings, with those she loved.

And not around the man whose love she could never win.

She rose and went to the window. The gray November day looked bleak. As she opened the window, she could smell rain in the air.

Tia stirred and looked up. "What does the weather look like?"

"Gloomy. The skies look as if they will open any minute now. I fear we are in for a stormy day."

Her sister sighed. "So much for a final ride about the countryside. Of course, that means the roads will be clogged tomorrow. Do you think Mama might postpone our journey home?"

She chuckled. "Mama has decided tomorrow is the day, so tomorrow is the day. You know how she is. Her mind becomes set upon something, and nothing ever changes it." Lia sighed. "I am already dreading how long it will take us to return to Millvale."

The journey to Cumberland had taken about ten days. This time of year, with inclement weather, it might be two weeks—or longer. Lia dreaded the long hours spent in the carriage each day, with only her thoughts to keep her entertained. More than anything, she wished to banish any thoughts of Lord Cressley.

"You are thinking of the viscount, aren't you?" Tia asked.

Closing the window, she returned to the bed, sitting on the edge. "Yes. I cannot help it. This is the worst pain in the world, Tia. To love someone and not have your love returned. I am miserable."

Her twin sat up, propping pillows behind her. "Well, he's a bloody fool for not seeing what a treasure you are."

Her eyes went wide at her sister's harsh words, but even Lia felt like muttering a few curse words herself. "I think he is like most men. Shut off from his emotions. I do believe he has the capability to love. Just witnessing him with Celia lets me know that." She paused. "But I think his feelings for her use up anything else left inside him. I adore the child, but I cannot waste my time on Viscount Cressley anymore. Let him do what most every man in Polite Society does. Wed for social status or wealth."

Taking Tia's hand, she concluded with, "As for me, I still have hope that I may find love. But what of you, Tia? Do you seek love?"

Her twin shrugged. "I truly have not given it much thought. I was so angry when Papa died and delayed our come-outs. I set aside thinking about the Season or men or my future and have merely been living in the present. I did enjoy watching Val and Eden's romance unfold and all the work we did on the fete. I have soaked up our time here at Traywick Manor. I suppose once the new year comes, I will turn my thoughts to the Season."

"What does instinct tell you now?" pressed Lia. "About love."

"I know it exists. Ariadne and Val have found it. Lucy, too. But you know I want to have a bit of fun, Lia. I am not quite ready to be a wife and mother as you are. I want to wear pretty gowns and dance at balls and eat Venetian breakfasts and go for rides in Hyde Park during the fashionable hour. I want to meet different people, both men and women. You are—and always will be—my closest friend, but I want to get to know other girls. I hope eventually to attract the right gentleman. It would be wonderful if we did grow to love one another, but that will not be a requirement for me when I wed."

"You sound so practical now. *I* am usually the practical one."

Tia laughed. "Here I am telling you that I want to soak up everything about the social swirl of the Season, yet you are calling me practical." She embraced Lia. "Oh, I do love you dearly, my sweet twin."

They rang for Esther, and Lia dressed first, with Tia telling her to go down to breakfast.

"I will join you in a few minutes. After all, there is no rush with the inclement weather. We will be housebound all day."

Lia went to the breakfast room, only finding Aunt Agnes there.

"Good morning, Aunt Agnes. You are up early."

"I could not sleep," her aunt replied. "I think I am already missing you, Tia, and my dear Alice."

"We have been at Traywick Manor for two months, and you and my cousins were at Millvale for several months before that."

"Yes, and this time together has been lovely, hasn't it?"

She finished making her plate and sat, a footman pouring tea for her. "Yes, I have enjoyed every minute of it. I must say that I have fallen in love with the Lake District and its raw, rugged beauty."

Her aunt's gaze met and held Lia's. "Anything else you might wish to mention to me?"

Aware of the footman and butler standing only mere feet from them, she said, "I believe I will leave a part of my heart in Cumberland."

The look Aunt Agnes gave her led Lia to believe that the older woman understood the hidden meaning in her words.

"You know you are always welcome to come and stay at Traywick Manor any time you would like."

She knew that, but she would never accept an offer to visit again, not with Viscount Cressley living so close by. Part of her thought that she would cull through her suitors, allowing anyone but those who lived in Cumberland to court her. Lia did not wish to wed a man who lived in this area because she did not want to take the chance of having to live in close proximity to Lord Cressley. Who would have thought she would choose a suitor based upon where he lived?

The others joined them, all but Mama, who liked to keep to her rooms for breakfast, and they lamented how they would not be able to ride today. The rain had started in earnest now, and Verina said it showed no sign of letting up.

"I thought you would be unhappy, confined to the house today, so I sent a note to Crestbrook," Aunt Agnes said. "I asked Viscount Cressley if he would allow Celia to come visit for the day. Keeping the girl entertained will keep you all very busy."

Lia only hoped she would not have to see anyone but Celia.

Celia arrived an hour later, escorted by her governess, who remained in the carriage. Aunt Agnes greeted the child when she entered the drawing room. Celia made a quick curtsey and went straight to Lia, wrapping her arms about her.

"I'm so glad I get to stay with you today, my lady."

"I feel likewise," she replied, her throat thickening with emotion.

Aunt Agnes said, "I invited Lord Cressley to come for tea when he retrieves Miss Celia. You are free to do as you like until teatime."

So Lia *would* have to see the viscount a final time.

The day passed quickly, thanks to Celia. They went to the music room, and Verina played the piano for them as they sang, teaching the young girl several new songs. Justina brought out a checkerboard, and they taught Celia the rules of the game. She caught on quickly, clapping her hands when she won a game.

Tia suggested they make some new clothes for Lally, and so they went to the sewing room, finding scraps of material. While Lia, Verina, and Justina sewed for the doll, Tia and Celia sat nearby, Tia reading aloud to everyone. Since the doll was small, it did not take long for three new gowns to be made, one by each of them. Celia took turns dressing Lally in her new clothes and thanked everyone for contributing to the doll's wardrobe.

All too soon, it was time for tea, and they went to the drawing room. The minute Lord Cressley arrived, Celia showed off Lally's new gowns to him. Watching him show such enthusiasm for a doll's clothes only tugged all the harder at Lia's still-broken heart. Fortunately, conversation was lively, and she did not have to speak to the viscount directly.

When the time came for Celia and Lord Cressley to depart, Celia hugged everyone goodbye, saving Lia for last.

Her eyes misted with tears as Celia said, "I will miss you, Lady Lia. You're my very best friend."

They embraced, and she thought the next time she caught sight of Celia would be a dozen or so years in the future, when Celia came to town to make her debut into Polite Society. Already, the child was a natural beauty, and Lia could only guess at what Celia might look like by the time she made her come-out. She wondered if the girl would even recognize her or recall anything about the special bond they had formed during Lia's visit to Cumberland.

They walked downstairs with Lord Cressley and Celia, with the viscount thanking her aunt for today's invitation. He addressed Mama, Tia, and Lia together, saying, "It was delightful to make your acquaintance, Your Grace, and your lovely daughters. I hope to spend time with you again come the Season next spring."

"You must call on us when you come to town, Lord Cressley," Mama said. "His Grace will certainly wish to meet you."

Lia winced, not wanting Viscount Cressley to become a family friend. She already wanted to escape his presence and try to heal her broken heart. She did not need him frequenting their London townhouse and stomping on her heart again and again. Perhaps she would address the issue with Mama and explain how she'd had feelings for the viscount and did not wish to be in his company.

Then he and Celia left, racing out in the rain, climbing into their carriage, and departing. Lia felt the final death knell, knowing nothing would ever come of their relationship.

Moving to Aunt Agnes, she whispered, "I have the beginning of a megrim, Aunt. I will not be down for dinner this evening."

Her aunt gave her a knowing look. "I shall have Larsen send up a tray to you. Just in case you feel like eating a little something."

"Thank you. I appreciate you doing so."

Lia retreated to her bedchamber and saw that Esther had done all the packing for their departure tomorrow morning. That gave her precious time alone, something she had not had a lot of during their time at Traywick Manor. She opened the window, seeing the rain had finally come to a halt. Because of that, she decided to go down to the stables. She slipped into her spencer for warmth and changed into the boots Esther had left out for traveling, then went down the back staircase used by the servants, cutting through the kitchens, where the staff was busy preparing the evening meal. Lia grabbed an apple from a stack sitting in a wooden bowl and slipped outside.

The air was quite cool but smelled wonderful after the rains. Lia inhaled deeply, thinking again how much she would miss this part of England, knowing the only time she would return to it would be when she read Mr. Wordsworth's poetry. She would view his poems with new eyes in subsequent readings, having now experienced the beauty of the Lake District firsthand.

In the stables, she greeted a groom and made her way to Orion's stall. She had ridden only him during her entire visit to Traywick Manor, and she had grown attached.

Orion chuffed, coming to her, his head sticking over the door to the stall. Lia rubbed his nose and then placed her brow against the horse, breathing in the scent of horse and hay.

Then she presented Orion with his treat. "I have brought you a little something. You have been a pleasure to ride, my dark beauty."

The horse nibbled on the apple in her palm. When he finished, she kept the core, kissing Orion. "Until we meet again," she said, tears blurring her vision as she hurried away and back to the house.

Esther waited for her in the bedchamber. "I thought you might feel better if you had a hot bath, my lady. The water will be here shortly."

"That is very thoughtful of you," she told the maid. "I believe you are right."

Lia luxuriated in the bath, knowing it would be a long time before she had another one so unhurried. Esther helped her to wash her hair, and Lia combed it, letting the air dry it. More water was brought when Tia arrived, and her twin also got a bath.

"Oh, this is a luxury I will miss when we are on the road," Tia said as she stood, and Esther helped rinse the soap from her.

"I agree. But before you know it, we will be at Millvale. And Eden surely will be increasing by now. Oh, it will be such fun to have a babe in the household."

Lia helped comb Tia's hair. Her sister had no patience for things such as this, and Lia found the task soothing. Afterward, they climbed into bed.

"Our last night in a comfortable bed, as well," her twin remarked. "I think inns deliberately have horrible mattresses and useless pillows in order to encourage travelers to continue on and not linger."

That caused Lia to burst out in laughter. She hugged Tia. "Oh, I am so glad we are still together. I worry about when we both wed. Most likely, we will live far apart and only see one another at the Season."

"Then we will have to investigate wedding suitors who live near one another," Tia said. "Ariadne and Lucy are neighbors. Perhaps you and I can find two decent gentlemen who live close to one another. We will wed them and see one another every day."

"I hope so," Lia said, knowing that would be next to impossible.

Tia took Lia's hand. "Goodnight."

"Goodnight," she echoed, wondering what the upcoming Season would mean to their futures.

CHAPTER TWENTY-ONE

RUPERT WENT TO the schoolroom, knowing Celia and Miss Wilson would still be at breakfast. His eyes were gritty from lack of sleep. Lady Lia had departed yesterday for Kent.

And he wasn't certain he would survive until next spring without being able to see her.

Yesterday, he had kept busy doing manual labor about the estate. He drove himself hard, wanting to bury himself in work, trying to forget the auburn-haired beauty. Even Holson had begged him to take a break, but Rupert had only pushed himself harder. He had returned to the house well after dark, going up in time to tuck Celia in for the night. She had wrinkled her nose, calling him smelly, and ordered him to go take a bath. Laughing, he had done so, all the while wishing Lia Worthington had been naked in that bathing tub with him.

His idea of waiting until the Season began and courting her as a gentleman was a sound one. He had been surprised when the Dowager Duchess of Millbrooke had given him permission to call upon her family when he did come to town for the Season. Deliberately, Rupert had not glanced to Lia because he was afraid to see how she might react to this. Poorly, most likely, because of the way they had parted. He was determined to make things up to her.

That is, if he could manage not to go mad before next April.

He had a little less than five months to wait before being in her presence again. Actually, he needed to go to town early so that he might be fitted for a new wardrobe. While the local tailor had done a fine job of creating everyday wear for Rupert, Burrows had no experience in sewing evening clothes for *ton* events, and Rupert would need plenty of those for the many social affairs he would attend. He wanted to be sharply-dressed—even stand out—because his heart told him Lia would be surrounded by a bevy of suitors. Anything he could do to pull away from the pack of callers would help.

Now, it was the second day since Lia had left Cumberland. Should he continue to count the days, or would that prove more difficult? Already, he'd had trouble sleeping. If he kept this up, he would look like a cadaver. He needed to eat right and sleep well. Keep his mind on sensible things. Work the estate and spend time with Celia, which was what he was planning to do now.

Rupert reached the schoolroom and stood in the doorway a moment. Celia was telling some story to Miss Wilson, who managed to look interested and entertained by the girl's chatter. The governess was a true gem, and he knew his niece would flourish under Miss Wilson's hand. Already, he had called in the governess and spoken to her about happy he was with the progress she was making with Celia. In turn, Miss Wilson had told him that this post was everything she had hoped it would be and that she would stay as long as Celia needed her. Rupert assured the woman that she would be employed until Celia's come-out ended, knowing it would be nice to have a woman's touch during that time.

Celia must have sensed his presence because she turned. Spying him, she sprang from her chair, coming to wrap her arms about his leg.

"Good morning, Uncle Rupert. I'm telling Miss Wilson about my dream."

He led her back into the schoolroom and took a seat, his knees almost next to his ears as he crouched in the small chair.

"When you finish your breakfast, I was hoping we might ride

together. That is, if it will not interrupt Miss Wilson's plans for you."

"I am always flexible, my lord. Miss Celia enjoys spending time with you. If you are available now, please take her with you."

"Can I ride Posey?" she asked. "Or am I going to ride with you?"

"Which would you rather do?"

"Ride Posey!" she cried. "I'm a good rider, just like Lady Lia."

Hearing the name was like a knife to his heart. Rupert smiled, though. "I want to see how your riding has improved. I am off to have my own breakfast, and then you and I can ride for a bit."

Rupert excused himself, making his way downstairs. As he sipped his coffee and ate eggs which seemed tasteless, he went through the post, finding nothing of interest.

Celia joined him, and he finished his coffee with a final swallow. Lifting her atop his shoulders, he strode toward the stables, having their horses saddled. Miss Wilson had continued the riding lessons, and she had confided that Celia already had more confidence atop a horse than most children of that age. Still, he knew that they couldn't ride too far, much less gallop.

They enjoyed walking their horses in the pale sunshine for almost three-quarters of an hour before returning to the stables. Celia took his hand as they returned to the house.

"Uncle Rupert, why do have on your sad face?"

Her question caused him to stop. "What do you mean?"

Her face scrunched up in thought. "Well, you just look sad. I like it when you look happy."

"I suppose I am a bit sad," he shared. "I miss Lady Lia."

Celia's eyes widened. "I do, too. Can we go see her?"

He smoothed her hair. "Ah, little love, Lady Lia lives all the way in Kent. We have told you it takes many days riding in a carriage to reach it. She has only been gone two days. She will not even be home for another week and a half. Possibly two weeks. The roads are in poor condition this time of year, so it takes longer to reach everywhere."

"But can we go see her?" his niece repeated.

"No, Celia. You must be invited to go and see someone. Remember how we were invited to go to the picnic by Lady Traywick? That is how things work."

Her bottom lip thrust out. "But I miss Lady Lia."

"I do, as well."

"Why can't she live here? With us?"

Rupert was afraid to say too much. He had already trampled upon Lia's heart. She might not even allow him to become one of her suitors next Season, so he did not want to get his niece's hopes up.

Then he recalled how she mentioned how her family all planned to take their children to the Season, so that all the cousins could grow up with one another and parents could see their own children. It had not occurred to him that he would be leaving Celia behind for the duration of the Season. Why, that would break not only her heart, but his. He would need to take her to town with him come next April. Thankfully, he had the efficient Miss Wilson to keep Celia on track with her studies.

"We will see her in London in a few months."

She brightened. "I know where London is on the globe. In the atlas, too."

"Lady Lia will be in London, starting in April. She is looking to find her husband. I will also be looking for a wife."

"Could you marry her?" Celia asked.

"I would like to," he said carefully. "But Lady Lia must also want to wed me in order for us to become husband and wife."

"Do you love her?"

The unexpected question caused him to stop in his tracks. Lia had asked a similar question, and Rupert had certainly mucked up his answer.

"Yes. I do," he said simply.

Celia thought a moment. "Then why do you have to wait to tell her? Why can't you go and tell her now, Uncle Rupert?"

Out of the mouth of a child came something so incredibly simple—yet so very right.

Why *not* tell her now? Why wait for months, having her heart harden against him and his break apart? They belonged together. They always would.

Scooping up Celia, he held her high in the sky, twirling about. She giggled, that beautiful noise that made his step light.

"You are right!" he cried. "I should go after her. *We* should go after her."

Rupert said this because he could not possibly leave Celia alone. It might take a couple of weeks to reach Millvale and a couple more to return. That did not include the time it would take for convincing Lia to wed him. Then there was the matter of the banns being read. Bloody hell, that would be another three weeks.

Setting Celia on her feet again, he recalled talk of a special license, something he could purchase that would expedite matters. He had heard someone in university mention that his older brother had wed by special license, some kind of dispensation granted by the Archbishop of Canterbury. All Rupert could remember was a place called Doctors' Commons. Yes, that was where something of this nature could be purchased.

Determination flooded him. He would have them go to Kent by way of London, stopping to acquire this special license. Of course, Lia might not want to wed him, even if he did arrive with the marriage license in hand, but Rupert could not wait for months, pining for her. He was a man of action.

Celia was jumping up and down, clapping, grinning at him. "We're getting married."

Quickly, he dropped to one knee, clasping her shoulders. Looking at her gravely, he said, "I cannot promise you that Lady Lia will want to wed me. I have hurt her. Hurt her feelings. She may not forgive me."

His niece looked at him, and with words far wiser than her years, said, "Just tell her that you love her, Uncle Rupert."

He would do that. He only hoped that would be enough to convince her they belonged together.

They returned to the house, and he took Celia up to the schoolroom. Miss Wilson sat at the table, perusing several books open in front of her.

"Miss Wilson, are you up for a bit of traveling?" he asked. "I would like my niece to accompany me to Kent. Naturally, I would wish for her lessons to continue."

A slow smile grew into a wide, happy one. "I would be delighted to continue with Miss Celia's lessons on the road, Lord Cressley. Travel is very educational in itself. I assume you are going to Millvale?"

Rupert couldn't help but grin at her. "Yes. Celia has convinced me that I should leave immediately and tell Lady Lia that I love her."

"That *we* love her," prompted Celia, causing both adults to laugh.

"I sensed that there was something between the two of you the minute I arrived at Crestbrook," the governess said. "I think it wise that you act quickly, my lord. Lady Lia's generous heart and beauty will attract many gentlemen. You do not want to be too late in expressing your sentiments."

"I agree. Can you have Celia and yourself packed and ready to leave early tomorrow morning?"

"Yes, my lord."

"Then if you will excuse me, I have other preparations to make."

Rupert quickly sought out Adam Holson, informing his steward that he would be gone at least a month and possibly longer.

"I know I leave Crestbrook in steady hands."

"Thank you for your trust and belief in me, Lord Cressley. I will not fail you."

Next, he called a meeting with Prater, Mrs. Prater, and Damsley.

"Miss Celia, Miss Wilson, and I are leaving tomorrow. We

will be gone approximately four to six weeks. Damsley, I will need my things packed, and you will accompany us on our travels. Prater, inform the stables and my coachman. Mrs. Prater, let Cook know of our absence."

He hesitated. If things did not work out as he hoped, all would be for naught, but he added, "I would also like the viscountess' rooms prepared in the event they may be occupied soon. Clean out any clothing which remains. Have new bed linens purchased. See that the carpets are cleaned and the furniture polished until it shines."

The housekeeper looked at him hopefully. "Might it be Lady Lia who comes home with you, my lord?"

"That is my fondest desire, Mrs. Prater. I cannot guess at this point if she will return with us or not. If she does so, I want everything prepared for her." Then his tone grew sterner. "But that is not to leave this room," he warned. "While the rooms are to be made spotless, do not say a word as to who might occupy them."

"Certainly not, my lord," Mrs. Prater said. Then her face softened. "But I will pray that occurs."

"I will need all the help I can get, from God and man, to convince Lady Lia to become my wife," he told the trio. "I do appreciate those prayers, Mrs. Prater."

Rupert left them, knowing his orders would be carried out. He escaped to his study, excitement building inside him. He had one chance now to make things right between him and Lia.

He only hoped he would not stumble again—because the rest of his life depended upon it.

CHAPTER TWENTY-TWO

T HEY FINALLY ARRIVED in London after a week and a half of traveling, and Rupert instructed his coachman to head straight to his townhouse. He hadn't had time to alert the Bowers that he would be staying there overnight, and Mrs. Bowers was a bit frantic at having no notice. Still, she and her husband were welcoming.

Once he had made certain Celia and Miss Wilson were settled, he took a hansom cab to Mr. Ousley's office, apologizing to the clerk because he did not have an appointment.

"Mr. Ousley is free at the moment, Lord Cressley," the clerk said, taking him back to see the solicitor.

"Why, Lord Cressley," Mr. Ousley said, clearly surprised. "What brings you to town? And how are you finding Crestbrook?"

"The estate is thriving," he shared. "Mr. Williamson, our longtime steward, has recently retired. He recommended Adam Holson as his replacement, and I believe Mr. Holson will be with us for many years to come. But I have something important to discuss with you, Mr. Ousley. I only just arrived in town an hour ago, and I plan to leave for Kent tomorrow morning."

"What might I help you with, my lord?"

"I am hoping to wed in the very near future. I know marriage settlements must be drawn up for that to occur. I also wish to purchase a special license once I leave here. Can you help me?"

"For the special license, you will need to go to Doctors' Commons." Mr. Ousley withdrew a piece of paper and jotted down an address, handing it to Rupert. "As far as the marriage contracts are concerned, it is usual to meet with the bride's father or guardian, along with his solicitor, and hammer them out."

He frowned. "I did not know it worked that way."

"How soon are you looking to marry, my lord?"

"If my intended says yes, as soon as possible." He paused. "I know you are a very busy man, Mr. Ousley, but is there any way you might accompany me to Kent tomorrow? That way, if Lady Lia agrees to the marriage, you would already be on hand."

"And who is Lady Lia's father?"

"He is deceased. Her brother is the Duke of Millbrooke. I suppose I would need his permission, or that of her mother, the Dowager Duchess of Millbrooke."

"I know His Grace's solicitor, a Mr. Creighton. We are old friends," Ousley said. "If Creighton is free, perhaps we might travel down to Kent with you tomorrow."

Relief flooded him. "That would be wonderful, Mr. Ousley. Please check with Mr. Creighton. I shall go to Doctors' Commons now and call again at your offices once my business there is complete."

"I should know by then if Creighton is free or not. If you will tell me what you would like written into the marriage settlements, I can go ahead and began a draft of the contracts. That will save us time."

"I am clueless, Mr. Ousley. What do they involve?"

Briefly, the solicitor talked to Rupert about everything from monthly pin money to dowries for any future daughters and provisions for any sons beyond the heir apparent. He also mentioned they would need to include arrangements for what would happen to his viscountess, should he predecease her.

"Since I have no experience, I will let you use your judgment, Mr. Ousley. All I want is to be generous in whatever you write up."

"Then I will speak with Creighton and begin the process, my lord."

"Thank you so much."

Rupert dashed outside, hailing another hansom cab and giving the driver the address which Ousley had provided to him. He easily found the offices, but he had to wait an hour and a half before he could see the archbishop's representative. Even then, after stating what he needed, it took another hour before he had the special license in hand since certain things had to be verified before the license could be issued. While it allowed Lia and him to wed on any day and time and at any place to their liking, it was only good for a month. He hoped not only would Lia agree to wed him—but that she would do it within the timeframe of the special license.

Returning to Mr. Ousley's office, he found the solicitor hard at work, another man and two clerks also assisting him. Mr. Creighton was the other solicitor, and he had brought one of his clerks.

"We have written up what we think is a very good marriage contract, my lord," Mr. Ousley told him. "I took your word and have been most generous in setting the terms. Mr. Creighton will tell you the same."

The Millbrooke solicitor said, "While I cannot leave tomorrow and go to Millvale with you, I have written a brief note to His Grace, informing him that I had a hand in writing these marriage settlements and that they are very charitable toward Lady Lia and any issue from the marriage. I have encouraged His Grace to sign the documents, saying they are in the best interests of his sister."

He looked to Ousley. "Will you be able to accompany me to Kent?"

"I can do so, my lord. I will bring a clerk with me so that if His Grace approves, copies can be made for all parties involved, as well as one for Mr. Creighton to keep."

"Then be at your offices by nine o'clock tomorrow morning,

Mr. Ousley. With a change of horses, we should be at Millvale by two in the afternoon."

"We shall see you then, my lord," the solicitor said.

Rupert returned to his townhouse and met with the Bowers, saying, "There is a possibility that I may soon wed. I would like the viscountess' rooms scrubbed from top to bottom."

"Of course, my lord," the housekeeper said. "Do you know when you might return?"

"I cannot say. I wish I could. I leave tomorrow morning for Millvale, which is south of Maidstone."

"Everything will be taken care of immediately, Lord Cressley," Bowers assured him.

He went to the schoolroom, where Celia and Miss Wilson were enjoying a last meal of the day.

"Is everything to your liking?" he asked the governess.

"Yes, my lord. I might need to purchase a few supplies for this schoolroom, but Miss Celia and I could easily hold lessons here."

"I plan to bring Celia—and any future children I may have— to town with me for each Season."

Her startled expression told him how unique the idea was, and he added, "It is going to be a new family tradition. I do not think it would do either Celia or me any good to be apart from one another for so many months."

Miss Wilson smiled approvingly "I think it a sound idea, my lord."

"Tell Bowers what you need for lessons. He can purchase it and have those supplies ready for when we return in the spring."

Rupert only hoped that he would be introducing his new viscountess to Polite Society when the next Season rolled around.

HIS BELLY CHURNED as his carriage turned and drove up the lane to Millvale. They had stopped twice for directions, the last time in

Willowshire, the local village. Rupert had seen the local church as they passed through and wondered if he would soon be standing at its altar with his bride or if he were on a fool's errand.

Hopefully, he would know the answer in the next hour.

He had left Celia, Miss Wilson, and Mr. Ousley at the Willowshire inn, telling Miss Wilson to order them some food. He would return as quickly as possible. Whether it was with good news or bad, he couldn't say. Celia had wanted to go with him to Millvale to see Lia, but if he were turned away by her, he did not wish for his niece to be a part of that humiliation. It would be difficult enough to contain his sadness from her if things did not work out as he wished.

His carriage stopped in front of an imposing house, larger than any he had ever seen. Then again, it was the house of a duke. As Rupert climbed from the vehicle, the butler came out to greet him.

"I am Quigby, my lord, butler to His Grace."

"Good afternoon, Quigby. I am Viscount Cressley. I have come to call upon Lady Lia."

"Won't you come inside, my lord?"

The butler led him inside and said, "Lady Lia is in the village with Her Grace and Lady Tia. But His Grace and the dowager duchess are here. Might you wish to speak to either of them?"

"Both, if possible."

"Then let me show you to the drawing room, my lord. I will let Their Graces know you are here."

Rupert followed the butler upstairs, almost feeling as if he marched to Tower Hill and certain death. At least he could explain to Their Graces why he was there.

He hadn't been in the drawing room more than two minutes when a muscular man a few inches over six feet entered and came toward him. He had emerald eyes and russet hair.

"Your Grace," he said, bowing his head in respect.

"Lord Cressley," the duke said, offering Rupert his hand. "You are a long way from home."

Expelling a long breath, he said, "I most certainly am."

The dowager duchess breezed into the drawing room, coming toward them. "Cressley," she said, allowing him to take her hand and kiss it. "I was wondering if you might show up."

"You were?" he asked, not able to keep the surprise from his voice.

"Well, you do love my Cornelia, don't you?"

"Most fervently, Your Grace," he replied.

"Come. Sit," she instructed, and the three of them took a seat.

"Mama seems to know more than I do," the duke said, eyeing Rupert with interest. "I was familiar with your name because it was mentioned to me by my sisters when they returned a few days ago. You are a neighbor to my cousin, I gather."

"Yes, my estate is next to Lord Traywick's," he said, nerves flitting through him.

"And you love my sister." The duke's tone was even, but he saw questions in the man's eyes.

"I may have mucked everything up," he admitted. "I do love Lady Lia. I told her I did not. She knows that I am fond of her. I cannot say why I did not admit as much to her."

Sympathy filled Millbrooke's eyes. "Love can play havoc with one's emotions. I almost made a mess of things with my duchess. Fortunately, we were able to straighten everything out between us." The duke paused. "And I am deliriously happy now." He smiled. "I am also going to be a father."

"Why, congratulations, Your Grace. That is wonderful news," he replied.

"Our little one will come in mid-March. Once Eden is able, we will come to town for whatever remains of the Season."

"And bring your babe with you," Rupert said, smiling. "Yes, I know all about the Marchioness of Aldridge's plans for the ten cousins. That they are to bring their children to town each Season and enjoy family time with both their own children and their cousins and their children."

"You do know our family secrets," the duke said. "Is that

something you might be willing to do if my sister accepts your offer of marriage?"

"Absolutely, Your Grace." He hesitated and then said, "I want you both to know how much I care for Lady Lia." He pulled the note from Creighton from his pocket. "This is from your solicitor. I met with Mr. Creighton and Mr. Ousley, my solicitor, when I stopped in town yesterday. Together, they have drawn up marriage settlements that are quite favorable to Lady Lia."

"I like that you came prepared, Cressley," Her Grace said. "You have a good head on your shoulders. And the fact that you know my daughter seeks a love match is also in your favor."

Worry filled him now. "I do love her, Your Grace, but I fear it may be too late."

The dowager duchess smiled evenly. "You came quite a long way, Cressley. You even took the time to have marriage settlements drawn up. Cornelia will be moved by that."

"I also purchased a special license, Your Graces," he informed the pair. "I am hoping Lady Lia might be persuaded to wed quickly."

"Hmm. Then I will go speak with Cook. I will let her know of the possibility of a wedding breakfast. If you will excuse me."

"The others are due to return soon, my lord," Millbrooke told him. "I will make certain that Lia comes to the drawing room so that you might speak with her alone. If you do not mind, I shall tell my wife and Tia you are here—and why. That way, they will be prepared for whatever decision Lia makes regarding your offer."

"Thank you, Your Graces."

"And Cressley, I will want to review those marriage settlements immediately if my sister agrees to this match."

"Of course, Your Grace. They are with my solicitor. He, my niece, and her governess are waiting at the Willowshire inn."

The pair left. Rupert roamed the room for a few minutes, walking from window to window, gazing out at Millbrooke. His pulse quickened as he saw a carriage coming toward the house.

He stayed at the window, looking down, and saw the duke go outside to greet its occupants. Millbrooke handed down his wife, who was obviously increasing, followed by Lady Tia.

And then Lia appeared. His heart sang with joy. He told it to be still, that she had yet to agree to wed him, but he could not banish the happiness filling him.

Rupert watched as the others disappeared from sight, entering the house. He waited, his heart beating rapidly, waiting for the door to open. For Lia to walk in.

When she did, her step faltered. Their gazes met. They both froze, unable to move or speak.

He was the first to come to his senses, striding quickly toward her. He reached her and took her hands in his.

"I have been a rattleplate. Utterly bacon-brained," he blurted out. "I love you, Lia. I truly do. When you asked me if I did, I lied to you. Or I was lying to myself. I cannot say. All I know is that I never thought of love being a part of my life. Now, I cannot think of anything *but* having love in my life. Having *you* in my life. Loving you every day of my existence and even beyond the grave."

She seemed speechless, so he continued to speak, hoping to convince her.

"I adore you, and I will show you every day just how much I love you. I will prove it in ways large and small so that you never need doubt me and my eternal love for you."

He choked on the final two words, tears swimming in his eyes. He had laid bare his soul to her.

Now, it was for her to decide if they had a future together.

Her fingers squeezed his. "I never thought I would hear those words come from you. I have loved you so much, Rupert. When you told me you did not love me, it was like a thousand deaths. I wanted to hate you. Hurt you. Instead, I simply withdrew inside myself. I have barely eaten. I cannot sleep."

Tears now welled in her eyes. "I did not think I could go another day without you."

He brought her hands to his lips, kissing her fingers tenderly. "I was a complete arse, Lia. I have put both of us through something awful. I beg for your forgiveness. If you can find it within your heart to forgive me—to love me, even a little—then I will be the happiest man alive."

"I never stopped loving you, Rupert."

He released her hands, pulling the sacred document from his inner coat pocket and handing it to her. She opened it and began to read it, her jaw dropping.

"What? Is this what I think it is?"

"It is a special license," he said solemnly. "If you are willing to forgo the calling of the banns, we can wed as soon as you would like. I also had marriage settlements drawn up. They are—"

But Rupert never finished his sentence. Lia jerked him down to her. Their mouths collided, and a fevered kiss began, a kiss unlike any other. They drank deeply of one another, their bodies flush against each other's. He could feel the pounding of her heart as it raced, knowing his did the same. They kissed. Laughed. Kissed while they laughed. And when he finally broke the kiss, the radiance of Lia's face was like the most brilliant rising of the sun he had ever seen.

"So, you will wed me?" he asked.

"Yes, you silly goose." She kissed him again. "I would say tomorrow, but Mama would object. Maybe in two days. Or three." Lia stopped. "No, Celia should be present at the ceremony. We must go back to—"

"She is here. In Willowshire," he said excitedly. "I brought her and Miss Wilson with me. She wanted to come with me to Millvale, but I was afraid you would not even see me."

Her hands cradled his cheeks. "You will probably get tired of seeing me."

"Never," he said, devouring her mouth again, taking pleasure in each kiss.

This time, Lia broke the kiss. "You must bring them to Millvale. I will go with you. They can stay here in the house. Val and Eden will not mind."

"I met your brother. He seems to be a good man."

"He is. And you will like Eden."

"Shall we go tell your family our good news then?" he asked.

"Yes."

Quigby lingered outside the drawing room, telling them the others awaited them in the library. The moment they entered, he saw the hopeful look on the faces of the occupants. Then Lia cried out joyfully, throwing herself into her twin's arms.

"I see that a marriage will take place," His Grace said. "This is my duchess, Lord Cressley."

The Duchess of Millbrooke had honey-brown hair and hazel eyes. She greeted him warmly. "It is an honor to meet my soon-to-be brother-in-law. Welcome to Millvale, my lord."

"Thank you, Your Grace."

Lia returned to his side. "Mama said not tomorrow but the next day. I am getting married!" she squealed. Then she sobered. Gazing up at him, she said, "I am wedding the man I love. The man I will continue to love as the years pass."

Though they were in front of her family, Rupert couldn't help it. He bent and pressed a light kiss to her lips.

Then Tia said, "Welcome to the family, my lord." She embraced him.

"We do not stand on ceremony," the duke said. "When alone, we prefer to address one another informally. I am Val. This is Eden."

"I am Rupert," he told them.

"We must go for Celia now," Lia said. "Oh, she came such a long way. Mama, may Celia and her governess stay here? I know it would be more appropriate for Rupert to stay at the inn in the village."

"And Mr. Ousley," he said. When she looked blankly at him, he realized she had cut him off with her kisses. "My solicitor. He brought the marriage settlements for Their Graces to review."

"I will come to the village with you and meet Mr. Ousley,"

Millbrooke said. "He is invited for dinner this evening. You, too, Rupert."

A warm feeling ran through him. In an instant, he had family. Family he could count on. Family whom he would become friends with. Family he would celebrate with over the decades to come.

"We should also stop at the vicarage and see if Mr. Clarke can perform the ceremony," Lia said. "Oh, there is so much to do!"

"Then move the wedding back another day," suggested the dowager duchess. "That will give us time to prepare for the wedding breakfast and invite our neighbors to the ceremony." She paused, brows arched. "Can the two of you wait that long?"

Rupert looked at Lia. She nodded. "Yes, Mama. Today is Monday. We shall wed on Thursday if Mr. Clarke agrees."

They returned to his carriage, the duke going with them. Rupert sat next to Lia, their fingers laced together. A calm settled over him. Optimism poured through him. He loved—and was loved in return.

Life did not get much better.

CHAPTER TWENTY-THREE

L IA GAZED INTO the mirror, pleased with what she saw. "Thank you, Esther. My hair has never looked better."

"I'm so happy you like it, my lady. And thank you again for asking me to go with you, back to Traywick Manor. It's a lovely place. I'm glad you're marrying the viscount."

She was happy. She was now the fifth of the ten cousins to wed. When they had returned to Millvale last week, they had learned that Dru had wed the Earl of Martindale two months prior. Dru had gone to visit Lucy after her wedding to the Marquess of Huntsberry, and she had fallen in love with one of Lucy's neighbors.

Just as Lia had done.

The door flew open, Tia rushing in, followed by a more sedate Eden. Lia stood and faced her sister and sister-in-law.

"You look marvelous!" her twin proclaimed. "Rupert is going to fall all over himself when he sees you."

"You do look lovely," Eden said. "More importantly, you look happy."

She reached for their hands and took them, squeezing. "I am wildly happy. I love Rupert so very much. It is wonderful because he loves me, too."

Tia grew serious. "You have the love match you have always desired. By this time next year, you might even be a mother." Tia embraced her, and all the love Lia had in her heart for her twin flooded her.

"Oh, I am going to miss you so much, Tia. Perhaps you can come to Crestbrook and find someone in the neighborhood to fall in love with."

"I have already spent two months at Traywick Manor, and no one came close to drawing my attention. No, I will wait for the Season and all it will bring. I will eagerly meet the many bachelors in attendance. Ariadne is right, though. While going to the Season and attending all the wonderful events will be incredible, the most important thing is that it will be a time of year when you and I will reunite once more, along with our siblings and cousins."

"You will have a start on being a mother with Celia to raise," Eden commented. "What a precious child she is."

Rupert and Lia had sat Celia down and told her of their plans to wed. She had asked the little girl to call her Aunt Lia, and Celia had been more than ready to do so. In truth, Lia would be the only mother the child ever knew, but she did not feel right being called Mama and taking the place of Celia's birth mother. Lia knew Celia would love and watch over any babes Lia had.

Mama entered the room and looked Lia over, nodding approvingly. "You make for a lovely bride, Cornelia. Come. It is time to go to the church."

The four women went downstairs, where Val waited in the foyer for them. Her brother smiled widely upon catching sight of her.

"You make for a most beautiful bride, Lia," he said, brushing his lips against her cheek.

"Thank you for everything, Val."

Her brother had met with Rupert and Mr. Ousley, his solicitor. They had gone over the marriage settlements, and copies had been made. Val had presented a copy to Lia, telling her that her betrothed had made certain she and any children they had would be well cared for in the future. While Lia knew she and Rupert would live a great distance from Val and Eden, she hoped each year when they came to the Season that Rupert and Val would grow to be friends. Already, things were very friendly between them, which was a good sign of things to come.

Val escorted them outside and handed up each of them into the carriage. Lia held hands with Tia the entire way there, wondering what life would be like without seeing her twin daily. At least she and Rupert would attend Tia's come-out Season, and she hoped her sister would find lasting love.

Mr. Clarke met them outside the church and told Lia that they could begin the ceremony whenever she was ready.

"Please start immediately," she told the vicar. "I am ready to begin the next chapter of my life with my groom."

Everyone gave her a final kiss and entered the church as Lia waited in the doorway. She was a bit sad that Ariadne could not be present, but she was not willing to wait any longer to wed the love of her life. She had already written to her older sister about her upcoming nuptials and promised that she and Rupert would be at the Season. She could not wait to introduce him to the rest of her family and their spouses.

Mr. Clarke nodded at her, and Lia made her way down the aisle of the church. Invitations had been issued quickly, and she saw many from the community seated in the pews. But her gaze focused on that of her betrothed, and she moved toward him, seeing his encouraging smile. He took her hand in his when she reached him, and the clergyman started to speak. Suddenly, Lia felt a presence by her side and glanced down, seeing that Celia had left her seat and come to stand beside her. She slipped her arm about the girl, and the ceremony continued, Lia and Rupert speaking their vows to one another and becoming husband and wife.

They returned to Millvale with all their guests. Mama and Eden had planned the wedding breakfast, and it came off flawlessly. Lia could not help but gaze down at the gold band on her ring finger.

Rupert leaned close, brushing his lips against her temple. "Do you feel the same as I do? That this is somehow a dream, and it might dissipate?"

"It is a dream come true," she told him. "This ring, an eternal circle, is tangible proof of our love for one another." Then she turned her gaze from the ring to her new husband. "But I know exactly what you mean. If this is a dream, then I hope never to awaken from it."

They would remain at Millvale through Christmas since the holiday was a little more than two weeks away. Eden had given them a suite of rooms in the east wing so that they would have some privacy as newlyweds. They retreated there now after bidding goodbye to their guests, and Rupert said he would give her time to prepare herself for their wedding night. He brushed a tender kiss against her lips, telling Lia that he would return in half an hour.

She rang for Esther, and the maid helped her from her wedding finery into a beautiful, filmy night rail which left little to the imagination. The maid helped Lia place her dressing gown over it, and she tied the belt, hoping Rupert would not be disappointed in her tonight. Mama had told her nothing about what was to come, so Lia's trust was in her husband as to what she should do.

He returned to the bedchamber, wearing a banyan and trousers, padding barefoot along the carpet. Her mouth grew dry as she caught sight of his bare throat and a glimpse of his chest.

"Are you ready to begin a new adventure with me?" he asked.

She had not thought of marriage as an adventure, but it would be with this husband of hers.

Smiling, Lia took his hands. "Show me all I need to know, Husband."

"First, I am going to show off my hair skills," he said teasingly. "I have learned much from brushing and combing Celia's hair. Come. Sit at the dressing table."

She did as he asked, and he undid the single braid she wore, brushing through her long tresses, his touch soothing.

"I love the shade of your hair. Such a rich auburn. I hope all our girls have hair this color."

Their gazes met in the mirror, and she asked, "How many girls do you think we might have?"

"Oh, a good half-dozen would suit me. And we should toss in a boy or two. After all, I do need a son to pass down my title to."

She rose, wrapping her hands around his neck. "You know how much I want children, and I believe you are going to be the most wonderful father. I see you with Celia. You have taken to fatherhood naturally."

"I knew not a thing about children when I arrived at Crestbrook. Celia made it easy for me, though. She was so loving from the start." His hands framed her face. "I hope we are blessed with many children and that they will always be close to one another. We will raise them in love and show them just how important family is."

Then his lips met hers, and the magic began.

They kissed for a long time, their kisses heated, desire shooting through her. He finally took a step back and slipped from his banyan, allowing her to see his broad, muscular chest. Fascinated by it, Lia placed her palms against it, moving them, watching the muscles jump.

"You are wonderfully made," she complimented, leaning in and pressing a soft kiss to his chest. Feeling him shudder, she gazed up. "Do you like that?"

"Very much. I would like to do the same to you."

She undid the knot of her belt and shrugged from the dressing gown. His eyes roamed her body.

"This is going to take further exploration," he said, slowly grinning. "Remember, whatever we do between us is for us. If there is any time you are uncomfortable with anything, tell me so. And if you like something—ask for more."

"I will," she promised.

Rupert removed her night rail and his trousers. They stood before one another, gloriously naked. The place between her legs pulsed. He stepped toward her, wrapping his arms about her, and

Lia was pressed against his heated flesh. They kissed, and then he led her to the bed. Esther had turned it back for them, and he scooped her up, placing her gently against the pillows.

What followed were things Lia had never imagined. Once they occurred, she could not imagine life without his touch. His hands and lips explored every inch of her. He spent a long time caressing each breast, causing hot desire to shoot through her. He replaced his hands with lips and tongue. He flicked his tongue over her nipple, and it pebbled in need. Then he took her breast into his mouth, sucking hard, bringing a rush of need, causing her core again to pound. His hands glided up and down her hips. Across her belly. He kissed his way down her body, and she realized where his final destination would be. It shocked her. Thrilled her. Consumed her.

He had her place her feet flat on the mattress, parting her legs before he feasted upon her. His tongue lapped at her, slipping deep inside, caressing her in an intimate fashion which immediately brought them closer together emotionally. Then something began building and spilled from her. Her hips rose as wave after wave of pure pleasure engulfed her. She heard cries and realized they came from her, and she called his name, again and again. With one last shudder, she grew limp.

Kissing his way back up her body, he reached her mouth and drank from it, again and again.

She took his face in her hands, saying, "I have not a clue what you just did, but it was the most wonderful thing ever."

He grinned like a schoolboy. "Oh, there is much more to come, love."

They kissed again, their bodies fevered, and Lia wanted more from him. She had never thought herself a greedy person, but her need drove her to possess all of him.

His fingers found the seam of her sex again, teasing it. "You are ready for me," he said huskily.

"I will always be ready for you, my darling."

She watched his shaft grow and stroked the length of it several times, listening to his groans as she did so.

"Enough," he said. "I wish to be one with you, Wife."

He touched the tip of his manhood against her core and then thrust quickly into her. She gave a small squeak of surprise.

"I will stay still a moment. Let you get used to me."

He kissed her deeply and then began to slowly move. She quickly caught on to the rhythm, her hips moving up to meet him, allowing him to drive deeper into her. His hands clasped her hips, helping each of them to thrust harder. The pace began to increase, finally becoming frenzied. Again, that feeling built inside her, and it was as if an explosion occurred. Lia clung to him as she shattered in his arms. He collapsed atop her, kissing her mouth. Her nose. Her eyelids and cheeks.

Then he rolled slightly, still within her, and they now faced one another, lying on their sides.

"I love you, Lia Cummings. I am mad with love for you."

"Will it always be this wonderful?"

He looked at her with such tenderness in his eyes that it caused tears to mist in her own.

"I believe each time we make love together, it will be better than the times before. We will learn what pleases one another, and our love will grow deeper as the years pass."

Rupert brushed a lock of hair from her face. "I am going to be one of those greedy men, Lia. I am going to want you every day. Even more than once a day."

Her palm cradled his face, her thumb caressing his cheek. "I had always thought greed was something bad." She smiled. "Now, I think being greedy in love is a good thing. Oh, Rupert. I am so full of joy right now. I do not know if I can be any happier than I am at this moment."

"And I think this is just the tip of our happiness, love."

Her new husband kissed her, and Lia believed in him. In her. *In them . . .*

EPILOGUE

Crestbrook—November 1808

R UPERT WENT TO his study, finally ready to write the letter he had promised to send over a year ago. His commanding officer had requested that Rupert write to him and let him know how he fared in civilian life. He seated himself at his desk and placed a fresh piece of paper in front of him. Dipping his quill into the inkwell, he began to write.

Dear Lieutenant-General Bond—

I hope this letter will find you since I know the British army is constantly on the march. Unfortunately, your prediction of the war widening proved to be true.

What the bloody hell was Bonaparte thinking, deposing the Spanish king and putting his own brother on the throne? At least his actions have resulted in giving England a strong ally in Spain. I hope you are part of this Peninsular campaign and that you find Wellesley to be the man to lead us to victory.

My brother's health had deteriorated rapidly by the time I reached London last year, and so I claimed the title after his death and have been Viscount Cressley for over a year now. I discovered Perceval had sired a child, and so I became an instant father figure to my five-year-old niece. Celia is a delight, and we took to one another instantly. Crestbrook, my country estate, thrives, as well.

I also can report to you that I am now a husband and

father in my own right. I wed one of the daughters of the Duke of Millbrooke. Lia (short for Cornelia) is the light of my life and my reason for living. I never knew romantic love before meeting my Lia, but I experience it abundantly every day.

Two weeks ago, my darling gave birth to twins. Mary is the elder by six minutes, and she has her mother's auburn hair and sweet spirit. Edward, our son, has a headful of dark hair, and both children have their mother's deep blue eyes. They are good babes and rarely cry—unless they are hungry. The pair of them can be louder than a cannon attack, demanding to be fed, when hunger pangs strike them.

I appreciate the life I have now and am filled with a deep contentment. Thank you for encouraging me to go home and face my responsibilities here. I pray every night for your safety and hope the tide of war will turn, with Bonaparte being defeated. If this war ever does end, I hope you might consider visiting us at Crestbrook.

Sincerely,
Former Major Rupert Cummings,
Viscount Cressley

He folded and addressed the letter before properly sealing it, wondering how long it would take to find its way to Bond. His commanding officer had greatly influenced him, and Rupert hoped the lieutenant-general would not lose his life during this war.

Leaving his study, he gave the note to a footman and asked that it be posted. He knew it would first go to London and then be sent on from there. Wellesley was gaining ground in Spain, and a majority of British troops were being located there in what was being termed the Peninsular War.

Rupert shook off his sudden gloom, relieved he was no longer in the military. He headed upstairs to the nursery, where he knew he would find Lia. As expected, she sat in one of the two rockers in the room, holding a babe in each arm.

Leaning down, he kissed her cheek. "May I steal a bundle of joy from you?"

She smiled up at him. "You most certainly can."

He eased Mary from her arms and took a seat in the second rocker. Lia had insisted on having two placed in the nursery since she sometimes came up and rocked one of the twins while the nursemaid rocked the other. Rupert found himself coming to the nursery often. Just as he and his wife couldn't seem to get enough of one another, they were the same about their babes.

As he gently rocked, he looked down at his firstborn daughter. She studied him with innocent eyes.

"Shall I sing to you, Mary?" he asked, and then he softly began singing a lullaby which Lia had taught him. She joined in, their voices blending together, and at the end, he said, "Mary is fast asleep."

"So is Edward."

Lia rose and placed him down for a nap, and Rupert settled Mary in the crib next to her brother. He had thought they would sleep separately, but his wife said that she and Tia had slept together from the beginning, and she wanted their twins to do the same until they grew a bit older. He watched now as the pair gravitated toward one another in sleep, Edward putting a protective hand over his sister's.

He slipped an arm about his wife's waist, and they watched their babes for a few minutes.

"Who knew my favorite thing in the world would be to watch them sleep?" Lia mused.

Smiling, he kissed the top of her head. "Well, I have always enjoyed watching you sleep. It is the same with Mary and Edward."

She leaned into him. "I never knew my heart could hold so much love."

Rupert lifted her chin and gave his wife a soft, sweet kiss.

"Shall we go downstairs? It is almost time for tea. Remember, your aunt and cousins are coming over from Traywick Manor."

"Yes, let us go down to the drawing room. But wait. Just one more minute," she said, gazing down at their sleeping twins.

"I will always wait with you, love. I want you forever by my side." He kissed her softly. "You complete me, Lia. I am whole because of you. Celia. The twins."

"I love you, Rupert. So very, very much."

They remained, watching over their children, and he knew they would continue to grow in love every day which came their way.

About the Author

USA Today and Amazon Top 10 bestselling author Alexa Aston lives with her husband in a Dallas suburb, where she eats her fair share of dark chocolate and plots while she walks every morning. She enjoys travel and sports—and can't get enough of *Survivor* or *The Crown*.

Her Regency and Medieval historical romances bring to life loveable rogues and dashing knights. Her series include: *The Strongs of Shadowcrest, Suddenly a Duke, Second Sons of London, Dukes Done Wrong, Dukes of Distinction, Soldiers and Soulmates, The St. Clairs, The de Wolfes of Esterley Castle, The King's Cousins, Medieval Runaway Wives,* and *The Knights of Honor.*